SKY BRIDGE

Also by Laura Pritchett
Hell's Bottom, Colorado

SKY BRIDGE

LAURA PRITCHETT

MILKWEED EDITIONS

© 2005, Text by Laura Pritchett

www.milkweed.org

Published 2007 by Milkweed Editions
Printed in the United States of America
Jacket design by Percolator
Interior design by Linda Koutsky. Typeset in Sabon 10/14.
Author photo by Stephanie G'Schwind
13 14 15 16 17   5 4 3 2
First Paperback Edition

ISBN-13: 978-1-57131-054-5
ISBN-10: 1-57131-054-1

Generous underwriting for *Sky Bridge* was provided by an anonymous donor.

Milkweed Editions, a nonprofit publisher, gratefully acknowledges sustaining support from Emilie and Henry Buchwald; the Bush Foundation; the Patrick and Aimee Butler Family Foundation; CarVal Investors; the Timothy and Tara Clark Family Charitable Fund; the Dougherty Family Foundation; the Ecolab Foundation; the General Mills Foundation; the Claire Giannini Fund; John and Joanne Gordon; William and Jeanne Grandy; the Jerome Foundation; Dorothy Kaplan Light and Ernest Light; Constance B. Kunin; Marshall BankFirst Corp.; Sanders and Tasha Marvin; the May Department Stores Company Foundation; the McKnight Foundation; a grant from the Minnesota State Arts Board, through an appropriation by the Minnesota State Legislature, a grant from the National Endowment for the Arts, and private funders; an award from the National Endowment for the Arts, which believes that a great nation deserves great art; the Navarre Corporation; Debbie Reynolds; the St. Paul Travelers Foundation; Ellen and Sheldon Sturgis; the Target Foundation; the Gertrude Sexton Thompson Charitable Trust (George R. A. Johnson, Trustee); the James R. Thorpe Foundation; the Toro Foundation; Moira and John Turner; United Parcel Service; Joanne and Phil Von Blon; Kathleen and Bill Wanner; Serene and Christopher Warren; the W. M. Foundation; and the Xcel Energy Foundation.

The Library of Congress has cataloged the hardcover edition as follows:

Pritchett, Laura, 1971–
Sky bridge / Laura Pritchett.—1st ed.
p. cm.
ISBN: 978-1-57131-046-0 (alk. paper)
1. Sisters—Fiction. 2. Colorado—Fiction. 3. Young women—Fiction.
4. Adopted children—Fiction. I. Title.
PS3616.R58S57 2005
813'.6—DC22
2004027334

This book is printed on acid-free paper.

MINNESOTA
STATE ARTS BOARD

NATIONAL
ENDOWMENT
FOR THE ARTS
A great nation
deserves great art.

for Jake and Eliana,
with love

SKY BRIDGE

PROLOGUE

That pickup is a piece of junk. Three different shades of white and roaring like the muffler was never part of the deal. But Tess, she's beautiful. Leaning out the passenger-side window, blowing kisses from her palm, her dark eyes dancing like they've finally decided to come alive again. "*Good*bye, Libby, good*bye!*" she's singing at me.

As if that pickup and man are going to get her somewhere. As if she's not leaving anything behind. As if she don't see me crying.

She smiles, she waves. As if *this* is the happy farewell she's been dreaming of.

Her dark hair is giving her trouble, shifting sideways from the breeze, and she has to stop waving long enough to catch up the shiny-dark strands with both hands, and something about that makes her laugh, and with her laugh everything starts to change. The truck roars louder and the gravel snaps as the tires start moving. Her hair flies from her hands again, her body leans farther from the window, and her goodbyes get louder.

I step forward. Bits of hay dust from the bed of the truck blow in my face, and the sun's setting behind her, and no matter how hard I squint, I can't see. Then she's gone. Just like that. And I'm still standing there, looking at the place where she just disappeared.

What's left is this: a couple of cows and a barbed-wire fence and pale grassland stretching on to meet the faint outline of mountains in the distance. The sky's streaked with pink and orange where the sun's getting low over those mountains, but by the time the arc of sky gets to me, it's a dark evening blue. A meadowlark's singing and there's the distant sound of pigs slamming the covers of their feeders, but all in all, it's pretty quiet until Amber starts crying.

This kid is cradled in the crook of my arm, looking past me and into the sky with foggy blue-gray eyes. One red arm wobbles in the air, the fist clenched tight, and from her mouth shoots a raspy wail, way too big for that newborn body.

A word comes out of me too, a breath of a word: "Please." It's the word that's been rising in my mind this whole time: Please, goddamn, *please*.

Please don't go.

Please change that look in your eyes.

Please look at Amber.

I stare at the space where my sister just was, and I realize that she was acting like, Hey, ain't-this-a-sweet-farewell? But underneath, the eyes were saying something else altogether: Keep your promise. Leave me alone.

I cover my mouth, sink down till my knees touch rocks, and bend over the baby, and I'm crying like crazy. Because that's when I know that my sister is leaving, and that she doesn't want this baby of hers that I'm holding in my arms.

ONE

 It's true: Every house has a few places that reach out and hold you. Standing spots, Kay calls them, and she says every home has one or two. That's why I always find myself leaning against the frame of the kitchen door and looking east, toward the alfalfa field that comes up a stone's throw from our door. In the summer, at least, that's where I stand, sometimes with my one-cigarette-of-the-day, looking out over the leafy alfalfa in its various stages of growing. Besides that green field and the stretch of blue sky, the only other thing in view is the circle of buildings and cottonwoods that make up Baxter's place in the distance. And the rutted dirt road that runs along the edge of the alfalfa, the one that connects our two houses.

Up close is the shed and burn barrel and Kay's car that doesn't run any more, and Kay's other car that hasn't run in so long that yellow-flowered weeds are growing out of it. There's a concrete birdbath that we once used for cigarette butts, but it fell over in a windstorm a year or so ago and nobody's picked it up yet. I'm quitting anyway and Kay mostly does her smoking over at Baxter's, so now it makes a nice little step for me to put my foot on.

Next to the birdbath is a line of wilty-looking yellow marigolds. Who knows why I put them in. I think it was my attempt to make this place seem a little more—I don't know, hospitable or something. I planted them when Tess was at the hospital in Lamar giving birth. I also put up blue streamers because all along we'd thought the baby was going to be a boy and I'd bought the roll in advance. But the tagboard sign I did in pink letters: WELCOME HOME TESS AND BABY AMBER!

The sign and streamers are in the burn barrel now—I stuffed them in there yesterday, after Tess drove off. If I turn a bit, I can see the streamers hanging over the edge of the black, sooty can. Every once in a while a breeze lifts them and they look like magical arms waving goodbye.

"Maybe I should have saved those for your scrapbook," I say to Amber.

She blinks her hazy eyes at that and keeps staring at my white T-shirt like it's the most interesting thing she ever saw. What gets me about her is that she clings to me like a tiny monkey. She's got her tummy to mine, and her little fingers clutch onto my shirt and her little legs curl against my belly. It almost seems like if I let go—just dropped the hand that's cupped around her tiny diaper—she'd stay attached to me somehow.

I flick the cigarette butt out at the gravel and rub Amber's back up and down, up and down. "Well, what the hell. We'll be fine, won't we? Basically, I can't be any worse than Kay, and I guess I turned out all right, even with a mother like that." I'm tilting my head down, saying this to her blond hair.

Blond hair. Ridiculous. All along, I thought Amber was a boy and I figured he'd look like us. I was hoping he'd take after Tess especially, with her straight dark hair, tan skin, tall body—Tess who doesn't need glasses, who's got straight teeth and a true smile. Not like me with my glasses and crooked teeth and

4

dull brown eyes and stupid thick, wavy hair—hair that sounds like a horse's mane when I brush it.

Amber, though, is fair, just like her father, Simon. She's got blue eyes and pale blotchy skin, and like her father she seems too wispy and empty to be real. That's how every day she'll be reminding me: Libby, things just don't turn out like you think they will. Daydream if you want, but expect the opposite to come true. And don't go feeling sorry for your heart when it registers the difference.

"Libby! You deaf or what? Damn." Kay's riding up on her horse, and only stupid Kay would be riding a horse. Every other ranch-hand around here drives a four-wheeler but no, not Kay, because Kay is Kay, and Kay says it'll be a cold day in hell when she sits on anything as noisy and ugly as that.

"Libby, I've been hollering. Didn't you hear me?" She reins the horse in. "What the hell's the matter with you? Are you cry-ing?"

"No."

"Because there's no use in crying."

"That's good, because I'm not crying."

"There isn't any point."

There isn't any point in talking to her, either, so I stare off into the sky behind her.

She squints at me and sighs. Then she takes off her sun-glasses and her beat-up fishing hat and slouches down on the horse like I've worn her out. She sits there a while, staring at me with that look that means that I'm a sorry excuse for a human and especially for a daughter. I look back. It's her hair that makes her eyes look so green, because it's more white than brown now, and she's got it back in her usual ponytail, low down at the base of her neck, and the wisps hanging around her face are bright white, and I wonder if she knows how beautiful she is—or could be if she didn't look so continually pissed off. It's not just her face, it's her whole body: ready to attack. She's wearing a maroon T-shirt covered with bleach circles, and her Wranglers are splattered with manure, and even though she's slouched down it looks like she's going to leap up and have it out with the world.

After she's done staring at me, she puts her hat and sunglasses back on. "Come on over. Baxter decided to work cows after all. We need your help."

I tilt my head toward Amber.

"Good god. Libby, you're not the one who gave birth. People have been carrying on with their lives with babies since the beginning of time." Then she adds, "We'll put her in some shady spot."

The horse is dancing all over the place, and Kay jerks back on the reins so much that Luz rears back a bit. When she gets the horse quieted down, she says, "She doing all right?"

I shrug.

"Well, that kid'll get her days and nights straightened out soon enough, then you'll get some sleep. Luz, you barn-sour old thing, damn, cut it out!" Kay turns the horse in tight circles, fighting the antsy of the horse and the horse fighting back. Kay wins, and finally the horse stands quiet, flaring her nostrils but holding still.

"Mom, I can't take a newborn baby out with a bunch of cows."

"You sure as hell can. Go inside and put on some shoes and get Amber a sunbonnet—you keep a hat on that kid—and get over to Baxter's."

I don't say anything at all to that, but still she throws in, "Quit being such a snot." Then, "Anyway, we've got the cows nearly done. Just help with the calves, just the record keeping.

You can hold Amber on your lap. Or she can sleep in her car seat. Whatever, just hurry up."

Well, that's what I imagined anyway—that I'd be like one of those women in Africa, like you see in magazines, with a baby strapped to me and the two of us doing everything together. So after Kay kicks Luz into a trot, I get us ready and drive over to Baxter's. This is where Kay has been working as a ranch hand since we moved here, which was right after I was born, and which is why we get free rent in the old, falling-apart brown house that sits on the edge of Baxter's land, at the corner of his alfalfa field.

I find Kay and Baxter by the corrals, both leaning against the chute and talking over the head of some tame-looking cow that's standing there, reaching her tongue into one nostril and then into the other. I can't get over that, how funny cows look licking out their noses. It makes me love them, and that's love for you—one little detail and your heart turns tender.

I haul Amber and her clunky car seat over to Baxter and Kay.

"Hey, little baby," says Baxter, reaching down with a stubby finger to touch her nose. "Look at you, you wrinkly sweet thing, you were up all night, your grandma says. Now that ain't no good. You be a good sleeper for your new ma, how about?" Amber flails her arm and watches all these words coming at her. Her right eye is squished down a bit, so it looks like she's attempting a wink, or maybe like she's already being sarcastic and making a face like I do when I'm thinking, *As if,* or, *Yeah, right.*

"Pretty as can be," Baxter says, backing up from her and looking at me.

I snort. That's a bit of a lie and we both know it. "She looks like a blond lizard, don't she?"

Baxter tilts his head, considering, and scratches at his white hair, shaved so close it looks like bristles. He's got a tan face

7

and green eyes, even lighter than Kay's, and even today, even working cattle, he's got on clean jeans and a soft blue western shirt with those silver snap buttons, and that's why I like him, I guess, because he always looks tidy and put together.

"Naw," he says. "She looks like an angel. *You* look like an angel, smiling like that. Like a proud mother."

"Baxter, she doesn't look nothing of the sort. She looks like a tired mother, scared shitless. Put her here, Libby." Kay points to a little nook in the corral in between the chute and a water tank. "You have to be at work at four?"

I nod yes to the four o'clock part, no to the dirt in the corral. "She'll get kicked there."

"No cow's gonna get past me into this corner." Then she sighs. "Please don't argue. Please try not to be such a brat. Please just do what I say for once."

I set Amber down. Kay scowls at me, I scowl back.

Baxter watches us and then says, "She'll be the youngest helper I've ever had. She'll grow up tough. Probably spend a lifetime giving her guardian angel gray hairs."

Kay thrusts the record-keeping book at me and says, "Let's get busy."

Baxter ignores her, though. "When my brother went to war, the Second World War, I asked my guardian angel to follow him. Promised I'd take extra special care of myself. That's why my brother made it back, you see. He had two beautiful ladies watching out for him. And look here, now I do!" He spreads his arms out toward me and Kay. "No! I got three!" This time he's raising his eyebrows at Amber and he's got a big delighted smile on his face.

What can I do except just roll my eyes at that, because that's Baxter for you, crazy for sure, but in a too cheerful, hokey sort of way, which is the opposite of Kay's sort of crazy. Most days I can't take the either of them.

8

"Libby, cow number is 56-X. Write it down," Kay says.

I move the syringes and bottles that are sitting on the edge of the stock tank so there's room for me to sit down. I push my glasses up, open the record-keeping book, and take the pen from the edge, where it's jammed in those rows of metal circles. I glance at the writing above to remind myself what it is I'm supposed to be writing down: cow number, sex, sire, vaccinations. Baxter needs these records so he can keep track of everything, even though he says the drought's gonna cause him to sell off the herd anyway, and pretty soon there's gonna be nothing left for him to record. In the notebook, he keeps a line called Miscellaneous Notes, which is my favorite thing to read, because it's here that Baxter keeps track of things like who he's treated for foot rot, who got a rattlesnake bite, what sort of coloring the calves from such-and-such a bull have, or even stuff like, "This cow looks downright sad," or "Prone to mastitis," or "Hooliganish," or "Good mama."

The notes I leave for him; the rest I'm in charge of and so I get busy writing. Maybe this isn't the most exciting way to be spending a morning, but Derek's at work, Tess is suddenly gone, and standing at home with the baby was no good, so I guess it's better than nothing.

Baxter says, "Live so hard that you give your guardian angel gray hair, that's how I see it. I like to imagine mine sometimes, blond hair streaked with gray, shaking her head at me and wishing she'd gotten assigned to someone else."

Kay gives a shot of 7-Way and dusts for mites, and Baxter punches a fly tag in the cow's ear and rubs some ointment on a ringworm circle. As he works, he leans toward me and talks. "That's what my mama always said. 'Child,' she'd say, 'Your guardian angel must be exhausted by now. I know I am.'"

I try to give Baxter a real smile, because he deserves that at least, and when he's satisfied that I've been listening he and Kay get to work. For a long time there's nothing but numbers being voiced into the air, flies buzzing, cows thrashing against the chute. One of Baxter's peacocks comes walking in the corral, his tail floating out behind him, and Baxter's donkey he-haws from somewhere far off. I think Baxter might have too much time on his hands; this place is always filled up with weird animals and it basically feels like a small zoo in the middle of nowhere.

When I'm not writing, I watch Amber. She's just a face, poking out of a blanket and mostly covered in a bonnet. She's sleeping and her mouth is in the shape of a little O and I hope she won't grow up ugly and stupid like me. And maybe that blond hair will fall out and grow in dark—that's what I'm hoping for. But I'd like it if her eyes stayed blue, even though the nurse at the hospital said they'd probably change.

I try to catch the feeling going on inside me. Because catching feelings is something I try to do. I get real quiet and find what I'm feeling and then *feel* it. Sometimes it's like, *Fuck this!*, and I let the zigzag anger crash through my whole body, even in my pelvis and feet and behind my eyeballs, and I feel like I'm going to fly apart. And sometimes it's the opposite and I think I'm going to sink so deep into myself, like I'm empty, and I start to collapse into this nowhere space that just goes on and on and on. But this time I'm watching a new baby girl asleep, a red face and a white blanket, and the problem is I can't tell what I feel. I want it to be a *Yes, yes, yes!* and a *Love, love, love!* but it's not. But neither is it *Oh shit, shit, shit!* or *Please no, please.* Whatever it is, is darting around so fast that I can't catch it, I'm just not fast enough.

"Goddamnit, Baxter, hurry up here," Kay says.

"Guardian angels," Baxter says. "Pay attention to them."

"She's not listening to you," Kay says. "So will you please give this cow her shot?"

I turn and look at Baxter and wait until he's pinched the skin on the cow's shoulder and stuck in the needle. "Baxter," I say. "Get serious. You don't really believe in guardian angels. You don't believe in that stuff."

I see a half smile flash across Kay's face, because she's always wondering too if Baxter is as dopey as he sounds or if he just wants to believe all the happy jabber that comes out of his mouth. It's a fact of life: It really bothers people when somebody is just too damn cheery; pretty soon you've got to wonder about the depth of their thoughts.

"Naw," Baxter says after a while, his face falling a little. "But I used to. And I wish I did, because I sure could use one right about now." His body pauses for a second, and then his eyes light up as usual. "And so could you. And so could that baby."

"And so could Tess," Kay says.

"And so could Tess," Baxter agrees. He's watching Kay walk across the corral with a whip in her hand, ready to chase in the last cow that's backed out of the chute and is standing by herself in a corner. Baxter's amused because of what Kay's mumbling, which is her usual rant about Baxter's damn corral system and he's such a cheapskate, it wouldn't take much to fix it up so things could run smoothly for a change and why's she always dealing with idiots? Everybody's pulling her into stupid situations and what the hell did she do to deserve to be surrounded by people without a glimmer of sense?

"Now, now," Baxter says to me, "Now, now, now. Kay's got it made and she knows it." He means that his cows are downright famous for being so calm and that Kay is lucky to be working with such a herd. There's nobody who loves his cows like Baxter. Everybody wonders why they're so cooperative and easygoing, and Baxter says it's an extension of his own calm disposition. That's how I learned that word, *disposition*. He's so darn proud of those cows, and even though he only rounds them up a few times each year he calls lots of them by name.

Kay finally catches this rare ornery cow and she and Baxter prod it forward, through the alley, and Kay twists the cow's tail and Baxter pounds her on the butt until she steps into the squeeze chute, where they catch her head. The cow stands pretty good after that, getting her shots and tags, though her eyes are rolling backward a bit and she looks not bitchy-mean, like Kay is saying, but downright scared.

Now the cows are done and it's time for the calves, and while I'm waiting for Baxter and Kay to bring them in, I try some quick sketches in the back of Baxter's book. First the corral fences from far away, and then a close-up, one weathered fencepost, and I try to capture the way the wood looks with cross-hatching. Then I draw Baxter's old white farmhouse, and then the eyes of a cow, and then Amber in her car seat, but none of these are good so I tear the pages out and crunch them up and jam them in the pocket of my jeans.

Finally the calves are in, and, as Kay likes to say, calves are a different experience altogether. They twist and back out of the chute, their legs get stuck between bars, and they snort and bawl and scramble out of everyplace they get put. Plus they have to go through so much. Ear tagging isn't so bad. But if they're not polled, they got to be dehorned, and right as they're coping with the pain of that, they're getting their shots. Then comes the worst part for the young bulls that Baxter don't want as bulls, and they've got some real thrashing to do.

Quite a few of the calves are jammed in one of the corrals and most are pretty big, though a few look new and flimsy and teetery. Kay flicks the whip in the air above the whole mess of them, moving them into the alley. When she gets one group in, she jams a manure-stained fencepost behind the last one's butt to keep them all from backing out. Then she pats the first one on the rump, trying to make it walk forward, but this bugger is going sideways and backward and Kay's cussing and I duck my head to hide my smile because it's nice to see Kay suffer now and then. Baxter's not helping her either, he's just leaning against the fence post and watching, a little amused too.

"Libby," he says. "You're pretty quiet. You okay?"

I shrug at that.

"Though you never do. Talk much. Look at that baby. All yours! You lucky thing, Tess doesn't know what she's missing."

I'm thinking, I do talk. But I've just learned who it's worth saying something to and who it's not. And the truth is, anyway, that my mind is flipping back and forth between being dead and screaming at me because what was I thinking, anyway? And I think I better keep myself quiet because it seems like if I tried to say anything I'd just blow apart.

"She's waking up." Baxter nods at Amber over the syringe he's filling up from a brown bottle and then mumbles something about the right number of cc's.

"I'll get her a bottle," I say.

"You will not," Kay says. "Wait till she cries. You need to stretch out her feeding times. She could go three or four hours. This every half-hour in the middle of the night is ridiculous. Just let her be. And if you hold her every second, you're never going to be able to put that kid down. I'm telling you, you're spoiling her."

"She's lonely."

"She's not lonely. She's figuring out the world. Leave her be."

Baxter clears his throat. "Libby, Libby, Libby. Listen here. You shouldn't go and lose the first thing that makes you smile each day. You hear me? Don't go and lose the *first* thing that makes you smile."

"Okay, Baxter. You've told me that a time or two."

"Which means, you got to pause and think about what it is that makes you smile."

13

"All right."

"I haven't smiled yet today," Kay says. "I don't think I will. I guess I got nothing worth keeping. Are you going to help me here or what?"

Baxter doesn't move. He says to me in a real quiet voice, "Adeline's what made me smile. When I woke, I was thinking of her and smiling." I don't say anything, but he says what's on my mind for me. "But I went and lost her anyway, didn't I?"

I wish I had words for things. Other people do, probably. But I've never been able to tell Baxter how sorry I am that his wife died, that I miss her too, that she made the best frog's-eye salad. Which scared me when I was a kid, till she told me it was made out of tiny pastas and whipped cream and no frogs were involved. When I was little, I used to wish that Adeline was my mom because she seemed warm and soft and calm, like she didn't have that need to hurt anybody, but mostly, I guess, because she seemed to actually like me. I never said anything about this to Baxter, and I can't now either. Stupid me, because this is my chance to say something if I only could think of it. Instead, I shrug and stare at Amber, who is staring at the air in front of her.

"I've been thinking of selling this place," Baxter says.

I look up, surprised, and I see that he's watching me, waiting for my reaction and nodding, like, Yeah, I knew that'd get her.

"That decided it, though—remembering my ma saying, 'Don't go losing the first thing that makes you smile.' This place makes me too happy. I lost too much already. I'll stick it out for a bit longer. I'm getting old, though. I'm getting old."

"You're not old, Baxter."

"Plus, a person's just got to rise to the occasion." He's always saying that, but he especially started up with that particular phrase right after Adeline died. Kay'd been worried for a bit, because for a while none of the bills were getting paid and the place was starting to fall apart. Kay had said that everyone needs a wife, including wives, and when you don't have that extra helper all hell breaks loose. But Baxter figured out how the bills got paid and the books got kept, and now it seems he's adjusted to being alone and I guess he rose to the occasion after all. "You do that, too, Libby," he says to me now. "Rise to the occasion."

"Sure," I say.

"And as long as I got Kay, this place'll run for a bit longer." He says it in a whisper, though, because Kay's coming up the alley with a calf. He winks at me, like this is a secret we should keep, and that's another thing about Baxter, he's always trying to make something special or secret when it's not.

A calf bawls, wanting his mama. The mama bellows back. Flies are landing all over me and, Jesus, it's like a million degrees out here.

Amber's staring up toward the sky. I should get her picture taken by a real photographer. Probably she needs a diaper change. I gotta move out of here. I gotta get some money. I wonder what Derek's doing right now at the rig. I wonder where Tess is, because she sure didn't tell me where she was heading when she drove off yesterday. I wonder if Amber is getting too much sun, because the doctor said no sunscreen till she's six months and that I was going to have to work hard at keeping a baby out of the sun in eastern Colorado. I wonder when my heart is going to quit hurting for Tess, and I wonder when I'm going to start feeling wonderful for Amber. I wonder how, exactly, I ended up here, because not in a million daydreams did I ever imagine this.

Last fall, Tess said to me, "Libby? You want to know something funny?" She was ready for school, in her Roper jeans and boots, with her hair curled and her dark eyes made up. It was one of her country-dress days. Other days she dressed up artsy, or scootery, as she called it, with her skirt with pleats at the bottom. She cared about that sort of thing and it drove her insane that I was pretty much a fan of jeans and baggy T-shirts. But anyway, this was one of her country days, and she said, "Lib, I have the funniest thing to tell you. You want to hear something really funny?"

"Sure." We were leaning against Kay's truck, and I remember it being warm from the sun, even though the day was cold. The snow was falling in little lazy circles, but neither of us had put a coat on. We were hugging ourselves with sweatered arms, waiting for Kay to come out of the house so she could drive Tess to school and drop me off at the store.

Tess was doing a little bounce number on her feet to get warm and she bounced up and down and she said, "I'm pregnant."

I think maybe I laughed, because she had said it was supposed to be funny, and also because it was surprising, and also because I didn't believe her. Then I said, "*What?*"

She pressed her lips together, blending in the pink lipstick. "I'm pregnant."

I looked from her face to her belly, where her sweater met the fabric of blue jeans. Her tummy was tiny, as always, and the sliver of it I could see was as tan and muscular as ever. "You're not pregnant," I said.

"I am."

"That's very funny."

She rubbed at her nose and looked away from me. "It's true. We weren't careful. Don't freak out. It happens. You know, it just happens. I don't want to ask him to drive me."

"Who?"

"Simon. I don't want him, I want you. To drive me to Denver. Or Pueblo, if they do them there. I've got the money,

16

I'll figure things out. But I want you to drive me."

"But Tess—"

"I've already thought about everything." She tipped her head up toward the sun and closed her eyes. "I wish I could go back in time. This is the first time I realized what people mean when they want to go back. You understand? I wish I could redo that instant. You remember what that health teacher always said? A moment of pleasure, a lifetime of pain. Only it wasn't even a moment of pleasure."

"Tess?"

"He wasn't worth it. The sex wasn't worth it. Of course it wasn't. At least I'm eighteen now, because otherwise everything would be more complicated. How come you never warned me?"

"What?"

"Warned me that just a moment could fuck up so much?" She looked at me and smiled. "I'm just teasing, Libby. Don't look so surprised. It wasn't your job to warn me, even if you are my big sister and all. Just joking."

I was looking at the icicles hanging from the house. They were dripping, and the drips made little plops and dings as they hit the stuff below: a hubcap, an empty five-gallon bucket, the fallen-down birdbath. The ground was muddy and filled with our footprints. The cement pad outside the door had wedges of manure from when Kay scraped her boots on the edge before walking in.

All of a sudden, the icicles quit dripping, like it had gotten cold enough to freeze them up again. I said, "Tess, are you sure?"

"The line was blue, Libby. Both times."

"No, I mean, that you want an abortion?"

"I don't like that word so much. There needs to be a different word." She looked at me sideways, squinting her eyes because of the flying snow, which was picking up. "Libby, please?"

A few geese flew above us, honking. Pigs were slamming at their feeder. The phone was ringing inside, which meant Kay would be a bit longer.

I asked her, "Please what?"

She said, "Please help me."

The sky was an enormous arc of gray-white, like dull metal. White snow spun by and everything got blurry and silenced. The world was hushed, just like the way things quiet down before something big bursts into the air.

TWO

Miguel Mendoza is standing out in the middle of the highway, in front of his trailer, waving his arms for me to stop.

"Miguel," I say when I pull the car over. "I gotta get to work. I'm late."

"Libby, thank God I didn't miss you. I got to get to work too. My car's broke down."

"Where's Juan?"

"With his *abuelita*. I was driving him in this morning and my car just stops, just dies, right there on the highway, and I hiked the last two miles with him on my shoulders—fuck—and left him at his grandma's and I called to have the car towed in and hitched back here, and now I'm very late for work. *Gracias a diós.*" When he's settled in the car, he makes a sign of a cross. "Now I'm carless in the middle of nowhere, *híjole*, that's just great. This is just not the right part of the world to be broke in. Good thing there's you. I figured you'd be heading to work. Shit." He rubs the sides of his face with his palms. "Fuck."

"I picked up a lady hitchhiking to Lamar last week. Her car was broke down too. Her daughter had just gone to the doctor for eating pennies." I have to say this loud, because by now we're going sixty and the windows are rolled down since it's burning-hell hot even though it's early June, and the wind is roaring around in the car, bouncing around and slamming into our eardrums. "The pennies were on the floor because her vacuum doesn't work. She was working extra shifts to pay for the doctor. She was hitchhiking to work because of pennies, a vacuum, a doctor, a daughter, and because her car was broke down. Hitchhiking all the way to Lamar, that's crazy. You smell like pot. Do you know anybody named Clark? Because that's the name of the guy Tess took off with. I don't know nothing about him. But Tess drove off with him yesterday and now I'm a little worried."

He looks down at his shirt and lifts it from his body a few times, like that will shake the pot smell away, and then stares up at the ceiling of my car and closes his eyes. "Tess left?"

"Yeah. She just drove off with this guy. I'd met him before, but I didn't really pay attention, because I didn't think he mattered. Because I didn't think he was going to drive off with her, you know."

"Who's watching the kid?" He's talking loud too and he leans way over to me so we don't have to try so hard, which helps the noise situation quite a lot.

"Right now? Kay. She's going to watch her while I'm at work. I took care of her all last night, though. She's mine now, I guess. Can you believe that? I have a baby."

I'm busy driving but I glance at him sideways in time to see his jaw, which is right next to me, tighten underneath his skin.

"Did Tess tell you she was leaving?"

I bite my lip. There's a lot of answers to that question, and I don't know which is most true. Yes. No. Maybe. She used to say she was leaving the minute she graduated high school. But sometimes, when I told her that maybe we could rent a place in Lamar together, she'd agree to that. When I said that maybe the two of us could move to Denver or something together, she'd agreed to *that*. And after she was pregnant, we talked through other ideas, too. People'll do that to you, sometimes—agree to all sorts of scenarios, and I don't think she meant to be confusing, it's just that she didn't know.

"I'm *un poquito* pissed off at mothers who leave their babies right now," he says after he realizes I'm not going to answer his question with anything other than a shrug. "And no, I don't know any guy named Clark. He from around here? From Lamar?"

"I don't know."

"What'd he look like?"

"I don't know. Tess told me yesterday, 'Libby, this fine gentleman is going to take me on a bit of a vacation,' and he said, 'Sure thing,' and she said, 'You know, I just got to get out of here for a while. I'll write.' He looked like a regular guy. He was big—not fat really, but big. He had black hair. They just drove off."

After a pause, Miguel says, "My *abuelita* always said that there's two kinds of people in this world, warm people and cold people. Sometimes they trick you. You think they're cold but you find out that underneath they're actually warm. They got a heart after all, and it's a heart that goes outside itself, into the world. Then you got the people who come across as warm, but underneath they're so damn cold and empty that it's just scary. It's true, you know. The people who seem warm but are cold. That's Shawny for you. That's Tess. From now on I'm only gonna deal with people who have some heat inside them—do you know what I mean Libby? *Me comprendes?*"

He's caught me by surprise—Miguel's not the sort to say something like this—so I say something dumb, which is, "I learned a trick, which is that you rub a baby's lower lip with

21

the nipple of the bottle and that's how you get her to suck. Probably you already knew that."

"I can't remember that far back." He says it slowly, as if he's thinking about it.

"Do you remember how a baby takes that bottle like it's the most serious thing, concentrating? Her eyes are always open, staring at my shirt, but it's like she's thinking of the milk, how it feels going down her throat. I think that's amazing. She's got the cutest toes. I can't wait till she starts fitting into the outfits I bought her, especially this one with pastel bunny rabbits on it. I got that one at K-Mart. Kay said to me, 'Lord, Libby, quit buying outfits because babies could care less what they wear,' but I said, 'That's half the fun, Kay. You're never wanting to have any fun,' and Kay said, 'Honey, it ain't going to be fun like you think, this isn't a baby doll to dress up. Save your money for stuff she needs.'"

Miguel smiles. "Kay's right, for once."

"Naw. I mean, I'll save money and all. But I can buy Amber an outfit or two. Or pictures, which is another thing Kay got all worked up about. At the hospital, I got the most expensive portrait package and she yelled at me for an hour. She said, 'Libby, who are all these pictures for?' and I said, 'Lots of people,' and she said, 'Libby, there are about four people on this earth that care that this baby was born,' and I said, 'That's ridiculous.' Because Amber's only a newborn baby once, you know. I got some extra pictures if you want one."

"Sure, okay."

"One of these days I'm going to get an apartment of my own and I won't have to put up with Kay hollering at me all the time. Besides, I don't know if she's the best person to be taking care of Amber, but I guess it will be okay until I figure something else out."

"You're gonna need her. I'd stay on her good side."

22

"There is no good side."

"Then whatever side that gets you through the day." He tilts his head and scratches at his hair. Miguel is not that much older than me, but already he's graying near the temples and his eyes are steady and look like they've seen a lot, or like maybe he's lived a long time before in some other life, but it's funny because his face is round and he looks like a boy, so all in all he looks like he's caught in a whole bunch of stages of life.

Miguel and I look at the car clock at the same time. It takes twenty minutes to get to town from here and I've only got four more minutes till I'm late, plus I gotta drop off Miguel, so I speed up to eighty-five. The wind's whipping in the car and the noise of it vibrates around my head from a thousand different directions. Some day I'm gonna have a car with air conditioning, mostly so that I can just drive in silence.

Pastureland spreads in all directions, burnt yellow with the sun, and from here it seems like maybe the whole world might be made up of flat land and sky. Everybody's sold off their herds so there's a lot less cows, but every once in a while there's a bunch around a windmill and stock-tank.

I pass a car loaded down with immigrant workers, who are probably heading to some job, and I feel sorry for them, because it's going to take them a long-ass time to get there in that piece of junk station wagon. Then I pass Mrs. Tribble, who probably shouldn't be driving anymore, because she goes about fifteen miles an hour down the highway and weaves back and forth across the center line and everyone around here knows to look out for her but outsiders and semi-truck drivers don't. Then I swerve around a dead cat that's been left on the highway, and then the road is clear again and it's just us, zooming through the middle of nowhere.

Miguel is looking out the window too, and keeps on looking while he says, "Stupid Shawny. I can't do this all alone."

I glance over at him, at the angle of his face I can see. "I'm pissed at her too, you know."

"No. You're not angry like I am." Then he nods at the building ahead, though I know that's where he works. It's right alongside the highway, a low stucco building that's been about a million things but is currently Lupe's Diner. The parking lot is gravel and pitted with huge potholes, which I swerve around as I get him to the front door.

"*Gracias por el* ride," he says as he gets out. "Juan asks for you. He's got an opinion on everything these days. He was throwing a temper tantrum because the moon was the wrong shape—he wanted it full instead of crescent. He doesn't get what he wants and he says, '*Rompiste mi corazón.* You broke my heart.' As if it's my fault. I'm not in charge of the moon, man. I wasn't in charge of his mom's life."

I start to say something and then stop. "Tell him I'll bring him some cookies, cookies with lots of sprinkles." Then I add, "With moons. Moons that are both shapes."

Miguel leans over and looks in the window at me. He nods and smiles, like he's considering something that he wants to say, and he takes a breath and does it. "We're the ones left behind. To work our asses off, no? Maybe we should have just taken off too, but now we can't." His voice isn't angry, though, it's just tired. "You know what we got left with? Hope. I don't know how to get rid of it. I don't even know what the fuck I'm hoping for. Shawny's *gone.* But still, I keep hoping for something. And even now, I look up at the sky and say, 'Shawny, *rompiste mi corazón, rompiste mi corazón.*' And you, you're going to miss Tess. I know how close you were. I don't even think she deserved your love, but she got it anyway, because that's the way it happens. I know you're going to miss her, and you're going to keep hoping." He shrugs at me, and he looks genuinely confused, and that's the face that stays in my head, even though time moves on, even though I catch my breath and then keep on breathing, and even though I nod, and then shift into gear and leave him behind.

Frank ought to give me hell. I wish he would, in fact, so I wouldn't feel so shitty for always being late to such a good job. But no, as soon as I park he walks out of the store with a big wave and smile, picks up a box sitting on the curb, and brings it to my car. I open up the trunk and watch him come in his usual bowlegged walk, box balanced on his round tummy and his smile half hidden by his big, bushy, western-style mustache.

"Sarah Price brought the swing—her baby doesn't need it anymore. And Betty Zigler wants to know if you want a toddler bed, because she's got one she's looking to get rid of, though I told her that was years off. She's the one who brought this box of baby clothes. I bet any storage space you and Kay had is already used up by now."

"That's true. You know, people don't have to—"

"Stuff's expensive, everybody likes to help. So, I heard Tess left." He winks as he twists the box into the car. "Word's already gotten around. Kay called, asking if I knew anything about this Clark fellow."

We walk back to the store to pick up another load. There's a bunch of baby clothes in the box I'm carrying, and Frank has three bags of diapers. "Really? That surprises me," I say. "That Kay bothered to call."

"Told her I didn't know him. I know most everybody out this way, but I suppose some escape my notice. I'll do some checking, though. Just happened to run into Chet Sanders, who knows a big, dark-haired Clark that works in Lamar, and he says he's a quiet fellow, hauls hay, works as a mechanic. I'll see if I can find out more."

"It's not like he kidnapped her or anything," I say. "She wanted to go. She asked him for a ride. I'm sure he's fine, she's fine. Everybody's fine."

"Well, doesn't hurt to check. With the baby and all, I thought she might stay. I guess I figured she had reason enough to stick around. But before that, I knew she'd be one of the ones who'd go. I can just tell about people. They either love this place or they don't. And most of you young kids don't."

I almost say, *Nobody* does, Frank, it's the middle of Nowhere, Colorado. It's just a matter of whether or not folks figure out *how* to leave.

I must be making a face that shows all this, because Frank says, "Now, Libby. This place has some real advantages, and you'll come to appreciate them more now that you're raising a kid. It's safe. It's small. And people look out for each other." At this, he swings his arm at the pile of stuff in front of us. "If you ask me, it's the last fine place to be."

I'd like to say something about how even I'm smart enough to see that it all depends on your perspective, because maybe he doesn't see it but all my old schoolmates are either doing drugs or working minimum wage or in jail, and for sure they're all bored as hell, hanging around and letting their lives go by, including stupid fucking me, and anyway, none of my day-dreams are here, in this place, and isn't that my brain's way of telling me something?

Frank says, "Remind me to call around to see who's going to supply night crawlers to the store this year. Everyone's asking."

"Okay."

"And Ed Mongers wants to know if anyone with an alfalfa field would be willing to let him keep his bees nearby, because blooming alfalfa apparently makes good pollen, good honey—something like that. I don't know, I can never figure out what that guy's talking about. I told him to talk to Baxter or your mom."

"Okay."

"Let me know if you need anything."

"Okay."

"You got a picture of Amber for me?"

"Yeah."

"Good. And put one in the back, too, and I suppose Arlene will want one. So, you were out working cows, huh? Kay told me to take it easy on you because you look about as shell-shocked as she remembers feeling, although you'll never say as much, and that you're going to need some time to absorb it all."

"Kay said that?"

"Your mom has a kind heart. She just doesn't like to show it." Then he adds, "I been there once, so shell-shocked I felt blasted to bits." As he says this, his eyes drift away from mine, toward the faint blue outline of mountains, and his eyes hang there long enough that he doesn't see the surprise in mine, although maybe he feels it, because he shakes himself loose from his thoughts and winks at me. He says, "But that's worlds apart. Because yours involves wonder, and that makes all the difference."

Ideal Foods. It's stitched right there on my blue apron, in white embroidery thread, stitched by Frank himself. Stitched right above *Santa Fe Foods,* which is what this place used to be called.

Ideal Foods.

Santa Fe Foods.

As Frank likes to tell the out-of-towners, the name of the store is right-on in both cases, because this is the most ideal place to be. And because if you know where to look, you can still see the wagon-wheel ruts of the Santa Fe Trail.

I think he might be making both parts up. I've lived here my whole life and never seen any traces of wagon wheels, though I've touched the secret petroglyphs that only the locals know about, mostly because those places are also our party spots. Seems like the earth pulls you to places the same way houses do, and certain spots are just good for hanging out, whether you're an Indian doing a drawing or a white girl getting drunk.

But if you ask me, this apron just looks insane: *Ideal Foods Santa Fe Foods,* like somebody couldn't make up their mind.

Sometimes I think that we're all so wobbly inside, like none of us can make up our minds about stuff, and we spend all this time waffling back and forth, which just confuses everybody. I imagine a whole room of people rocking back and forth, like they're physically acting out what their minds do all day, and we all look like a bunch of crazies, bumping into each other all because we can't seem to line up and walk straight, because there's these other possibilities that must be considered. It makes me a little sad, actually, because I think we're doing it for the right reasons and it's hard when you're trying to do the right thing but you don't know what it is. And probably it doesn't matter. People would come in here no matter what the store was named.

I straighten my Ideal Foods Santa Fe Foods apron and scrape the manure off my shoes before heading out front. I love this job. Mostly because it's just me and my mind and my daydreams, and time gets filled up, and so does my heart, and even though my life isn't what I pictured, at least I have this, meaning that if I can't have the life I want, at least I can have a job where I can daydream about the life I want.

Always, I start with the ice machine in the back room, where I shovel ice cubes into clear plastic bags that say ENJOY POLAR ICE! They have these pictures of white bears on the plastic and I have a long tradition of talking with them, though I

28

do it in my head so that people don't think I'm crazy. I tell the first bear, *I hope Kay is taking good care of my girl, and probably she's not, and what should I do about that, you cute thing?* I say to one, out of the blue, *You're a fucker.* I say to another one, *You think Derek's going to leave me or what? Because Tess said he would.* I say to another one, *There's no way Tess can make it out there, she's just a girl, well, she's eighteen, but she's a girl.* I say to another one, *I'm sorry I called your buddy a fucker. I'm sure you're all nice enough.* I tell one, *You'll end up in a cooler with beer at John Martin Dam.* And you, I tell another, *you'll be packed around some newly dead fish.* I say to the last one, *What? You think I'm crazy? Not everyone talks to pictures of goofy-looking bears on plastic bags?*

After the ice come the milk jugs, which I pull forward so the rows look full and neat. Eggs and butter, pulled forward. Plastic bags and paper bags, restocked. Floor by the cash register, swept. Then I clean the table up front, which is there for people who want a bite to eat in the store. The poker table, it's called, since that's what it gets used for, especially when the sheriff comes in with the volunteer EMT guys after a call and they need a game of cards to get whatever crash or drowning or death out of their system. So there's the poker table, and then I clean the smudges off the glass door, and then more restocking. Then I clean the meat room, which is where Frank grinds hamburger and slices ham. It's this part that takes so much time— wiping the chunks of bloody meat from the machines, taking the slicer apart and putting it back together, wiping down countertops and cleaning the huge knives in the sink. The chemicals I mix in the water smell so strong that my eyes cry all by themselves and I'm always worried that anyone looking through the window to the meat room will think I'm drowning in sorrow. All this I've got to get done before eight, which is when I need to restock and straighten again so that I can start cleaning and mopping at nine, so that everything's set to go for the morning by the time the store closes at ten.

Just like I figured, Derek walks in right when I'm in the meat room, right before my break, right when I'm smelling and looking my worst. I wipe my face with the back of my hand and straighten my blue apron as I turn around to see him.

His face is burnt red and a farmer's tan shows around the neck and sleeves of his turquoise T-shirt, which reads C.A.T.S. COLORADOANS AGAINST TEXAN SKIERS. Who knows why he bought that shirt, since he never skied in his life, but he has a thing against rich people, and a thing about outsiders moving to Colorado, and I guess he thinks Texans are guilty of both, so he harbors a special resentment against them. Although not really, because Derek never gets worked up about anything; wearing a T-shirt is about as far as he'll go.

I can tell he just got off from work at the oil rig—we joke about that, how a guy named Derek works for a rig—because he's still got on his torn-up jeans and boots and a haze of oily dirt covers his arm hairs and he smells so bad I have to bite my lip to keep from making a face. He looks too skinny, like he's still a gangly kid or something, waiting to fill in and grow up.

"Hey, you," he says, poking his head into the meat room. "Take your break yet?"

"Nope."

He tilts his head toward the door. "Come outside."

I look at Frank on my way out, and Frank nods, so I take off my apron and bunch it under my arm as I follow Derek out the glass door. We sit on the sidewalk, our feet on the parking lot. My arms prickle as the air-conditioned cool leaves my skin and the warmth seeps in, and it smells like heat out here, like dust mixed with air that's burning.

I reach over to scratch Derek's back. "Tess left. Last night, just drove off with—"

"That guy? I knew it. I *knew* it—"

"Really? I didn't know it."

"Like, left, or *left* left?"

"I don't know. She had two suitcases. And I don't know where she got those, I never saw them before."

He's silent for a long time, then he says, "She wasn't kidding, was she?"

"She'll come back. Anyway, it doesn't matter. I'm not worried."

"Wow, she really left you with her baby. Why didn't you call me?"

"Didn't want to bug you."

"You didn't want to bug me?"

"She just needed a bit of vacation. But I wish she would've held Amber more. Like at the hospital. I should have given her the baby to hold more. And I wish she would've told me she was leaving. Well, she kept saying she might, but I never took her serious."

He pokes at his work boots with a stick, jabbing off little bits of dirt from the edges. "He's dealing drugs. *They're* dealing drugs."

"No way, Derek."

"Why else would some guy start stopping by the house of a super-pregnant woman every time he got back from some 'delivery,' and why would Tess ask you not to mention him to Kay?"

"He delivers stuff, Derek. He's a truck driver. When he came back from trips, he wanted to see her. Tess is beautiful. He was— I bet they're— You know, after she feels better–"

"Naw, drugs or wetbacks—"

"You shouldn't use that word."

"Drugs or wetbacks, I'm telling you."

"And you should know better than anyone that it's best to keep Kay—what's the word? Uninformed about boyfriends. I tried to keep you apart for as long as I could. And even now, you still don't like Kay."

"Your mom introduces me as your no-good boyfriend. 'This here is Derek, Libby's no-good boyfriend.'"

"See?"

"She doesn't like me."

"She doesn't like anybody."

"They're dealing drugs."

I press my hand to my forehead. "Derek, sometimes you say the dumbest shit. No way would Tess get involved in that."

"Then where'd she get that money she left you?"

"From wherever."

"Five hundred bucks? From wherever?"

"Just drop it."

"Libby, I'm sorry to say this, and don't get all pissed off, but sometimes I think you act stupid because it's easier. You just refuse to see things so that you don't have to deal with them."

"The whole *world* does that, Derek. Anyway, I'm never going to use that money, I'm going to pretend I don't have it. It's for Amber. I don't know where Tess got it, but it's not from drugs."

He sighs, meaning we got to change the subject before we get into one of our fights. "Who watched the baby last night?"

"I did. She cried a lot, but that's okay." I'd like to tell him more, how freaked-out I felt, or how it's crazy that there's always something to do—boil water, change a diaper, feed, burp, walk, and then all of it all over again—and how that keeps surprising me. How I don't know how to get a onesie over her head, or how tight to pull the diaper around her tummy, or how hard to thump her back to get the burp to come. How I don't know if I should wrap her tight in the baby blanket, because it seems too claustrophobic. And how I didn't know about how light and hollow she'd feel, how much she'd squawk, how red-faced and blond-haired and angry she'd be.

But I'm trying hard to do what I promised, which is not get so wrapped up in this new situation that I forget about him. So instead I say, "How was work?"

"Same." He tucks in a pinch of chew and tilts his head. "Wish I'd get off day shift. I get off when you go on. You going to come by tonight?"

I look up at a car pulling in the parking lot. "I don't know. Amber and all. Can you come to my place?"

"Maybe," he says. "I'll see how I feel."

I tug at his shirt. "I'll do my best to seduce you if you do."

But he doesn't smile. "I don't know what Tess was doing anyway, sleeping with Simon."

"I don't know."

"He's a jerk."

"There was nothing better to do."

"Tess has always been too damn wild. Plus she felt like she didn't exist or something if she wasn't using her body. Do you know what I mean? She was never *not* sleeping around."

I giggle as I do Tess's chant: "I like the boys, uh-huh, uh-huh, I like the boys." I can picture her exactly, her arms above her head, her lips thrusting in a dance, her dark hair whipping around her head, laughing as she teased herself.

"But *Simon*?"

I shrug, because that is indeed a mystery. Simon was a proud member of the Cowboy Christian Fellowship, organizer of revival meetings at the rodeos. Not because there's anything wrong with Jesus, I guess, but because Simon never stopped to consider Jesus much; he was more interested in telling people that he was riding broncs for the Lord, and anyone knows that just doesn't make any sense. And because he'd do things like give us bumper stickers that said GOD ANSWERS KNEE-MAIL. And because he actually asked us to donate money to him so that he could buy a Harley Davidson, and he gave us little cards on which he'd written: "Psalm 18:10 reads 'He flew upon the wings of the wind.' Please help me do the same." Which is just to say, as Kay put it, this religion wasn't coming out of anyplace true, it was just the worst and saddest kind of dedication, because it didn't involve any thought.

That's how it was with Simon. He was the sort whose talk couldn't be trusted. He was wispy. For example, he sure changed his tune about abortion when it came down to his future and suddenly he wasn't so against it anymore.

What Simon really wanted was for his parents not to know. In fact, that was the one good thing about having the baby, Tess said—that it kept Simon from getting out of it completely free and clear. At least he had to fess up. Not that it mattered much, because after his parents found out they signed him up for classes at the college in Alamosa and sent him over there early for summer classes. They said he told them he wanted no part of anything. So Tess did what they asked, which was to put that she didn't know who the father was on the hospital papers, because otherwise the government would subtract money from his paycheck for child support and all and it wouldn't be fair for a kid to follow him around for the rest of his life, especially since he wanted the abortion too. "They got a point," Tess had said. "There's no need for him to get sucked into Libby's Situation." That's what she called it, Libby's Situation. I said I didn't care, go ahead and leave off Simon's name, because we were going to be just fine ourselves. But Derek knows about all this, so I don't say anything. But then it's quiet for a while, so I say, "I wonder if he ever thinks of her?"

"Who?"

"Simon. If he thinks of Amber."

Derek shrugs. "I doubt it."

"I thought he might come back."

"You did?" Derek sounds surprised, because this is something I've never told him.

"Well, I thought he might come back and hold Tess's hand when she gave birth or something. I think Tess did too, because those last few days, when she was home and not feeling so great, she kept looking around, like she was expecting someone. Every time a car pulled in our drive, she'd heave herself up and look out the kitchen window to see who it was."

"Who was it?"

"Well, you mostly. Sometimes it was Clark."

" Just stopping in to check on his new girlfriend? His about-to-give-birth girlfriend?"

"Derek, shut up. You know what I keep thinking about? How when Tess went into labor she asked the nurse to have me wait outside. 'She wants to do it alone, honey,' the nurse said. I thought maybe Tess would let me in. I can see her not asking Kay, because she'd likely get yelled at the whole time, but I thought maybe Tess'd want me there. How come you think she didn't want me?"

Derek shrugs. "You got me."

"She was in there such a long time, Derek."

"I know."

"Twenty-six hours."

"Yeah."

"I had no idea it could take so long, did you? And finally they called me in and someone handed me a baby and said, 'Here's a little *girl*,' and I looked at Tess and she was sleeping, or pretending to. Her hair was all knotted up and there were bruises under her eyes, and there was throw-up on her nightgown and she smelled like blood. Blood and throw-up. I was so surprised. Because Amber was a girl, and because she was so blotchy purple, and because Tess wasn't smiling and lit up. I kept thinking, *Naw, this can't be right, this is just not what it's supposed to be.* I'm just realizing that now. How surprised I was then."

Derek spits his chew out on the sidewalk, then drinks some water from a bottle he's got near him and spits that out too. "Libby, you're a mother now. That doesn't surprise anyone except you." Then, like I knew he would, he adds, "You just have to agree I ain't got what it takes to be a decent father."

"You keep saying that. You don't have to be."

"Okay. Just don't ask."

"I'm not asking."

"You and me, we were smart enough to be careful."

"Yeah."

"So it doesn't seem fair."

"No."

"She's the one who messed up."

"It'll be okay, Derek. You'll see."

"The problem with Tess is that you were always taking care of her and she let you. She used you."

"No she didn't."

"She did so."

"Drop it, Derek. And anyway, it'll be okay because this morning I helped Kay and Baxter, they were working calves. Amber slept in her car seat the whole time. Babies can adapt to anything. It'll work out."

Derek snorts. At first I think it's at me, but I look up and see Ed Mongers' old orange VW bus pulling in the parking lot. There's two kind of folks around here, as Derek likes to say, the ranching kind and the escape-people-hippie kind, and Ed Mongers is this second kind and Derek's not mean about it, he just finds those sorts amusing. He nods and says, "Howdy," when Ed walks by us, but sort of like he's being ornery, and Ed says, "Hello there," back with a smile on his face, and he surprises me by winking at me, like he knows we're all teasing each other just a bit. He's got on jeans and a T-shirt and so if you didn't know Ed you'd think he was just like everyone else, but everybody around here knows that he lives in a house that's U-shaped and made of tires with slanted windows on one side and extra tires piled all around. There's a crummy-looking greenhouse behind it, and a bunch of white boxes that I guess are for his bees. He sells honey at the store, and I hope that's not his only income, because there's just not that many people out here that eat a lot of honey.

"I ought to go back in."

Derek nods and looks sideways at me. "Want me to take a look at your car sometime?"

"It's not making that noise anymore."

"Tell me if it does."

"All right."

He hangs his head and rubs his thumb and finger across his eyes. I can tell how tired he is because he winces, like he doesn't have the energy to keep his eyes open.

I say, "You should look for a different job. Or make them promote you to driller." He shrugs his shoulders at that, though, so I add, "You going to go home and sleep?"

"Maybe rent a movie."

I run my hand down his back. "Sneak by later if you can."

"Amber sleeping in your room?"

"Well, yeah. But I can move her over to Tess's space."

"Well."

"Derek, she's what, a week old? That's not old enough to know what's going on. Believe me."

"What if she wakes up crying?"

"You're just inventing something to be mad about."

"No I'm not."

"Because you think she's going to ruin our lives."

"No, I think maybe it will be hard to have sex with a baby hollering."

"Just give her a chance."

37

"I'm giving it a chance." He touches my nose, and then kisses me on the lips, a soft kiss, and then his lips are on my neck. He's smiling as he kisses because he knows I don't like it when he kisses me that much outside the store but that I do like it, of course, because one thing Derek knows about me is that his kisses drive me crazy, they really do, they send me spiraling in a new direction every time, and he likes to kiss me just to see me change the way a person changes when they go from existing in life to being caught somewhere magical instead.

Finally he stops and hugs me, and then he pushes himself to his feet and walks to his truck. He's wearing Rustler jeans, since they're the cheapest kind and they get tore up so much at work. Usually I wish he'd get a better brand so he'd look nicer, but this time the sight of those skinny legs in those cheap jeans just makes me feel sorry. Sorry that he probably won't ever have any better. Sorry that his life isn't a little easier, a little more fun. Sorry that he's feeling bad about us, about something that wasn't his fault. Sorry that we're together but that we both suspect it's not love. Sorry that we were just kissing and now we have an ache that we can't do nothing about. I feel so sorry that it's not until he's out of sight for a good long while that I can turn and head back into the store.

Here's a smart thing I learned from Tess: If you want someone to keep a promise, you tell the whole world about that promise.

Telling the town about our deal was Tess's way of making sure I wouldn't back out. That was smart, because maybe I did want to change my mind a time or two. Then I realized I couldn't. Not unless I wanted to leave town. Not unless I didn't care if I ever faced these people again.

"All I asked her to do," Tess would say at the start of every conversation, "was drive me to Denver for the abortion."

And I'd say, "Tess, that's enough now."

And she'd say, "Libby, I can tell the story if I want to."
She'd rub her white T-shirt, stretched tight over her big belly,
and say, "But no, my big sister wouldn't do that for me. No,
Libby had another alternative. She wanted me to carry the
baby. If I carried the baby, she'd raise it. Sounds noble, don't it?
But she don't know what she's in for." Then she shot me a look
that meant, Now that everyone knows they'll hold you to it.

My favorite response to this conversation came from Frank.
What he said to her was, "Tess, your sister is a noble gal. She'll
be a good mom. Noble." He kept saying that word over and
over, like maybe he hadn't used it before and wanted to test it
out. Later that week, he gave me a raise. That's pretty much
how it went—once Tess was really showing and Kay had been
informed, everyone in town found out and after that they were
generous with me. They weren't with Tess, which is maybe why
she made plans to hightail it out of here after the baby came.
But for me, doors got opened and people patted me on the
back. When I mopped the floors, people'd stop to ask how I
was doing, had I decorated a room yet, was I pretty excited?
They said things like, "Aw, you're a good kid, Libby," or, "You
got the makings to be a fine mama."

All that made me believe I could do it. It was nice, you
know, making people proud because I'd done the right thing,
but also having them sympathize a bit, because the thing I
promised wasn't so easy.

Stupid me. I thought Derek would feel that way too. I
should have realized long ago that he wouldn't, and that anyway, all that attention would never be enough.

THREE

It shouldn't be this hot. Something is wrong. I feel like the old-timers and their croaky *In all my days here, it ain't never been like this,* but it's true. It's never been like this. Even I remember how on summer afternoons the clouds would boil up and send down rain. Now the heat feels dangerous, like it's pressing down to suck away the life of this earth—and even worse, it's doing it quietly, like an evil thing waiting for us to not notice so it can pounce.

Kay's note says, "Amber was up most of the evening, so probably she'll sleep good tonight. Hot, isn't it?"

The hot part is true, but the other part is turning out not to be the case.

Amber is screaming her head off, maybe because the heat makes it feel like her lungs won't work. I've got her at the edge of the tub, about to give her a bath—her first bath, in fact, even though I haven't scrubbed out the tub with Borax yet. Which is something I meant to do, but later, because her first bath would be in the kitchen sink, but the kitchen sink is full of dirty dishes because the dishwasher suddenly broke and I can't hold a crying baby and do dishes at the same time, and I can't clean out a bathtub and hold a baby at the same time, and so this baby is just going to survive in this gross tub.

Baths are supposed to be good for calming a colicky baby. Besides, the back of Amber's sleeper and the back of her body are covered in yellow crap, pretty much all the way up to her neck, and I have no idea how a tiny baby shits with such force.

I don't know *how* to give her a bath, though. She's slick and kicking, and I can't tell if the water's too warm or too cold, or how much of it to put in, but finally I get her down in the tub, with my hand cupped behind her head. She looks scared when I put her in the water, and her arms clutch at the air, like she's looking for something to hold. Since there's nothing, she braces her arms like she's holding air, like she's fighting hard to hang on to even that. I run my finger down her forehead and nose to calm her. She keeps still and stops crying, thank god, and she looks like she's busy feeling whatever it is that she feels.

"Good idea," Kay says. I turn around to see her standing behind me in her pajamas, which consist of her white, baggy underwear. She's got her arms crossed over her chest and she's leaning against the doorframe, slender and muscled, light blue veins crossing underneath her white skin.

"Sorry. I tried keeping her quiet."

When you look at Kay, you can't help but notice how beautiful she is, even if you don't want to notice a thing like that. Being pretty is the last thing on Kay's mind, and it ought to be the last thing on anyone's mind, according to her, because it's just one more example of a ridiculous world where everyone is hell-bent on seeing what doesn't really matter, basically so that they can avoid seeing what does, which is the fucking *inside* of people. All this came out in one of her recent drunken rants, in her gone-berserk tone of voice, and what I was thinking at the time was, *Kay, there aren't that many people that* want *to see the inside of you, believe me.* But all I'm thinking now is, *Kay, you are so pretty; you and Tess both have that, like it or not.*

Kay yawns. "When'd she lose her umbilical cord?"

"Yesterday. I forgot to tell you. I saved the stub in her memory box."

"Libby, that is—"

"Disgusting, I know. But it seemed crazy to throw it away since it's the part that was attached to Tess, after all."

She sits down on the toilet seat and her bony knees bump my side. "I remember bathing Tess. Just like this. Same tub, same kind of night." She grabs for her toothbrush and starts brushing, and I know from the smell that it was whiskey and Coke that she'd been drinking before she fell asleep. "She thinks she's so good, so brave, that Tess. But you know, one of these days she's not going to feel superior to anything anymore. That's when you know you've grown up. You quit feeling superior." Then she taps her knee against my back, like she's playing. "I was pretty smart once. Then I wasn't. I don't remember some of my life, your life. That's crazy. That's wrong." She sighs and looks out the window across from the toilet, then leans sideways over to the sink and spits out the toothpaste. "I was busy with something else." After a bit, she says, "Some of my boyfriends, they were all right, don't you think? Remember Sy? He was the one with a motorcycle. He was nice."

"Yeah."

"And Grant. He fixed up this place a lot."

"He built me my bookshelf," I say.

"Did he? I don't remember that. But then there was T.J. He was no good."

"Look at how much Amber likes the water."

"Give her a few weeks and she'll be lying there, kicking and splashing and smiling. Libby, I always wanted to ask, if any of those boyfriends, did they—"

I wondered if she'd ever ask this. Probably because she has enough reason to. With some of her boyfriends it was something floating on the air, and she should have known that, and she should have been wondering all along.

"No. They didn't," I tell her, which is the truth. They did something else, though, which was to keep me and Tess confused about who was staying and for how long and whether or not they'd like us and how strict they'd be, but that's not what she's asking and so I don't bother. Besides, some things are too hard to explain.

She runs her finger across the scar that's down low on her neck and keeps her other arm folded underneath her breasts. "That's good. Because I wonder what's inside Tess, buried so deep." Her eyes go a little empty; they always do that whenever she's thinking something quiet, and I noticed that about her once, how her eyes are either empty or fierce and there's not much space in between.

"She just wanted to leave. That's all. That's all it is. She just didn't want this baby, and she didn't want to stay with us." I wish Kay would leave. I hate that feeling of being closed in, of a body pressing into your space when you don't want it there. It's hard to shuck somebody off, to say, Look, back off, please.

"Tess left me a note, you know. 'Don't come after me this time. I'm eighteen. I can leave if I want. Don't worry any, blah, blah, blah.' Jesus, you girls."

"I bet she comes back."

"I bet she doesn't."

"She said she was just getting out of here for a while."

"She's gone for good. And that's too bad, because a kid needs her mother. Needs a father and a mother, but at least her mother."

I can tell what's coming now. Something about her tone of voice has shifted again, and that means that one of her big, long, loopy rants is coming, and I put my head down on the edge of the tub, which is cool and hard, and I keep my hand on Amber and start to zone out.

"Only a mother can love a kid through all that hard work. Once it took every last ounce of goodness in me not to throw you out the window, Libby. You just kept screaming. You were the damndest colicky baby that ever lived. I was at a hotel. I even opened the window. I even stood there, looking at the sidewalk below. You'll want to do the same thing."

"Jesus, Kay. I will not." I say this to the white hardness of the tub.

"Yes you will. When it comes, just don't do it. Last night, Amber was crying forever and you were so tired and you thought, *Man, I hate this baby.* Didn't you? You thought, *Maybe I wouldn't hate this baby if it was mine but right now I goddamn hate this baby.* And you thought, *I'm going to kill this kid if she doesn't shut up.* I'm just saying the truth. That every mother in the world has thought it. They just won't say it. Just don't take the next step. Don't ever do it."

I bite my teeth together until my jaw hurts to keep the tears from coming, the stupid tears from I don't know what. Being tired, being yelled at, being so hot.

"This kid's going to make you tough," Kay says.

"You've told me," I whisper.

"You're a bit slower than most, that's for sure. But you still gotta learn that the world is a hell of a lot harder than what you could even imagine."

"You've told me."

"Getting older is basically a process of getting tougher, of dealing with new kinds of pain."

"You've told me." I sit there with my eyes closed, my hand underneath Amber's head. My back is killing me, staying in this position, but I don't bother moving.

"Kids will tear you down. Then, if you can, you build yourself back up again."

"Okay."

"It's not hell, Libby," she says. "And in fact it can be great. I'm just saying it's hard. You're going to break. I just don't wanna see it happen, I guess—see you break like that."

It's a moment of too much said, too much nice, Kay offering this last bit, and so to make up for it she starts up with one of her usual rants: two dumb daughters, one who won't leave, the other who won't stay around, and what sort of daughter runs off, just disappears in a truck with some guy, and how come I don't know nothing, she's my little sister for god's sake. Her voice gets louder and she's leaning closer to me. How come I didn't stop her? How come I don't have the courage and strength to do one goddamn thing right? She ought to call the police, because for all she knows Tess is flopped dead in a field somewhere, and it's sure as hell going to be my fault when Tess dies. And you know what else, this baby ought to be having breast milk, because it's the formula that's causing her to cry all night. And furthermore I got to realize my horsing around days are over and that I'm not going to know what hit me. Two dumb daughters. The two dumbest daughters a mother could ask for. One that won't stay around, the other who won't leave.

Tess used to say: Libby, would you *please* tell me what you do in your mind all day? You daydream like nobody I ever met. You live in your head more than you live in your life.

I'd say: Leave me alone, I'm thinking.

She'd say: About what? A different life?

And I'd say: No, a different me.

The last time we had that conversation, she said, Well, sister, it's Real Life that you need to focus on now.

She said:

One, Derek is going to leave you.

Two, You're going to have your heart broke. Not by Derek, but by this baby. You're taking this baby so you'll have something to love, something that will love you back. But you know what? It's not going to fill you up, it's not going to make your life complete.

Three, You're going to end up just like Kay. Pissed off that you wasted your time on this earth.

She said, When we were kids, you'd take me down the road, to get me away from Kay, and you'd play make-believe with me, and we'd pretend to be in other families, in other places. Kids do that because they're kids. But you never stopped pretending. This is our world. This is *it*.

She said, Libby, this baby isn't going to be like you imagine at all, if you've even bothered to try to imagine it real. I feel so sorry for you. But this was your idea, remember that. You got to start *thinking,* and you've got to let go of the idea that you're something special to somebody, because none of us are, and if you don't, if you don't stop dreaming about that, you're going to end up all snap-snap-*snapped* to pieces.

I light a cigarette and say, "All right all right all right already."

But it's not all right, and Amber keeps crying.

If I could get a word in edgewise, I'd say, Kid, night hours are longer than day hours, that's an actual fact, and one of the things I could teach you is about how certain truths—sixty-minutes-in-an-hour and all that—just are not the *truest* truth.

But she's hollering so I don't even try, I just pace around outside with her cradled in the crook of my arm.

It seems like a few days ago that Kay was yelling at me in the bathroom, but it was just earlier tonight. This night just keeps expanding, and there's nothing to stop it, and it's three o'clock in the morning and it's going to be forever until the sun comes up.

Crickets are chirping and there's some animal rustling near the burn barrel—a raccoon I think, because I heard it doing that purr-chatter thing that they do—and the occasional car roars down the highway. But I can only hear these things when Amber pauses for a breath, which she doesn't do all that often.

"Blah, blah, blah," I say to her. "Be quiet. Go to sleep. Please. Because I'm going to drop dead in about a minute."

She cries some more, a high-pitched wail that bursts against my eardrums.

"Look, it's a good thing Derek didn't come by, because this ain't how you should be acting when he does. Would you like him as a father? He doesn't want to be, though. And I don't think I want him to be either, although sometimes I wonder if he'd be better than nobody. And that makes me feel like a real shit."

I throw my cigarette down and twist it in the earth with my toe and then cart Amber inside to the fridge for a beer, and then back outside. When I'm not drinking it, I balance the bottle on her tummy. When she quiets down for a bit, I take my turn in the conversation. "Your crying is really damn irritating, that's the truth," I tell her. "Listen to this. Once I honked the car's horn at a deer that was crossing the road and the horn got stuck—this was in an old car of mine. It just kept on honking, and I had to drive thirty miles with that noise, one big long honk, till I got to Derek's place, and he climbed under the car and cut the wires that lead to the horn, and, kid, you are worse than that. But probably you're crying because you feel like shit, so I'm sorry. And no matter what, I won't throw you out a window. Kay's right about some things, and I guess I'm glad she just says them. I do hate you sometimes."

She looks at me like she's listening, for once, so I take my chance and start talking fast before she decides to change her mind. "Derek and me, we stay together because there isn't anybody else coming our way. I keep trying to figure out how to love him, but I just can't. Derek is good. He's nice. He's a regular good-guy, and I don't know why, but I just don't love him." I lower my voice and say another thing I'm not sure about, but I want to hear out loud. "I'm not sure I love you, either. Not yet." She's spitting up white goo now, and I wipe it from her face with the corner of the blanket. "Maybe I didn't mean that. Sorry. I'm sorry! Listen, one thing I'll do for sure is get you braces if you need them. That way, you won't be ugly like me. You'll have improved chances. Too fucking much depends on how you look, kid, although maybe by the time you're grown humans will have grown up about this, although I doubt it. Kid, you seem to actually be listening. Good. Listen up. I've got things to tell you. I try to imagine you older, a blond-haired girl with braids and blue overalls, but I can't picture what your face looks like, or what it feels like to hold your hand, or where we're living and how things are going for us. It's hard for me to picture. What do you think about that? I think that's a bad sign."

She's quiet and looks like she's listening, so I drink beer and tell her any dang thing I can think of. How Tess was always my best friend, except for Shawny. How I never stopped to consider how much I loved them, because I just did. How I was counting on that to be true with her too, but so far nothing has cleared up. That I'm afraid of the dark, there's not so many mosquitoes this year, and that those bright things she's staring at are called stars. How I'm not really fond of the president of the United States, because he seems to have less going for him than even me. How my father's been gone since I was three and I have no idea where he is. How my parents used to be Baxter's ranch hands, but then my father left and Kay stayed on. How I spent my whole life wanting out of this brown house in the middle of an alfalfa field and never once did I figure that I'd be raising a kid in the exact same place. How probably I should call social services because she's not mine legally right now, and that's something I should take care of. And I would have, except that I didn't know Tess was leaving. But that maybe I won't bother because there's too much paperwork and anyway, according to Kay, all social services wants to do really is follow you around and figure out how to take your baby. How probably I should meet some other moms so that I don't feel so alone. How I haven't told anybody how much I'm missing Tess—so much that my heart feels tired from the ache.

Then I loop back to Derek, because I figure I gotta work this one out somehow. I tell her how we've been dating for two years now, and how sometimes he gets out of a nice sleep, drives here, and then gets back up and goes home again, and how he must think what we do is worth all that effort, which I appreciate. I for one wish he would just stay the night, because what could Kay say, given her own track record? But Derek has some weird sort of pride, and he doesn't want "to be beholden to Kay," meaning, he doesn't want to spend the night in the house of someone who doesn't like him.

I tell Amber that Derek has never given me flowers or taken me to a show in Denver, and sometimes he's yelled at me for no good reason and once he said, "Lib, I'm not going to tell you you're beautiful, because you're just not," and when he said that a sudden shock of hurt went blasting through my heart. But one thing he's done is to come through my window and stay with me. I don't care if it's just the sex he wants, which is what he jokes around and says, because it fills me up too. Sex is something to learn about later.

49

Although not as much later as she might think. Because I was only four or five when I first understood something about sex—climbing up a swing-set pole and this feeling shooting like sparks between my legs, and I hung on till my arms went numb to keep this new, wonderful feeling there. I thought it was just me until Shawny told me that she felt the same thing if she pressed herself against the top of the footboard to her bed, and I've always wondered at that, how kids know about the things a body can do, and the things a body can want, the things a body can desire like crazy.

A car's parked out on the highway, between me and Miguel's place, headlights out. I've been watching it the whole time. That's the truth, of course, that while you're doing one thing you're busy noticing another.

I'm guessing: people making out, out of gas, need to rest, lost. What are the reasons somebody stops a car in the middle of the night? I can't see the car all the time, not through all that dark. Only when another car passes on the highway—mostly it's semi-trucks this time of night—I can see a quick glimpse of taillights, the glimmer of glass windows. It's parked facing away from me, like it's heading into town.

Sometimes when I'm at the store, to pass the time I freeze the world in my eyes. And I just try to notice things, like, Martha's got oranges in her cart, she's got a band-aid on her pinkie finger, one of her socks has been turned pink in the wash, three jugs of milk are gone, one carton of eggs, Frank's hair looks softer than usual, Barry is writing his check with his left hand, the plant hanging above Arlene has six dead leaves. I watch the way Arlene's face flickers with something sad, how Frank is pretend-jolly, how Martha does in fact seem happy, like she's filled up with a secret joy.

Then usually I start feeling sorry for myself. I can't help it. I think, *Nobody sees me the way I see them. Nobody even cares to see me.* Then I talk myself out of it. I say, *Well, that's okay, you see you, and that's all you have anyway.* And then I think, *Yeah, but I'm not enough. I'm lonely.* And then I think, *Ah, shut the fuck up. That's the way the real world works, welcome to it. And every other person on the planet is feeling sorry for herself for the same damn reason.* Then I replace three milk jugs and one carton of eggs.

I think I started noticing stuff like that after I killed the four baby ducks. Kay had given them to me—the softest-yellow, cutest things—and I fed them bits of bread and dipped their beaks into water to help them drink. I kept them in a cardboard box at night and took them out to the lawn to wobble around in the day. After about a week, I put them in the stock tank for a swim. Then I went inside for some reason, and I got busy, and I forgot about those ducks. When I came back, their bodies were floating. They'd been too little to jump out, and they'd gotten tired of swimming.

It makes me sick to think about it.

I'm so sorry about those ducks, so sorry that they suffered. They were probably peeping that whole time, hoping somebody'd come and help them. Peeping and peeping, getting scared and more scared. Tired and more tired. Jesus. I can't think about it for long. I want to hold them again and say, I'm sorry. Oh man, am I sorry.

I don't know what to do with all the pain in the world. There's just so much bad, it freezes me up when I think about it. Right now I'd like to scream, Amber-shut-the-hell-up! But the only thing I got going for me is that I never want to add to the meanness that's already out there. And I want to make sure I *see* things.

So I hug this baby to my heart and I watch the car, how the red lights blink, how it swerves back onto the highway. I lean against the doorway and stare into the night and drink my beer and hold her and tell us both that this time I'll be listening, and watching, and I won't forget to pay attention.

Shawny had a gun, from a cousin who had a whole slew of them. The cousin traded the gun for a kiss. The deal was he got to kiss her for as long as he wanted, which turned out to be a pretty long time, but she got the gun.

It was an old, scratched-up Colt .38, a quiet soft blue, and it was the color that made the kiss worth it, she said.

We were alone the night she showed it to me. Kay was at the bar, Tess was with a boyfriend, and me and Shawny had been home drinking seven-and-sevens all night. Shawny was crying off and on, since the night before her boyfriend had dumped her. We'd all been to a bonfire party, and this boyfriend was sitting in the bed of a pickup with another girl on his lap. He'd kiss the other girl and look at Shawny and smirk at her, and she'd look back. She'd just lost her virginity to him the month before and it was killing her to stand there and watch, but she did, and that's the thing about Shawny, she was strong and sure enough to stare right at hurt and not look away.

When I came into my room with new seven-and-sevens for us both, Shawny was sitting cross-legged on my bed, holding a gun in her lap.

"Whoa, shit, Shawny," I said. "Shit."

"I like to hold it," she said.

"Shawny, what the hell?"

She waved her arm at me, pushing my words away. "The safety's on. Calm down. Do you know where you should point the gun if you're serious about killing yourself?" She pointed the gun to her temple and held it there, smiling at me.

"Shawny, put it down."

"Everyone thinks it's here, but no, it's not," she said. "Usually it gets you, but sometimes there's just brain damage and you can live."

"Please Shawny, please. Put it down. I'm not joking. We're drunk."

She put it in her mouth, and around the barrel of the gun her words were garbled. "Not here either," she said. "Same problem." Her eyes were lit up with a kind of smile, and her teeth clacked softly against the metal. "Do you want to know?"

"No, I don't. I don't, Shawny."

"Here," she said, tilting her head up, so that she could aim the barrel at the roof of her mouth. "So it goes right up into your brain. For sure, you'll die this way." She put up her hand to stop me from coming closer.

"It's not funny, Shawny. Put it down!"

"If you come any closer, I'll flip the safety and pull the trigger."

"Shawny, it's not funny."

"Then you'll have a big mess to clean up." She took the gun out of her mouth and pointed it back at her temple, and tilted her head toward it, and smiled. "The least people can do is kill themselves outside." She smiled and looked at me with the saddest sort of eyes. "Suicide is like falling in love. Did you know that?"

"You want a drink? Because here's your drink."

"When you try to explain why you're in love with someone, you give a big long list of everything you like. He's cute, he's got green on the inside of his brown eyes, he makes me laugh. Whatever. But everyone knows you also mean this mysterious, extra element. *That's* the thing that makes it love. With suicide, you could also give a big long list of reasons: My parents are fucking assholes, the world is a piece of shit, my boyfriend was just sitting in the back of a truck with another girl. But if you understand killing yourself, you know it's the mysterious element beyond. It's the extra thing that matters. That other stuff doesn't really matter at all. I'm not sure people realize that."

"Shawny, maybe I should call someone."

"Don't come closer to me. If you know about this extra thing, then you can do it. Kill yourself. Just like if you know about the extra element in love, you know you're in love. You either know about it or you don't." She shrugged. "I know about it."

"Shawny, we're young. And you know, everyone says we're so hormonal and emotional and—"

She smiled one of her sad smiles and her eyes were watery and blue and looking into nowhere. "Don't do that to me, Libby. That's a lame-ass thing to say."

"I'm not trying to be lame."

"Well, don't make this less than it is."

For a while I watched her. Then I said, "I just want to sit next to you. Can I sit next to you?"

She made room for me, and at first I sat on the edge of the bed next to her, but then I put the drinks down on the floor and leaned over and rested my head in her lap. It was the strangest thing. All of a sudden I didn't care what happened. I was too hazy and calm to care—too drunk, too tired.

She stroked my hair with her free hand, and every once in a while touched her finger to my temple, the same place on her own body that still had a gun pressed against it.

"Bet your arm is getting tired." I was trying to make a joke of it, to make her smile.

"That's the thing," she whispered. "I hold it up until my arm is shaking, till I can't—I really can't—hold it up more. Or until the roof of my mouth gets raw." I didn't move my head, but I could tell she was crying. "That's messed up, isn't it?"

When I didn't answer, she grabbed my hair, hard, and yanked it back toward her stomach. "It's messed up, isn't it? Isn't it?!"

"Hey! Shawny!"

She pushed my head back where it had been and held me down. "Never mind, you don't have to say it. I know it is." Her voice was calm again, back to a whisper. "Here, I'm going to do something. Don't move. Just feel."

There were tears sliding out my eyes from how much my head hurt, a circle of pain where she'd pulled my hair, but I bit my lip and closed my eyes and concentrated. The gun wasn't cold or warm, which made it feel like nothing. It felt like it was already part of my skin except for a hardness, a force against my head. But I knew she didn't mean the feel of the gun. She meant how it felt to be her, or someone like her, who was that ready. That sure.

I breathed out. "Life is so, you know, unexpected. And things can change. And they can change in big, good ways. Shawny, please don't— "

"I'm not going to pull the trigger. On you."

"That's not what I meant."

"There's a perfect space for it on your skull, isn't there? It's like a gun belongs there."

"Shawny, if you're not around, you'll never know about the big, sudden turns."

She said, "I'm counting on that." Then she put the gun to my lips, but I kept them tight against the barrel and wouldn't let it inside my mouth. Then she put the gun to the side, and I turned my head so I could stare at it, and we were both looking at it, and she said, "That's what I'm counting on. I'll wait as long as I can."

FOUR

A person shouldn't raise a kid in a place like this, I know that.

I walk around with Amber in one hand and try to clean up the place with the other. Pick up Kay's coffee cups, stack the mail, wipe the counters. It doesn't help much; it'd be so much easier to start someplace new. In an apartment in town, mice wouldn't leave black shit everywhere, spiders wouldn't fill the corners with webs, the freezer would actually freeze things, the cat litter box wouldn't be stinking. The carpet in the living room wouldn't smell like pee, the wallpaper wouldn't be peeling, the countertops wouldn't be all stained.

I'm not awake yet, so I'm feeling pissy. Amber got me up too early. It's not her fault but it's still too damn early. Fuck you, I say to everything: the pea-green carpet, the brown couch, the sticky kitchen table with its white top and made-in-the-seventies gold zodiac signs. Fuck you to the pile of laundry that's not clean anymore because the cat's been sleeping in it, and to the cat's full litter box, and to Tess's cat.

My dream house is a two-story thing, with wood floors, peach-and-gray furniture, cream-colored walls, a big grassy lawn, a white picket fence, flowers all over the place. Not too big, actually. Not too fancy. But tidy and clean and pretty.

It's like there's too much to do so I can't start, which means there's nothing to do and so I'm bored. I walk into my room and slide onto the bed and put Amber on my tummy. It's nice here. I painted the walls a light peach and put down a gray carpet remnant, which I got new and which covers most of the green stuff, and I keep the spiders knocked down and everything has a place.

When we were kids, Tess and I were always fighting about sharing a room, mostly because Tess was a slob. One night Kay'd had enough and she nailed up some boards and a big hunk of plywood, and then most of the room was separated. My half of the plywood got painted peach. Tess left hers alone, even though it had a spray-painted fluorescent orange streak across it.

Amber's stuff has all been in my half of the room, but now that Tess is gone I guess I could move everything over. I could paint her side pink or something, to match the flowers on the bassinet, which is real cute, lacy and all. But I don't have any paint, and no energy to go get paint, and I'll get around to it but not today. And so why even start cleaning the place out? I can't even move her stuff over because the white dresser with a changing table on top is too heavy, and since I can't move it till Kay helps I might as well not do anything.

Once Derek asked me to move in with him. We were lying in his bed after sex and I was looking across the bedroom into the rest of his cruddy trailer, at his piles of laundry and empty beer cans stacked into a pyramid on the coffee table. What I thought was, *No way*. What I said was, "Derek, you don't want me and all my junk in here cluttering up your life," and he said, "Yes, I do," and I said, "Naw, you don't." What I'm thinking now is, *Maybe that was my chance*.

Because how can it be worse than this? I can't believe that I pay for this—pay Kay two hundred a month for rent. I gotta get my finances together. There's rent, car payment, car insurance, gas, half the groceries, and now diapers and formula. And I'd like to get the long distance back on the phone now that I have someone to call if I ever hear from Tess, but Kay turned off the long-distance service a long time ago to save money and I can't even call out of here, which is ridiculous. Maybe I should get a cell phone, but my paycheck comes in at about two hundred a week after taxes, so it's supposed to be one paycheck covers the car, one covers food, one covers rent, and I'm supposed to live on the rest and save to get out of this place and so there's no way I'm going to get a cell phone. Shit.

I wish there was something to do. Derek's at work. In high school, I would have called Shawny, but Shawny is dead. And of course there was always Tess. By now, I'd have gone and pounced on her bed and we'd get ready to go lie in the sun, or drive in to Lamar, or at least watch a movie.

I close my eyes and send her a thought, a message. *Ohmygod Tess, I miss you. What if you're not safe and please come back. Tess, call me. Tess, your baby!*

Time just goes on and on. When Amber bursts into her series of waaaa, waaaaa, waaaaaas, I take her on a drive. First to Lamar, and I drive down by the park to see if any moms or kids are out, but there's just a bunch of teenagers hanging around in their falling-down pants, acting stupid because there's nothing better to do. I drive on to Derek's place, which is on the other side of Lamar, even though I know he's not there. In the screen door of his trailer, I leave a note:

> D on't you think
> E verything could be
> R eally a grand adventure?
> E asy to say and hard to do, but here's a bunch of
> K isses for you

Derek doesn't have a good name for that sort of thing. And he doesn't even like it; he thinks name poems are something little girls do. Which is true—I've been doing them since the second grade. But I argue that all this has made me smarter, because for one thing his name has taught me a bunch of "K" words. There's not many of them and I was having trouble right off the bat, so I hauled out the dictionary and learned things like *kisan*, which means peasant, and *kith*, which means friends, or somebody who feels like kindred. Which got me to thinking, as I told him, who are my kith? Maybe kisans, or knights, or knaves, and questions like that maybe are my koan, which, as I explained to Derek, is a question that you think on for a long time.

My koan is this: Do I love him or not?

I make myself a list to try to figure things out.

One, Love is when you miss a person when you're not with them and you're happy when you are.

Two, Love is when he's in your daydreams.

Three, Love is when you want to protect him.

Four, Love is when you pay attention.

Five, Love is that extra, mysterious thing.

I look at Derek's trailer. I look at Amber. I chew on my fingernail and look off at the sky. I don't know. I don't want to be alone. But I also don't want to pretend that Number Five is there when it's just not.

HAVING GOOD TIMES IN DURANGO, the postcard says. There's a picture of the other part of Colorado, the part with snow-topped mountains and trees, and Tess has drawn herself in, a little stick figure sitting on the top of a mountain.

Her tiny handwriting fills the other side:

Hey, I got a job first thing—clean hotel rooms and
waitress—free room and min wage. Come visit! I'll pull
a cot into my room and show you town. My boobs hurt
like hell but the meds help. I can drink all the beer I
want again! It feels so gooooood to be away, to be free.
P.S. How's your little baby?
P.P.S. I'm sorry. And I know that being sorry is
never going to be enough.

There's something else inside the post office box, too. A letter addressed to me from Simon Frazier.

Need to talk to Tess. It's important. Have her call me.

That's all it says, in scratchy guy-handwriting that tilts backward on a torn-out piece of lined notebook paper.

I stick both letters in Amber's car seat and I think, Man, kid,
you just *happened*, one moment of sex and look at all the
things going on because of you: Tess writing me, and Simon
writing Tess, and on and on. The health teacher was always
telling us that more kids are born to single moms in rural areas
than in inner cities, contrary to popular belief, and that a third
of the girls in the room would be pregnant before we graduated, and that she wanted more than anything to keep that
from happening, because it was easier to prevent a baby than
raise one, but that it was going to happen anyway because it
was easier than we thought to make a mistake, and she was
right, it did happen.

And furthermore, one little baby happening was probably
what killed Shawny, because it's all related in this weird way
that confuses me. Shawny left school and moved to California
with Miguel, and about a year after the baby was born she
went outside, into their back yard, and took a gun to her

mouth, to the inside of her mouth, and pulled the trigger. Postpartum depression, her mother told me. Stress, her father told me. And I thought, No: she was waiting for something to change. And something did. And it wasn't enough to compensate for Number 5, that extra element. And then Shawny could know for sure that even a big change wasn't enough. Not even a baby could fill that empty space, and so in a way, the baby did kill her.

And it's all related even more, because I was missing Shawny like crazy when Tess told me she was pregnant, and Miguel had just moved back to Colorado with his son, and of all places he moved back into Shawny's house—the one she'd grown up in—because it was empty and available and cheap. And I had to drive by that place all the time on the way into work, and I had to watch while kid things appeared on the lawn, and I had to keep hoping that someday I would drive by and, huh, Shawny would suddenly be there too, and then I'd realize, Nope, she's not ever going to be there. And then Tess told me she was pregnant. And that she wanted an abortion. So maybe Amber is alive because Shawny killed herself because of Juan and my sister left because Shawny killed herself and now Tess is writing me a postcard from a mountain town because of all of these things.

None of this makes any sense, but all these elements are connected in my mind, and if I hold it in my brain I see a web of connections, and electricity seems to be zapping from one to another, binding them together.

On the drive home I go the back way so that I can cry hard and not get in a wreck, and there's Ed's place and his tire house and his bees, and there's the pig farmer who has the pigs I always hear when they're slamming the metal covers of their feeders, and there's the gully where old-timers used to dump their trash and where Shawny and I used to go look for treasures, like old blue bottles or old forks or ceramic jars and evidence from other lives, and I bet those gone-for-good people had their own troubles and I know I'm not the only one but still it really hurts, it really does hurt to have your sister send you a postcard about her new life that doesn't include you.

It's not fair that Tess didn't tell me, in that real, honest way, that she was leaving. She knew that it wasn't fair too, which is why she didn't say a word until she handed me Amber, climbed into Clark's truck, and yelled "Goodbye, Libby, goodbye." Waved and smiled, and surprised me with that look of hers, the one that meant she was leaving, heading straight out, and that whether or not I chose to believe it, it was her final goodbye.

Miguel is sitting outside my house, leaning against the screen, and Juan is standing next to him, throwing rocks at my marigolds. Juan looks like his father—thick black hair that stands up a little, a round face, dark eyes that look like they've seen too much.

"Thought we'd come on by to see this *nuevo bebé*," Miguel says when I get out of the car. Lucky for me that even when I've been crying there's not much evidence and no one can ever tell.

"Lib-eeeeee," says Juan. He hugs my legs and then backs up so he can throw a rock at my knee.

"Ouch! Cut it out, Juan. I was just going to make you some cookies."

"With moons?"

"With moons. Do you want to see my baby? She's asleep." I kneel down and turn the car seat so they can see Amber's face. The wind is blowing, as usual, so I have to turn it so dust doesn't blow right in her face.

Juan considers her for a minute. "I'm not a baby. A baby is zero years old. I'm two." He holds up three fingers. Then

62

he bends down to pick up a rock, so I hold up my hand to stop him.

"Throw 'em at the flowers," I say. "The flowers can get knocked to pieces for all I care."

"She's cute," Miguel says. "*Qué linda.*"

"She's ugly."

Miguel shrugs a little. "Okay. Most babies are. But beautiful too, because you can imagine the possibilities."

"That's a nice way to think of it."

For a while, we watch Juan throw rocks at the flowers and we talk kid stuff: Juan's potty training, Amber's yellow shit, the time Juan threw up in his baptismal water, Amber being up all night.

Then Miguel says, "There was a car last night, parked between your house and mine."

"Yeah, I know! You saw it?"

"It was closer to your house. He let out a dog."

"Who let out a dog?"

"It was a VW bus."

"Ed Mongers doesn't have a dog. At least, I don't think so. I never saw one."

"Doubt it was Ed. Other people drive those things too, you know."

"Someone left off a dog?"

"I was out anyway, with a flashlight, checking my—"

"—marijuana?"

That causes him to pause. "You know about that?"

"Yeah."

"Okay, anyway, I was watching this car, and then a guy gets out, dumps a dog, and drives off."

"Where's the dog?"

"At my house. She's a mutt. Pretty ugly, actually. She ate a bunch of grass, and then walked inside my house, onto the carpet, and threw it all up."

"Are you going to keep her?"

"No."

"*I* want a dog. To protect me. Is she nice?"

"I don't know. You want me to bring her over? If she's no good, I'll take her back."

"And leave her by the side of the road?"

Miguel shrugs. "I'll take care of it."

"Why would a guy drop off a dog? People are mean."

"And stupid."

"Mean and stupid," I agree. "They allow pets at the new apartment complex in town. I just called them. Actually, I couldn't find the number, so I had to call Marsha."

"Marsha the sheriff's wife?"

"No worries." I wink at him. "I don't know her all that well. But I asked her who to call about renting one of the apartments where she's living now. She gives me her landlord's number and says, 'You want to hear something funny? This housing development is called the Preserve. And isn't that funny? They take a farmer's field, build it up and call it the Preserve. Actually, it's the Preserve at the Meadows. She said it made her embarrassed to live there."

"It would me too."

"*I* want to live there."

"So, you moving?"

I shrug. "I had some money saved, but then my car broke down last winter and needed a new engine, and I bought Derek a pair of ropers for his birthday, and pictures of Amber, and now it's all gone. I hate myself. I really do. I got to get out of here. I do."

He's listening, at least, so I go on. "I wish I knew where my dad was. I'd say, 'Look here, you bastard, you owe me about a million bucks for all the child support and birthday presents you never sent, so pay up and help me out for once.' Amber's awake. Look, Juan, the baby's awake."

Juan wanders over and takes a look. "Let's throw her in the trash can."

"Juan!"

The boy covers his mouth and giggles. "Let's give the baby a cookie."

We all stare at Amber, and she stares back at us, and then out from her mouth gurgles white spit.

"Ick," says Juan. "That baby needs to go in the trash."

"The landlord said rent's four hundred a month, plus utilities."

Miguel leans over to catch up Juan in his arms. He pulls him back into his lap and tickles him, and Juan throws his head back and laughs and squiggles free.

"I have half my last paycheck and forty bucks Baxter gave me for helping out with the cows. So, what's that? One more paycheck to cover rent. Plus the deposit. And phone. And hookups."

"And then my only neighbor will be gone," Miguel says. "I wouldn't blame you, though. I'll be moving in one of these days too. But don't forget about the diapers, the formula. More expensive than you think. The father isn't helping?"

"No. And you will have a neighbor. You'll have Kay. You can have her."

Miguel laughs. "*Ay, mi amiga.* Your mother is okay."

"If I move, though, I'll have to find a babysitter in town. Driving twenty minutes here to drop her off with Kay and then twenty minutes back into town—forty minutes twice a day—that won't work. If Tess comes back, we could move to town together."

"What's Derek say?"

I shrug. "Derek doesn't say anything because he's in the middle of his seven days on. At the rig. I haven't seen him."

He nods. "They got him still as a worm?"

"I hope they promote him to driller."

"But the pay's good."

"Yeah, twelve."

"Hard to leave twelve."

"Worms are good," says Juan. "Butterflies are good. Crickets are good. Ants are good. But red ants are bad. Wasps are bad. Some spiders are good. Some spiders are bad."

"He's figuring out what's safe in this world." Miguel says over Juan's list. "What hurts, what doesn't."

I laugh because ain't that something we'd all like to figure out? Then I show him Tess's postcard. Miguel reads the last line out loud and then looks up at me and waits for me to say something.

"I don't need Tess anyway."

Miguel tilts his head at me, because he knows I'm lying, and then he rubs his hand over his face and then holds his palms in front of him and speaks to them. "Libby, what do you do— How do you survive it when—when you realize you *do* need somebody and they're just not there?"

I have to stay silent to that one, because answering will make me cry all over again. Because I've been wondering myself. At first I thought that maybe it was best to fill that space with someone else. Like maybe instead of Tess, I'd find someone new. But then I figured out how you can't really do that. It's not the same. And you just go on hurting.

"Miguel, do you ever hope that other people are pissed off or sad too, because then you're not the only one? Or do you ever yell at imaginary people? Like: 'Fuck off, I know my mom used welfare and WIC, and I'll probably do the same, and I'll probably never have my act together, but look at me! What am I supposed to do? I know our house looks like shit, and probably I won't go to college after all, and I'll never be a nurse or an artist or anything else, but I don't know how to make it differ-

66

ent. And I'm sorry about that, but either teach me the rules of this game or fuck off.'" I say all this to the sky and then look at him. "Do you ever do something like that?"

Miguel's been staring at his palms this whole time. "That sounds a little familiar, I guess. I didn't know you wanted to be a nurse."

"I don't. But it's a job. I *want* to be an artist. I draw pretty good, you know. But nobody pays for art. Do you think there's something wrong with me? Because sometimes I dream that the world gets screwed up somehow, a bomb or disease or war. A 9/11, but bigger. I want that to happen. No I don't. But yes I do. Because if everything gets crazy, if everybody's life gets messed up, then I could find a way in, somehow. Then I'd have a chance. I don't really want that. But it's like, if something big doesn't happen, I don't see a change. And I want there to be a change." I can hear my voice getting a little wobbly, so I bite my lip and tell myself to shut the hell up.

"You want there to be a level playing field," he says.

"Exactly. That's a good phrase."

"My family—my cousins, for example, in Mexico—they say the same thing, sometimes. They say, those *bolillos*, those *gringos*, they start someplace easier. It makes it hard for them to like you. They want the playing field leveled too."

"I don't blame them."

"Some people'll never know about this. Because they had enough from the get-go."

"I guess it's not their fault. But still, I hate them."

"Doesn't matter whose fault. It just means that some people are never going to understand some things. What it's like, *por ejemplo*, to cross rivers and deserts and suffocate in the back of semi-trucks to get to a place to work your ass off. What white person will walk for days in a desert just to get a lousy-ass job? In Mexico they call it *la lucha*—the fight. The fight for work. That's what *I* see, is how hard *la lucha* is, and how the crossing can scare a man, and how he goes on in the face of that fear, and how he trusts, and how he hopes. What you *gringos* see is people taking your jobs, taking over your language, using up your space—"

"That's not what I see."

"I know. But them, out there. Big bomb, yeah. Because then they'd be brought down a notch, closer to us."

"Cat, *gato*, cat, *gato*," says Juan, chasing after Tess's cat, who bolts under my car and hides. Juan gets down on his knees to throw more rocks and one pings off something under my car.

"*Ya, hijo, déjalo en paz.* Don't throw rocks at the cat." Then to me he says, "Funny, how you've got to teach a thing like *be gentle* or *be kind*. They don't come naturally."

"You want that cat? You can have it."

Miguel says, "I was cheating on her. Shawny."

"I know," I say softly. "She wrote me."

He nods, slowly. I can see he's surprised. We've talked about Shawny a little in the year since he moved back, but we never talked about this. He says, "She was being so mean to me, you know. She wasn't happy there and I was sick of her complaining. Will you tell me, what she said?"

"She wrote, 'I think Miguel's cheating on me, the son of a bitch.'"

He laughs softly. "That sounds like her. She was always calling me a son of a bitch. I wouldn't have done it if I'd known, it's not like I ever thought, huh, I better not cheat or she'll kill herself."

"That's not why she killed herself."

He looks away from me and shrugs. "You don't know that." He clears his throat. "You said before, about the pot—"

"Kay saw it. She was riding over there, fixing the fence. Don't worry. She doesn't care. She said it looks very green and very healthy. She also said you were an idiot, but that's okay, because

68

she calls everyone an idiot. It's her favorite word. But you're less of an idiot than the law, she said. It's all relative, she said."

"You sure about that? She won't say anything?"

"That's one good thing about Kay. She doesn't really believe in the world's set of rules. She thinks everyone ought to come up with their own."

"Oh, look," says Juan. "A roly-poly that's snailing around." He picks it up and stares at the ball in his hand and then throws it at Amber, who's sleeping again. It misses her and goes flying by my shoulder into the grass.

"*Ya, hijo, por favor!*" Miguel puts his head in hands.

"Don't hurt bugs," I say. "Please." I turn to Miguel. "Kay said, 'As long as he's not smoking it around the kid, I could care less.'"

"I don't smoke around Juan."

"Well, then. But be careful. Ann Gayton—remember her from school?—she got arrested last month."

"I know."

"That's smart, that you're growing it down by the ditch. Shawny and I used to play there, in the ditch banks."

"I know, she told me."

"Kay said you put it between the water and the Johnson grass, which will hide it, and makes it look wild. She said you're sure as hell going to get all scratched up, though, by the edges on that grass."

"I do."

"Kay's the only one who'll see it, though."

Miguel nods. "I'd work two jobs if I could. But I can't, not with a kid. That's why the pot. I need the extra money. I've got some family coming in this summer."

"And what, you need the money for them?"

He shrugs.

"What, cousins? Illegals?"

He nods to both questions. "From Oaxaca. They'll be staying with me for a while. If *la migra* don't get them at the border."

"I don't know anything about that stuff. Except that Baxter hires them. I mean, I guess I know they're here. I just never thought about how they *get* here."

"It's bullshit, that's what to know. The INS could care less about them once they're here since there's work to be done by somebody and, no offense, but you *gringos* sure aren't going to do it, and you sure don't want to pay more for your food, which is what you'd have to do if you were paying enough to make it worth it. *La migra's* just a show. That's the one thing to know."

"What's I-N-S?" says Juan.

"Letters of the alphabet," says Miguel. He makes a face at me like, Ain't it sad what this kid's going to have to grow up and learn about?

"How many relatives?"

"Fifteen or so."

"Fifteen? All crowded in at your trailer?"

That makes Miguel laugh. "You don't know what crowded is. Fifteen is fine." Then he adds, "You just can't know some things, not ever, not even if you try."

"I hate the world for not knowing. About my life. So I bet *they* hate *me*, for not knowing about *their* lives."

"I think so. I think that's the way it works."

I bite my lip and look at him. Miguel was never meant to live alone, that's what Kay said. When he moved back to Colorado, after Shawny died, it surprised us all that he moved back into the place where Shawny grew up. He didn't move in with his mother, in Lamar, which was strange. Kay figured it was because he had some real pain to get through. Maybe he also moved out here, I'm realizing now, because it's easier to grow pot in the middle of nowhere. But it could also be that Miguel likes to be alone; because it seems to me he's got a quiet sadness about him that needs some space and time by itself. So I ask him, "Will that be nice? To have family here? Because, does it get lonely for you?"

He doesn't say anything to this, but I see his head nod a little. He says, "Libby, you're one of those people I can trust." I don't know what he's talking about exactly. His pot, maybe. Or his relatives. But it isn't until after he's gone that I realized he maybe meant being lonely. Because that seems like one of the biggest secrets of all to keep from the world.

We were just kids, flying kites on a day with a good breeze. Tess and I were out in the alfalfa field and we were so little and so it was amazing that we got them up in the first place, and that we kept them up, and it was making us laugh because it was new, and hard, and we'd done it. We didn't intend to get off the road and go out into the alfalfa, that's just where the breeze and kites took us.

Our kites were the regular triangle cheap kind, pink, and they were bouncing through the air, and I was so busy watching mine, which is why, maybe, I didn't hear Kay drive in or hear her walk up to me. One hand grabbed my arm and the other slapped into my head and she put out her foot and pushed me forward so that I'd trip. My hands hit dirt and my face hit a plant and the air got knocked out of me all at once. My body went from being happy to being full of hurt, all in one instant. Kay was screaming about us trampling some of Baxter's good crop, stupid idiot girls, what the hell were we thinking? At the same time, she was pulling in the kite, which had fallen and was bouncing over the alfalfa plants now, and then she was breaking the sticks and wadding it all up into her palms. I was scrambling over to Tess before Kay could get there, and I led Tess out of the field and we tiptoed all the way, which was our way of saying *See how careful we're being?* and I disappeared us down the road for a good couple of hours.

We went home earlier than we normally would have, because there was a storm boiling up over the mountains and the clouds were green. *It's a hailstorm*, I thought, and sure enough it was, a huge one, so bad that Kay made us get in the center of the house, away from the windows, and covered us with a blanket. She stood outside the blanket with her arms wrapped around us and hugged us till it was over.

When the thudding noise stopped, we walked outside and the whole world looked different. The windows broken, paint chipped off the north side of the house, the garden crushed, all the green turned white. The hail had also knocked one of Baxter's peacocks out of the tree, a male that used to roost in one of the cottonwoods near our place. Kay was standing over the dead peacock, looking at his bright body covered with globes of white and his long tail feathers floating up in the breeze, and she was saying, "Look at this, will ya? Will ya look at this?"

It was beautiful and crazy-looking, but I was more interested in looking at the alfalfa, at all the bent and broken stems jabbing out from the ice, at the whole field that had been knocked flat. I was wrapping my arms around myself for warmth and I was thinking, *Man, a few footsteps were nothing at all compared to the way the world can come crashing down.*

Here is something I know: some people pay attention to the world in a different way. An alert way. Because they know about danger. It depends on where they started, on how much their world got crashed up in the first place.

I wish I would've told Miguel before he left: Pay attention. *Ten cuidado.* Be careful. Because pot and illegal relatives—it just seems dangerous, like how you get too caught up in a pink triangle in the sky and so you don't see the danger coming up from behind.

F I V E

The cops' "well-being check," as they call it, came today, although Kay said, "Well-being my ass. She might be alive, but did they ask her how her heart feels?"

It was the Durango police that tracked Tess down after Kay called them, which was after I showed her the postcard. Tess confirmed that she was eighteen and there of her own free will. That she was employed and housed and fine. That she didn't have a phone number, that she didn't want to be contacted, and that she had that right. So the police called back to say the "well-being check went well."

"Kay's got a point," I tell Derek. "I bet they didn't ask Tess, 'So, you never cry yourself to sleep at night? You never miss your baby and your sister? You're really well?'"

Derek stands there, watching me water the garden—a ring of water around the small tomato plants, a ring around the cucumbers. The water's coming out in sudsy spurts because Kay hooked a hose up to the washing machine pipe, which runs outside, and told me anytime I run a load of laundry I need to water the garden at the same time to do my part in what she calls drought mitigation. According to her, we all got to figure out how to live better and to realize we live in a desert.

Finally Derek says to me, "You're a lot angrier at Tess than you think you are."

"I'm not angry at Tess."

"Yes you are."

"I'm not."

"Well, you are. I don't know why you need that pointed out to you."

"I'm not angry, I'm sad. I can tell the difference. I just can't believe she's gone, that she has a job, that she's staying away." Since he doesn't say anything, I add, "Then Kay wanted me to call Tess at work, because we got the name of the restaurant. I said, 'No, you call.' And Kay says, 'No, you do it.' It was like we were both kids. Ridiculous."

"You won't call her because you're mad at her."

"We don't have long distance."

"You could come use my phone."

"I don't want to."

"Exactly." He cocks his head at me and says, "Do *you* cry yourself to sleep at night?"

I don't answer that, which is my answer. As if I'm going to say that sort of thing out loud.

He says, "We haven't seen each other much lately."

I say, "I'm waiting for you to leave me."

I feel his body sway back. He blinks at me for a minute and then sighs. "So you gonna keep Miguel's dog or what?"

Ringo, which is what I've decided to name her, is standing next to me, eating grass. She's some sort of wacky-looking mutt, mostly Australian Shepherd, black and white and brown, and her main activity is eating grass and throwing it up.

"Yeah, I'm going to keep her. She doesn't seem to be the smartest dog in the world, though."

74

"I wonder what jerk dropped her off like that."

"With a note that says, 'Somebody take care of this dog.' No sé."

"You learning Spanish?"

"*Pues, sí*. From Miguel. That way I can teach it to Amber. Listen: *Te amo, mija*. And when she's crying, *Ay, qué te pasa, pobrecita?* And when the dog's barking, *Ya, cállate perro*."

"Well, what about me?"

"*Mi amor*."

He smiles like he really loves me, in a tired sort of way, but he doesn't say anything back.

I say, "Miguel's been coming by some, in the mornings. It's nice to have someone to talk to. It's like—well, it's like we became friends suddenly. After Shawny, it seemed like we didn't want to see each other for a while. But now he comes by and we talk kid things. But that's not weird for you, right?"

"Not unless it's weird."

"It's not. Anyway, there's a girl coming later this summer. A friend of his cousin's. This girl, she's pregnant. Miguel is going to marry her." I see Derek's eyebrows shoot up. "I know, that's a huge thing, that's crazy. To marry someone just so they can be legal? I don't know why, exactly. Or why her. But I thought maybe it was to save her. You know? Like he couldn't save Shawny, so he's going to save this other girl. Alejandra, her name is. She's coming with a whole group. Miguel's a little worried about it."

"I would be, too. He's going to *marry* her? What if he hates her?"

"It doesn't matter. I mean, it's not for love. They'll figure some arrangement out. Right now, this group is crossing the border. The border's the hard part."

"I bet."

"There's a *coyote* to help them cross. That's why Miguel's growing pot, to pay for the *coyote*. And then another *coyote* for inside the border. Because the buses have been hot lately, that's what Miguel says. Baxter hired two of Miguel's cousins to help for the summer. And the others will get hired out somewhere. I don't know how it works, exactly."

"Stay out of it." Derek reaches down to pick out a little weed and tosses it to the side.

"I am. But I am collecting food and clothes and stuff. So if you got anything. Don't give me that look. It's just food, clothes. Which I'll drop off at Miguel's. Nothing illegal about that."

"I've got some things, I guess, but don't be stupid, Libby. Don't get involved, it's serious stuff, it's jail time. But more than that—"

"I know, I know. I'm not an idiot—"

"—it's dangerous. You don't realize how messed up people can be."

"Yes I do."

"No, you really don't." He sighs at me like, Drop it. He's been untangling the hose to make it reach farther so I can get to the bean vines on the far side of the garden. "You know, there's a guy at the rig who got a girl pregnant. The girl's only sixteen. No way can she be a good mom. She's giving it up for adoption. They even met the people, some nice couple living in Colorado Springs who can't have kids and have been wanting one forever. Isn't the world messed up, that people who want kids can't have them and people who don't do?"

"Yeah, Tess was always saying that too."

I know what we're both doing here. With my story about Miguel, I'm saying, See, people do big things for someone else, like get married. Which is crazy, because I don't think I want to marry Derek, which is probably why he doesn't want to marry me, but still, here we are. And with his story, he's saying, See, people do big things for someone else, like give up a baby. And

I don't even know why we're saying either, because probably we're just going over the possibilities because we have nothing better to do.

We look at each other and shrug, which isn't enough, I know, but it's the best we can do.

He smiles one of those sad sorts of smiles. "Baby's sleeping, right?"

I don't even get a nod in before his hands are holding my waist, and he's taken the garden hose from my hand and dropped it in the dirt. I hear myself laugh, because he surprised me, and he pulls me down, right there, right in the grass next to the garden, right in sight of the highway, although not quite, maybe, because of the way the bushes are situated, and I laugh again and Derek whispers, "You have a nice laugh." We fold into each other to keep it there, the burst of surprised joy, before it wisps away.

Kay clears her throat at the same time I feel Derek's elbow in my side.

"Ouch! Amber, where's Amber?" At the same time, I'm looking down to check that my clothes are on. Thank god we got dressed before we fell asleep.

"She's inside, still sleeping," Kay says. "I just checked on her. You should try to keep her up in the day. She'll sleep better at night."

I'm trying to blink my eyes awake. Derek and I are both sitting up now, and Derek seems alert enough but I'm still in a haze. Derek and Kay are ignoring each other, as usual, pretending like the other one isn't actually there, and they're trying especially hard at this moment, because the world loves to pretend that sex doesn't really happen.

"Hello, Derek. Hello, Libby," Baxter says, tipping his hat at us as he walks over. "Kay and I are stopping by to get some supplies. Building a guzzler. Stores water at ground level for the wildlife. I want to get some interesting work in before we cut hay." He's got a straw cowboy hat on, beat-up and stained, and the same light blue western shirt. "Late hay this year. Going to be a lousy crop. Ah, well. Quail, you know, won't drink at a trough. They need low-lying water. Going to plant some deciduous trees and berry producers, like sandhill plums. Honeysuckle bushes too. Gives the songbirds nesting spots, shelter for the antelope and deer and that sort of thing."

"Sounds nice," I say.

"Sounds like a waste of money and time," Kay says, but she doesn't mean it. She starts poking around the garden then, bending down to finger the cucumbers and tomatoes, which are just about to take off and do some serious growing.

"Sounds like good hunting," Derek says.

"Nope, no hunting allowed. Not on this one little spot on earth. Libby you look tired. My mama taught me one thing that has proved to be immensely useful. When you look at someone, try for a second to feel what they're feeling. Like you, I could tell lately that your eyes sting, you got a queasy feeling in your stomach. Right? From being tired. It won't kill you, but it isn't easy."

Derek reaches around to scratch my back and gives me a wink, which means, I guess, that Baxter is a funny man, full of all kinds of tidbits, including kindness.

Baxter sits down next to us and keeps talking. "I remember Kay after she first had you. She got up at three-thirty in the morning to deliver papers. Her route took more than an hour; she drove forty miles to all ends of this county. She'd get home before you and your dad woke up. That was tired, too."

I glance at Kay, who's picking spinach in the shady part of the garden. "Baxter, if she did that all for her own piece of land, it was all for nothing."

"Sometimes you win, sometimes you lose. Either way, you rise to the occasion."

I try not to scowl at Baxter. People should realize that when a person first wakes up, the last thing she needs coming at her is a bunch of chirpy words. I yawn and get up to go get Amber. As I'm leaving, I hear Baxter talking on—about how he's expecting two nationals, as he calls the illegals, to help with irrigating and fixing fence and haying. When I come back, with an awake and newly diapered Amber, he's still talking, now about the heat, which has just risen over a hundred, and how he ought to put in a swamp cooler for us, and that maybe it'd help the baby sleep because he heard she's been up a lot.

I shoot Derek a sympathetic glance, but he looks all right, listening patiently, nodding his head now and then.

I sit down next to him and put Amber in my lap. "Patty-cake, patty-cake, baker's man," I whisper, bringing her two tiny feet together. "Bake me a cake as fast as you can." I bring her toes to her nose, bring her arms to her feet, doing the stretches that the magazines say to do. She flexes all around, but it's not just her muscles bending so much, it's more like her whole being hasn't hardened in any way yet. She doesn't make any noise, but she spits out white goo every once in a while.

Derek's watching her and I try to watch him. The look on his face is this: I could decide to love this baby.

I look away fast because that hurts. I know love is sometimes a decision and that Derek's good enough to try. He's considering it. But jeez, it seems near impossible to love somebody else's kid, and you shouldn't have to talk yourself into it, and you shouldn't be asked to try.

Baxter says, "Remember, Libby, once we were working cows? And I was looking at a lump on the jaw of a calf, and it was a rattlesnake bite sure enough, but before I said anything you were already handing me a syringe to stab her to get the poison out, and then you handed me another of penicillin and another of glucose. You knew what you were doing."

"That was years ago, Baxter."

"But the point is, you ought to be a rancher. No, now don't snort like that. Actually, I've been talking to Kay. How about you quit your job and come work for me?"

I don't know if he's joking or what, so I say, "I sort of like the store."

"She likes the store." Kay says it snotty-like, from where she's standing near the beanpoles. "I wonder if she'll like it in twenty years. You got to think ahead, Libby. You going to support that daughter of yours on five-fifty an hour?"

"Six," I say.

"Six," Kay repeats. "Libby, start thinking! Kids think only in the here and now. But they're supposed to grow out of that Baxter, aren't they? Libby here missed the boat."

"I'll pay you seven," Baxter says. "Keep books, clean house, feed the horses, general stuff. Flex hours."

I don't know what to say to that. I don't need Baxter's help. Plus I *like* the store. That's where I get to connect with the outside world, meet people—that's my only chance. I look at Derek but his eyes tell me nothing and he shrugs to confirm that.

Baxter's saying, "Adeline gone and all, I need the help. Just took me some time to realize that. Plus I'm starting up a few new projects that will keep me extra busy. Like this guzzler."

Kay says, "Why don't you fix up your damn corral system first?"

"Upland birds and coyotes need a place to get water."

"Coyotes," Kay snorts.

"Anyway, seven an hour. Think about it."

I nod and look up at the sky. No clouds, nothing. The problem with Baxter's offer is that it means I'll be here forever, doing the same thing. I can't tell him that, though. I can't say, Look, you have a life that I don't want.

Kay looks at me and is shaking her head. "Kid," she says, "you gotta get your act together. You call social services yet?"

"No."

"Why not?"

"I don't have their phone number."

"Look in the damn phone book! Get off your lazy butt and get it done, Libby. I'm not going to hold your hand. You need to get Amber legal."

I don't say a thing, and all I'm thinking is, *I gotta get out of here.*

Kay hates my silence, it drives her crazy, and she's about to start in, but before she gets going Baxter clears his throat, and he's an expert at changing the topic just at the right moment. "You know, when you get older, you want to impart some information before you go. And I'm growing old—"

"You're not old, Baxter—"

"—and I'm not feeling so good, and that makes me want to talk, and I got something I want to tell you. I've been wanting to tell you, and I even asked Kay. Something about your father. I just want to go ahead and say it. Okay?"

"Okay."

"Oh good god," says Kay. "I don't need to hear this."

"Your father," Baxter says again, but he pauses and follows Kay with his eyes. She's walking off toward the house, grumbling about having to go to the bathroom, there isn't ever even enough time to go to the bathroom, and why's she got to work for such a talker, could they please just get to work? When she's gone, Baxter starts up again. "Your father was a good worker, knew a lot about horses, was a fine roper, and so was your mom. He came out here to work for that company that makes pistons for John Deere tractors, as you probably know, but that place was like a sweatshop and eventually he found me. Like I say, he was a good worker. Sometimes people's lights burn out, though, and I don't know how that happens. I myself am burning at one hundred watts, bright as can be. But your father, his light was burnt out. One day, Kay comes to work all beat up." He clears his throat and pauses for a minute, and Derek and me are staring at him like, Jesus, where'd this come from? Because nobody around here mentions my father much, and there's no telling when something's going to finally come spewing out of a person's mouth.

"She looked real bad," Baxter says. "She was pregnant—not real big yet, but showing and all. In those days, she did a lot in the house too, though I realize now she hated it. Kay wasn't meant for indoor work. No one with any sense is. Anyway, I didn't say anything, but I asked Adeline to speak to her, which she would have done anyway. Adeline told her, I guess, that if Kay wanted help getting away, that we'd be there. And I guess Adeline said, 'Hon, don't let him hurt your babies. He's not hurting Libby, is he?'

"Well, Kay never answered that question. And she never asked for help. But maybe having that baby made her strong. One day Kay marches over here and says, 'He's left. You can ask me to leave too and I'll understand. But I'm as good a ranch hand as him, probably better. I'll get Libby in day care, and this kid too, when it comes. I'd like to stay here. It's our best shot.' And I said, 'Well, we'll give it go.' And that was that."

He pauses to look at me in the eye, which I take as an opportunity to look down at the grass, which I start pulling.

"So, one day I was driving the tractor down to bale some hay and I saw a truck pull in your driveway. It was your father, all right. So I headed on over here. He was crying, standing there all by himself. Crying like a baby. He said he missed you and all. He said, 'I miss Libby running up and hugging my legs and putting her little feet on my boots and asking for a dance.'"

"I remember that, I do!" I say it before I can stop it; it just comes floating out of me.

Baxter pauses a moment and says, "He said to me, 'You think I'm any good for them, Baxter?' and I said, 'Nope,' and he said, 'I don't think I am either. Don't tell them I stopped by, how about?'

"So I didn't. I sometimes wondered if I did the right thing, promising that. But then I remember his eyes. Eyes will tell you everything about a person. I'm sorry that you grew up without a father, though. I'm getting old. I wanted to tell you that story before it was too late."

"Jeez, Baxter. Plus you're not old—"

"I am. I am. Right now I'm still at one hundred watts. But one of these days I'll be down to sixty, and then forty. Then out."

I bite my lip and finally get something out. "Not for a long time, Baxter," I say. "I hope not. You're too ornery to die." That's not exactly what I meant to say, because really, the truth is, it seems like getting to the end of life isn't so easy—to know you're just going to disappear—and how do we get through our regular lives, anyway, when the truth is that we're wondering about love, and death, and things that are on the verge of smashing us to pieces?

"Well, I haven't treated my time on earth shabbily, I can say that for myself. That makes it better. Now, there's one more thing," he says. "Kay. She had some tough years. Boyfriends and boyfriends and more boyfriends, and I don't suppose all of them were kind." His voice is soft and low. "Maybe she didn't do right by you all the time. Maybe I didn't, either, by not paying attention. But people change, I believe they really do. Look deep inside your mom and you'll see a lot of courage, a lot of care. She is bitter, though, your mom. People can get behind pain like they're leaning into a wind and it supports them after a bit and that's what happened to Kay. She's probably just needed someone to prop her up while she got out from under the wind, the pain. Now that you're a mom, I think you ought to try to re-see Kay. Just try."

I glance at Derek and then back at the grass, and then at Baxter and back down.

"Now, if you can suffer but not be bitter it'll change you into a real human. A soft human. And now I'm done. That's enough of this. But I been feeling lately like if maybe I just said a few things I'd feel a whole lot better. Now, let me hold that baby." Baxter takes her from me and starts talking to her. "Hey, baby. Jeez, you're as light as a kite. I don't know much about babies. But you're looking good, you sweet thing. Now, tell me what you think about this. I'm thinking of putting up a sign, out by the highway, in the middle of nowhere. It'll read, If You Lived Here You'd Be Home by Now. Do you think that's funny?"

Derek and I laugh a little, but Amber starts crying. Baxter looks worried and hands her back to me.

Kay comes back out of the house and for a minute there's all of us talking past and through what Baxter has just said, and I wish it could always be like this, like a regular family having a conversation, only this is a weird family because nobody is exactly with anybody in the usual sense.

Right as Baxter and Kay are ready to leave, Kay turns to us all and says, "I heard a story from Lola over at the bank. She said she heard that in some other country some couple was put in jail for defying the government and to punish them the officials put their baby in the next cell. They had to listen to their baby cry, listen to it starve to death."

There is a silence as we all absorb that. Then Baxter breathes out, "Kay, now there's no need to be repeating stories like that." And I'm thinking, *I know why she's doing this, she can't stand us talking nice, she has to make every conversation a little mean or else it's scary to her.*

Kay looks so hard and she says, "Sometimes I think we're just animals, and then I can understand something like that. Like a baby fox. A baby fox might lose its mother and cry and cry till it dies. That's the way it goes. But then I think, damn, that was a *baby*, crying and just wanting milk. Then I can't stand to hear things like that."

Baxter looks up at her. "Kay, I can't either."

"Think of that baby, crying and crying."

"Come on, Amber," I whisper. "Let's go inside."

As I'm making my move to get away, Kay says, "Put in your two weeks notice at the store. Or cut back your hours. You could do both jobs." I shrug, but she stays after me. "Frank will understand. Just tell him soon so he has time to find someone else." She pauses for a breath and says, in a softer voice, "A well-being check, my ass. But it's a nice idea, isn't it? Well-being check. We could all use one of those."

The map shows the route clear enough, I guess. La Junta. Walsenburg. Monte Vista. Durango. From flat land to mountain, over the Sangre de Cristo and San Juan ranges.

I trace the route with my finger and tell myself that it can't be *that* hard, that I can do it. But it *does* look hard, and I can't. It's far and complicated and my car would probably break down, plus how am I supposed to get there with a baby that needs something every thirty minutes?

Missing someone hurts more that I thought. If only she'd call and say one damn real thing, that would be enough. Silence is so hard. I think maybe it's the meanest thing on earth.

I don't know how to love her less.

Maybe I will eventually wear out.

And I'm figuring something else out, too, which is that if you can't get what you want, you end up doing something else, just to get some relief. Just to keep from going crazy. Because when you're sad enough, you look for ways to fill you up. Which is why, maybe, I finally got around to calling the community college in Lamar and asking for application materials. "Financial aid materials too," I threw in at the last minute. The lady at the other end of the phone was busy and tired, so I didn't bother her with my story, which I realize is not special anyway, except that it's my life.

I called social services too, and they can't fit me in for a few weeks, but at that time, the lady promises, they can see about which services are applicable to my situation. If I'm going to legally adopt this baby, she said, I'd need to get my sister's permission and the father's too. I said, "What if there's no father?" And she said, "There's a father." I said, "Nope, there's no father." She sighed and said, "Come on in and we'll get it figured out." She sounded like she was tired of dealing with girls who did dumb things.

I sit with the map in front of me, staring at the impossible. Amber is right next to it, on her back, and I tell her, "It's 'cause of you I can't go." But I know that's not true. I wouldn't go anyway. It's me that's the problem. So I play patty-cake and itsy bitsy spider, because that's easier than thinking about directions my life won't go.

Ed Mongers is a slow talker, and when his sentences *do* make it out they're all in circles and stops and starts, with long pauses, and then a bunch of words all packed together. It takes him a good twenty minutes to explain that he has honey bees, and that bees like alfalfa, and that he'd sure love to swap us some honey in exchange for letting him keep his bees out here.

We're standing in the driveway and his eyes keep flicking from Amber to me to the house to the alfalfa field. Amber's nestled in my arm, and she opens and closes her mouth, like she's tasting air. She's got that white curdy stuff on her tongue, and I think it's cute, how she sticks out her tongue and then closes her mouth to think about that air for a while, and then does it all over again.

Ed has sand-colored curly hair that's graying near his temples, and small round glasses, and it looks like maybe he hasn't shaved in four or five days because he's got whiskers that are just at that length where they go from being bristle hard to soft. I guess he's in his forties, but it's hard to tell, and there's no doubt that he's good looking. But he also looks worried, and he keeps scratching the blond-brown whiskers on his face, or touching his glasses. He says, "They're Italian bees, which is a *friendly* kind. Flowers bloom in *waves*. Alfalfa will bloom in late July. The *first* wave comes in June, but the earliest batch of honey goes to the bees. The spring honey flow is *no good,* anyway, since it's mostly from leafy spurge and tastes too strong. Italian bees are *not* aggressive."

"Oh, okay. They don't bite? Because I've got a baby here and all."

"Sting," he says. "And I see that, that you have a baby, and I am surprised, because I see you at the store, and no, bees don't *like* to sting, and they won't unless they feel threatened. But we all lash out, don't we, if we feel threatened? And you were never pregnant."

I blink at him. "Oh, right. This is my sister's baby. I'm raising her, though. I'm adopting her."

"Oh." He draws it out, like a long breath, and nods. Then he looks at me closer. "I didn't know that. I'm out of the *loop.* You shouldn't give a baby honey. Not till they're *one.* I read that in my beekeeping magazine. But after that, it's a natural sweetener. It's very healthy. Why? Perhaps I shouldn't ask that. I mean, but taking someone else's baby—"

After a second I say, "Oh. My sister, Tess, didn't want it. She was going to get an abortion. I told her I'd raise it. We thought it was a boy. But it wasn't. This is Amber. She's almost three weeks, now."

"She looks like she's floating in space."

"I know! That's what I was just thinking, I really was. And like she's tasting air."

"Yes, that's right. That's what it looks like."

We both stare at her for a minute, and then I say, "Where do the bees live? In those white boxes?"

"Hive bodies, they're called. Bees are the most *amazing* creatures, really. I think it's amazing that you would take your sister's baby."

"Oh. Well, thanks."

"That's a *whole* different way of operating in this world. A lot of people, they don't want to take the hard way. I wish the world was *different*. I wish people wouldn't use plastic bags, or so many chemicals. Because, did you know that plastic bags *never* disintegrate? Never, *ever*? And those chemicals, they don't go away. Of course they don't. Did we really think they would? But those are all hard things. And I understand. Because the world is difficult enough, sometimes, and it's *too hard* to be worrying about every single thing. So we look for easy, convenient ways. My*self* included. I mean, don't think I think I'm so great. But that's why I moved out here. To get away and think about how to *live* life. To try to be of consequence, but I couldn't do that in the mainstream. Anyway, I don't think you took the easy way. Really? You live out here? And you work at the store? And you're raising your sister's baby?"

This guy is crazy; I never had to listen so hard in all my life to figure out what a person's saying. When I'm sure he's done talking, I nod a bunch of times, like I'm agreeing with everything he said, and I add, "Um, okay. You can keep the bees out here. I think that would be nice."

"Libby, I need to repeat something to you. That's a fine thing that you're doing."

"Thank you." I say it in a normal voice, but the truth is that it seems so kind, him saying this, that tears float into my eyes.

"I think it would be nice for my bees to live out here."

"Well, it's really okay with me if they don't bite."

"Sting."

"Sting. But I guess it's not really up to me. This is Baxter's land. My mom's his ranch hand."

"Oh, yes. I know. I already asked Baxter and he said I could, but I wanted to ask *you* too. Because I'd like to put them pretty close to the road here, so I can get to them okay. I have to check up on them. Make sure they're healthy, don't have mites, and watch for when they swarm."

"Whatever. Okay."

"*Thank* you, Libby."

"No problem, Ed."

He smiles. "I'm glad you know my name. I wasn't sure you did."

"Well, I've seen you at the store. I like the drawing on your honey jars."

"I did that myself."

"It's real nice. I like to draw too."

"Art is what gets us beyond what is real. It makes reality more real. It also shortens the distance we gotta travel to see how connected we are. That's what art *should* do. I'm just now teaching myself photography. Set up a dark room in my bathroom and everything. Listen, can I ask you a question?"

"Sure."

"Where'd your sister go?"

"My sister?"

"Yeah. Where'd she go?"

"Durango."

"She drove up?"

"She caught a ride."

"Brave, just going like that. Or not brave. Depending. She just went up, got a job?"

"Yeah, waitressing and cleaning in a hotel."

"Nice dog you got here." Ringo's bouncing her head against Ed's palm, wanting more attention. Ed made the mistake of petting her first thing and now Ringo won't leave him alone. That's what I like about this dog: She makes it clear she wants some love.

"*I* like it here," he says. "I don't even lock my doors at night."

"Me either. In fact, we don't even have a lock." As I'm saying this I'm realizing that maybe I shouldn't, but Ed's just nodding.

He says, "You probably know Baxter pretty well, huh?"

I shrug. "I guess. I've been living here my whole life."

"Can I ask you something else?"

"Sure."

"You don't have to answer."

"Okay."

"Is he expecting a group of *ilegales*? Illegals?"

I look at him, surprised. He catches my eye and is telling me, I think, to go ahead and talk, so I do. "Yeah. But look, he pays them good. He takes care of them, unlike some people around here. Because I know that some people, they don't. But not Baxter, really. The workers send money home to Mexico and I don't see anything wrong with—"

"Oh don't worry. I'm not going to—"

"Everyone hires Mexicans here—"

"I know, I know. Believe me, I know. I help them out some. Don't worry. If the *coyote* is charging them too much—well, I just make sure they don't get taken advantage of. Last *coyote* I was dealing with was charging his *pollos*—"

"His what?"

"That's what they call the immigrants. *Pollos*. Chickens. And the *coyote* transports them. Not a very comforting image, is it? Ha! Anyway, he was charging his *pollos* three bucks for a pack of ramen noodles."

"Oh."

"Three bucks! How can a human being do that?"

"Ed? Are you involved with this stuff?"

"Oh, Libby, there's a whole *network* out there." He lifts his hands and waves his fingers at the air, like he's pointing to invisible things that I should see, and then he gets wide-eyed and smiles at me. "It's exciting. It's sort of like the underground railroad. People helping, not for money, just because it's right."

"And you're part of that? You're a *coyote?*"

He bobs his head around like, Yep, yep, but then he says, "Not a *coyote*, exactly. I'm just a person who helps. And I'm waiting for this group of guys to come in. Actually, there are several groups coming in. And I'm worried they're out there somewhere—" He waves his hand to the west and shrugs. "They never got picked up. Wondered if Baxter knew anything. But I don't know him well enough to ask. I don't know *you*, either."

"I don't think Baxter knows anything. He just hires them when they get here. I don't know anything either. I don't."

Ed pushes his glasses up his nose and then rubs his jaw. "Well, I can trust you. And thank you. If it's okay, I'll bring my bees out sometime next week."

"All right."

"One more thing, just so you know. Sometimes a person can

hollow out the middle of semiful of alfalfa and put *ilegales* there. Or there's a false floor. They make a lot more money than hauling hay." His voice is softer now, and he's looking at me in a serious way. "There are other ways, too. I don't know how this group is coming. I'm just worried about these people—I think that maybe they need some help. I wish I knew. But what I really wish I knew was how to get out there," he says, sweeping his hand across pale pastureland and far-distant mountains, "and here," he says, touching his chest, "how to get the heart and the world to see the other." And then he looks at me and says, "That's part of understanding this life, isn't it, and," and he looks at Amber, "aren't you *excited* to see her do that?" Then he says, "I assume what I told you was in confidence." Then he says, "Yes, my bees sure will like it out here. I'm going to go now, but I'll see you again soon."

As I watch him wave and walk over to his orange VW bus, I lean down to whisper to Amber. "What do you think about Ed Mongers and his Italian bees?"

She flails her arms and looks up at me with hazy, blank eyes and then opens her mouth to taste air. Life, she seems to be saying, tastes pretty darn interesting.

Shawny used to tell me that we were made from the same patch of sky.

I knew what she meant. Because the difference between a friend and a real friend is that you and the real friend come from the same territory, or the same place deep inside you, and that means you see the world in the same kind of way. You know each other even before you do.

How Shawny was at eleven, which is when she moved here—that's how I remember her. Feathered blond hair, freckled face, riding her bike over to my house. She got off her beat-up bike, looked right at me with these steady blue eyes, wiped the back of her hand across her nose, and said, "My mom and dad and me just moved here and you're my only neighbor. My name is Shawny. If you come over to my house, there's a ditch bank where you can dig out holes and make caves. We can find treasures from that old dump to put inside the caves, to fill them up." She shrugged. "It's pretty fun."

Then she looked around the place, sizing it up. She got me on her bike seat then, and she stood up and pedaled us all the way to her place. I think she wanted me to see it because she knew that neither of us would have to be embarrassed—we were both poor and she was an expert at avoiding her dad like I was at avoiding Kay. Having someone like that—someone you don't need to hide things from—already makes you a different and higher class of friend.

Eleven, twelve, thirteen, fourteen, fifteen, sixteen, and at seventeen Miguel Mendoza moved to town and Shawny got pregnant. In between, we'd had ups and downs and periods where we'd loved each other so fiercely we had to see each other every day and other times when we let go of each other a little. Always, though, we kept ourselves open to each other.

I don't think there's all that many people who come from the same patch of sky. It's rare bumping into one; and it's Ed that's making me think about the word *friend*, and how you get there, and whether it's worth it, and how it might hurt, and how it felt to have someone like Shawny in the world, the two of us with our hearts all tangled up, doing something simple like making caves in the earth, like hollowing out the earth, and filling them with treasures.

S I X

Watching Arlene is like watching a fish die. In those final moments, after it's done flopping and fighting, it rests, waiting for the end, still and alert, but knowing what's coming. And every once in awhile, it flops its tail, one last surge of hope, and then it gives up again, and that's how Arlene is, making a small attempt and then sinking down and letting go.

I'm bagging while she cashiers and, surprisingly, she even has a line of three people, who have all taken to talking about the weather and wishing for cooler days and some rain.

Arlene's made up today, wearing black jeans, a western shirt, and she's curled her bangs under. She's hoping, I think, for some man to come in and buy groceries and notice her—just notice her as he leaves. And it makes me sad that every time a man comes through she tries to hold his gaze—like this older fellow who must be an out-of-towner because I don't recognize him and because he's buying worms, which means he's fishing at the dam. It makes me sad that this guy doesn't even look up. Just signs his credit card receipt and leaves.

"Well, anyway," she says when he's gone, "thank god Frank put air conditioning in here. Bank said one hundred."

"Wish my car had air. Baxter and Kay might put in a swamp cooler at the house, though."

"Saw Derek last night." She says it casually as she rings up Mrs. Sterling, who's dirt poor and counting coins in her hand and who probably wishes someone would notice her, too.

"Yeah?"

"With Shelley Patrick. At the movies."

"Oh." And then, "Really?" and then, "He called me to go the movies. I couldn't, though. Nobody to watch Amber. Although I could have taken her. But I was afraid she'd squawk the whole time. He and Shelley are just good friends. I'm glad he still went."

When Mrs. Sterling leaves, Arlene touches me on the shoulder. "I guess I just wanted you to know."

"Sure. Thanks."

I'm trying to act like I'm not surprised, but maybe she sees right through me, because she says, "Hope that doesn't hurt you too much."

"I don't have the time or energy to be hurt."

Arlene gives a tired smile. "I remember that. Having to get out of bed five times to warm a bottle. Oh, god, I was tired. Of course, that doesn't last forever and it sure is worth it."

"Everyone says that." What I'm wondering is, do people all say the same thing because it's true or because they just want to believe it's true? Because it could be that being a mom is too hard and when you get right down to it it's not worth it, but you can't say that out loud, because the world is terrific at lying to itself about all sorts of important things.

Arlene starts ringing up another customer but keeps talking to me. "Right now, all she does is eat and sleep and cry. I know it. But just you wait. Someday soon, something inside her is going to go *click*, just like a light being turned on. Then, in those eyes, you can see a person unfold. She'll smile soon. Then she'll say 'Mama,' and then she'll wave goodbye. I know it takes

95

awhile. Everyone used to say to me, 'They grow up so darn fast!' and I remember thinking, *What? Seems to be taking a long time*, but then suddenly I realized my kids were in kindergarten and I thought, *What? How'd that go so fast?* There were just so many hard times, it sometimes felt like it was taking forever."

She looks up at the clock above the door. "Like this job. I wait for time to slip away so I can go home. Life isn't supposed to be about waiting."

She waits, though, until the customer pays and I'm done bagging. When we're alone, she says, "That's how I figure if my life's any good or not. Whether I wish time would speed up or slow down. It makes me cry when I think about it too much. Because I wasted my life wishing it would speed up." She's looking out the glass door like she's not paying attention to me anymore. Then she turns back and touches my cheek. "If you need some help, let me know."

"All right."

"I guess I could watch Amber some night and you could go out."

"You don't have to do that. As Kay says, I'm not entitled to any help."

She tilts her head and considers that. "Well, all I know is that you're a beautiful kid, Libby."

"And you're a beautiful lady, Arlene."

We both smile, because we're always saying that to each other, and isn't it funny that we keep saying it even though it's a lie, and so it's not a nice thing to say? It's supposed to be, but really it just hurts the both of us.

I'm in the chip aisle, watching the gray ropes of my mop push water across the floor, when Simon's parents walk up. At first all I see is two sets of shoes that stop by the slick part of the

96

floor: cowboy boots and old-lady tennis shoes. When they don't move, I look up and there they are. I don't know *how* I know who they are, exactly, except they were probably at the same basketball and football games I was, or maybe at the store, or maybe in Lamar, and it's just the sort of knowledge that's seeped in without anyone ever telling me. Plus not too many people are as fair and blond as his father, who's staring right at me. My eyes sting from tiredness and from bleach, but I manage to look back at him without squinting.

He clears his throat and rubs at the back of his head with his big hand, which is covered with blond hair. He's wearing a shirt that says RATTLESNAKE FEEDS AND SUPPLY and old jeans, and in his face—it's a nice-enough face, a regular face—I see a little of Amber. "I'm Harold Frazier. And this is Dottie," he says.

Dottie smiles and nods. She's wearing a pink handkerchief over her permed gray hair, and something about her looks weak, like she's been rolled over by life, like maybe she's had all the strength pushed out of her.

"We're Simon's parents," Harold says.

"Yeah," I say. "I know."

"We needed some groceries."

"Oh, okay." I step back a little to let them pass, although there's plenty of room.

"Well, and to see you." Harold clears his throat again. "You're Libby, right? We wanted to ask you how the baby's doing."

I look around the store before looking back at them. "Amber's doing fine. Thanks for asking."

"She's pert-near a month, now, huh?"

"Almost."

Dottie leans forward a bit. "That's about when they start to wake up a bit. Does she look around a lot? Is she alert? Are you putting her on her back to sleep?"

I don't know what to think about these folks. Part of me

wants to push them away, because, man, they didn't give Tess the time of day and acted like she and her baby were the biggest mistake on earth. On the other hand, part of me wants to pull them in, because they're Amber's grandparents, after all, and here they are, standing in front of me looking old and sorry. "Of course I put her on her back," I finally say. "She's a very healthy baby. I have pictures in my purse. You want to see?"

"Yes," says Dottie. "We really would."

When I come back with my wallet, they're standing just where I left them. Harold's got his arms crossed, and Dottie is tugging on her pink handkerchief.

I show them the one from the hospital, and two I've taken since then. "I've got extras of these," I say, handing them the hospital one. "You can keep it."

"It's just like I heard," Dottie says. "She looks a lot like Simon."

"That's what people say. Although it's hard to tell too much, I think. See the nose there? That's Tess's nose."

"Well, I'll be," says Harold. "I'll be. A little baby girl." Then, "You live in that house on the Baxter place, right? The one off the highway?"

"Yes."

"With your mom?"

"Yes."

"And you're raising the baby?"

"Yes."

"Probably it's nice to have your mom there to help."

"Sure."

"It's a hard thing to do alone."

"Well, I've got Kay."

"I know Baxter a little. Surprising how little, though. It's just that we've only been here two years, and we live way on the other side of the county."

"Yeah, that's what Tess told me." I say it only because

there's a long pause, and it feels like I ought to say something.

He opens his mouth and closes it, opens it and closes it. He looks like a fish struggling, too—a fish right before the Arlene stage. "We're good people," he suddenly says. "You don't know us and we don't know you, so me saying that doesn't mean much. But we are. We were—we were very angry at Simon. We had hoped—well, we didn't want him getting tied down before he got to accomplish some things."

"We love him so much," Dottie whispers.

"And I must admit, we were angry with Tess. All along, we'd told him—well, we weren't in favor of—her."

"Shhh, now, Harold," Dottie says. "We just have been wondering. If we did the right thing. It's hard. Knowing this baby is growing up right across the county."

"Well, we were just wondering about the situation, exactly," says Harold. "Could you explain, maybe? How is Amber and what are your plans for her?"

They're having real trouble talking, these two, and usually I want to jump in and help people like that, but for once I stay quiet and watch them fumble around. But I can't take it after a while, and finally I start talking to help them out a bit.

"Well, I'm Amber's mother. Tess wanted an abortion. And so did Simon. But I argued with them both, and the result is Amber. And she's beautiful. And I'm a good mother. I'm going to give her everything I can."

"Oh honey," Dottie says. "I don't doubt it. What we came here to ask you, and I hope you'll be open to the idea, is if we can meet her."

I shrug. "We could meet in town sometime."

"Sure," says Harold. "Or maybe we could come by the place? We'll be out that way Friday night for a Farm Bureau meeting."

"We're so sorry," says Dottie. "I should have called you sooner. I should have gone to the hospital. We should have."

She shrugs and looks down at her feet.

"We had a real busy spring," Harold says. "We lost the fellow who's been helping us run the ranch. By lost, I mean he died. He—the place—well, never mind. It's not important to you. But it's been a real hard time for us, this spring. The drought and all, you know. Sold off most of the herd."

"We tried to forget about the baby," Dottie says. "But that didn't work."

"We're good people," Harold says.

"You probably need to get back to work," Dottie says.

"We'll call you. And see if we can't take you and your baby to lunch."

"Harold, we should let this girl be. We should get some groceries. There's a store, not as nice as this one, out our way. Usually we go there. But it's smaller and I think we should come here more often. Don't you think so Harold? The fruit here looks fresher."

"Yes," says Harold. "It's not too much farther to come here. Nice to meet you, Libby."

"We're real sorry," says Dottie.

Harold takes out his wallet and holds out a few folded twenties. I back away, but he thrusts his arm out farther.

"Thanks," I mumble.

He nods and then leads Dottie away. From the back, I'm surprised at how old they look. They're bowed down a bit, and Dottie leans against Harold. It looks like they're out of energy, and something about seeing them for real, instead of glaring at me in my mind, makes me feel sorry for all the times I hated them for turning away.

I'm surprised Kay's up when I get home from the store. At first I'm relieved, because I want to tell her about Simon's parents, but as I get closer I figure out what's going on, which is one of her Gone-Berserks, as Tess used to call these moments. She's sitting at the kitchen table, her head on her hands, her hair hanging loose, sobbing.

I ought to get to my room, but I can't just leave her there like that. "Hi," I say, and I sit down in the chair next to her. "Hey there. Hey. Whatcha doing up so late?" I try to sound cheerful, like maybe there's a chance for a good, happy reason. I bend down to pet Ringo, who's come up to wind herself around my legs and lick my hand. I wait. Kay doesn't say anything though, just keeps her head on her hands and shakes a bit harder. I roll my eyes, since she can't see me. "Don't cry."

"Give me one reason not to." She looks up at me, smearing her tears across her face with her hand, and she looks so ugly right now, with her blotchy face and snot coming down her nose. "Give me one reason! *One* reason!"

I look at her and shrug.

"Something's going to change here. I did my share, Libby. I did my share. Don't you go and mess everything up. Don't you do it!"

"Okay."

"I am so tired. You've wrecked up my life."

"Did Amber cry a lot? I'm sorry."

"You made this decision, you figure something else out." And then she's yelling again, a long thing about how I've disappointed her because I don't think very well, how come I'm so slow, how come I'm what she ended up with? I know to ignore her till she gets it all out, and when she does she jumps up and starts moving stuff around the kitchen, pretending to do dishes. She throws silverware into the sink, runs water, pours in bubbles. I'm afraid the noise is too loud at this time of night, and even if it doesn't wake up Amber, it hurts my ears.

"What kind of life do you think I've had? Hard. Not much to recommend it. But one thing I've never done—"

"All right, I said I'll figure something else out."

"One thing I've never done is to unload my problems on someone else. A person just does not do that. Not a mother to a daughter, not a daughter to a mother, not a sister to a sister."

"Okay."

"Keep your problems to yourself!"

"Okay."

"I wish that's how the world worked. That there were people we could hang our problems on. There is *no* such person. You got to learn to not even ask."

"I'll find a babysitter for nights."

"Your dad left. Tess left. Baxter told me today, 'Kay, we're getting up there in years, gotta face it, we gotta do this last part right,' and I said, 'Damn, Baxter, we're supposed to be able to rest now. When's it going to end? When's it going to let up?' I was just done with you girls. I was done raising you, and now this." She looks still for an instant, but then Amber cries from the other room and a wave of something fierce and mean crosses her face. "This is not my problem. This is your fault, your problem, you fix it, you let it crush *you*. You got no light going inside you, Libby. You're dead and dark inside. And so is Tess. You've always both been that way." She throws silverware, which is still sudsy, into the drying rack.

"I'm going to go get Amber."

Before I get out of the room, though, Kay throws in, "Tess made a mistake. But you made a mistake too. A big, big mistake. Why'd you do this? Why? You can't see it from where you're at, but you're not up to this. You're just not."

The minute I've got Amber in my arms I start up a daydream, the usual one about a man falling in love with me. He tells me, 'You've got so much love inside you. You've got so much good inside you.' And the look in his eyes proves to me that he can see it, and so, for a minute, I believe.

The night Tess and I sat down to tell Kay, it was one of those windy spring days, the sort of wind that reminds you of the power of air. It was the kind of wind that brings down tree limbs, smacks dirt and pebbles into windows, makes the house shift.

Tess asked Kay to sit down, that we had something to tell her. Before we could even get a word out, though, Kay said, "Damnit, I knew it."

Tess said, "There's something—" and cleared her throat.

It all happened in a split second, Kay leaning forward, saying, "Damnit, I knew it," talking at the same time Tess did.

Tess kept going, though, and finished her sentence. She said, "—that I want to tell you. I'm pregnant."

Kay leaned back and said, "I knew it. Goddamn—"

"I'm sorry."

"Anytime my daughters ask me to sit down at the kitchen table, I know it can't be good. I *warned* you—"

"I know."

"I knew you were pregnant, but I didn't want to know it. Oh, damn—"

"I'm due in June, June second—"

"Oh, good god. That soon? Tess, Tess, Tess."

All that talking went back and forth, lightning quick. Then there was a long pause, and Tess finally said, "Here's the thing, though. I didn't want it. I don't want it. I was going to have an abortion."

"Uh-huh," said Kay. "Why *didn't* you?"

Tess tilted her head at me, because it was my turn to talk. I opened and closed my mouth, but no words came out and Tess stared at me hard, but still no words came so she glared at me before turning back and looking at Kay. "Libby wants him."

"What?"

"I wanted an abortion, and Libby said, No, no, no, that I couldn't, that she wanted the baby, that she'd raise him."

"That is the—"

"Dumbest thing ever, I know. That's what I told her."

"It's not dumb," I said.

"It's a dumb idea, and I still think so. Only she talked me into it and now it's too late to back out."

"Like hell! You'll raise this baby yourself."

"I won't."

Kay stood up and slapped Tess across the face and the sound crashed through the room, even above the sound of the wind. "You goddamn will."

"Kay!" I jumped up.

Tess just sat there, though, with a blank face, far inside herself.

"Don't hit her," I whispered. "And anyway, why can't we all be happy about this?"

Kay looked at me and squinted her eyes. She really lost it then. She stood up, pushed her chair backward, turned to me with a red blotchy face and her eyes shiny green. "You fucking idiot girls! Do I want a grandkid just after I got done raising you? Oh, I see. I see what you're thinking. No, no, no. Don't you ask me to—"

"I won't ask for your help."

"Oh, Libby. You might not ask, but you'll need it." She ran her hand across her face, and held her face in her cupped hand. "You'll need my help."

"I won't—"

"You will." Then she started crying and walked into the other room. Tess and I sat at the table, looking down, tracing the zodiac signs with our fingers or looking at each other and rolling our eyes, because we didn't know what else to do. The wind was howling and making the glass in the window clank back and forth, back and forth. We sat there for a long time, and when Kay came back she said, "Listen. I'll do some. I'll do some. Maybe if we all help some it will work. Maybe it will work. Right, Tess? We'll all do some."

"Right," Tess said.

"Right," I said.

I bit my lip and smiled, because that's just what I'd imagined us saying in my daydreams. And so it seemed like for once a dream was going to come true.

SEVEN

 Mornings are soft, and that's enough to make me love them. If I were married, mornings are when I would stay in bed and curl up in the arms of my husband. They're when I would feel how much I loved him. And I would feel soft myself, and in love with my life. Then the day would get hectic and hot and full, like they do, but there would be the memory of a quiet morning holding me together.

This morning is like the fuzzy purple blanket Amber's on, like the daydream of love in my head, like my heart feels. Nothing real yet. Nothing hard, or tight, or hot, or hurt.

Amber and I are resting outside so we can get the morning sun, because for once it's cool enough to want the sun. I wish we were on a green, evenly mowed lawn, but this scraggly mixture of dry crabgrass and pebbles and cigarette butts isn't so bad in the mornings. I wish I could have slept in, like I used to, instead of Amber waking me up at five-thirty. But a meadowlark is singing—Crazy Meadowlark, I decided to call him, because I never heard a bird belt it out so loud—and Amber's awake and she's looking straight up, not at me exactly, but straight up into the sky.

I'm daydreaming—the usual one, about a man who's feeling very quiet and still inside, and me feeling very quiet and still inside, and we're coming together, direct and honest and true, and it's a dream I could stay in for a good long while, so I scowl when a truck pulls into the driveway. In an instant, though, I see that it's the beat-up three-shades-of-white thing I last saw Tess in and my insides whoosh up and I say "Oh!" before I can help it, and I'm looking, looking, trying to see past the glare of the sun on the windshield to see inside.

The driver's side door opens and Clark climbs out. But Tess doesn't swing out of the passenger side, even though I'm staring at it hard, wishing like crazy.

Finally I turn my eyes to Clark, who's walking toward me. He's wearing jeans and a red T-shirt, scratching his black hair before he puts on a Colorado Rockies ball cap. "Hey, Libby." He stands above me, staring down, and jams his hands into his jeans. "And hi, baby."

I nod at the truck. "No Tess?"

"No Tess."

"Oh."

"Just me."

"Oh."

"What's that kid's name again?"

"Amber. Is she okay?"

"Tess? Yeah." I wait for him to say more, but he doesn't. Instead he stares down Amber. "Cute. She was three days old last time I saw her. She wasn't as cute then."

"You wanna sit down?" I shift over to make room for him, but he doesn't move and I don't know how to ask him what he's doing here, so I pat the blanket and say, "So— Tess is in Durango?"

"Yep."

"And you're here?"

"Yep. I had a delivery to make up there. She said she wanted to get out of here for a while so I gave her a ride." He sits down, not on the blanket but on the dry grass beside it, and bends his knees and rests his arms on them. He smells a bit, like sweat and grease. "She's at a little resort, waitressing and stuff."

I wait, but when he doesn't say anything else I say, "Yeah, I know. She sent a postcard."

"Well, then. You know as much as I do."

"And you're back here, working and stuff?"

"Yeah, at Sammy's."

"What's Sammy's?"

"Shop in Lamar. I'm a diesel mechanic. Fix semi-trucks and stuff like that. But also I do some driving for a fellow who ships alfalfa. I'll probably be hauling that, in fact," he says, nodding at Baxter's field.

That makes me pause but I don't know what to say, so I say something else, which is, "Tess never told me she was leaving, you know. Not till the day you picked her up."

He looks at me and nods. "I know it. I know that must have been hard. Have you called her?"

"No."

"Are you mad at her?"

"We don't have long distance on our phone here. Plus she'll call here when she wants to talk with me."

He looks at me and tilts his head. "I'd be pissed if I was you. I'd be mad at me too, maybe. But look, I just gave her a ride out of here. We met at a party, and I stopped by a time or two, and one time I told her I was driving up to the mountains and she asked for a ride. Thought I'd do her a favor. I hope it was. But I don't need to be checking on her. She's a big girl. Me keeping tabs on her wasn't part of the bargain." He touches Amber's feathery-soft head. "So I was just driving by, out this way anyway, and I thought I'd stop in. You've been on my

108

mind a little. I wondered how you were doing with this baby and all. Plus Tess told me to give you something. I've been meaning to drop it by for a while now. Sorry." He walks back to the truck and comes back with a little package wrapped in newspaper. "Tess told me to check in on you. She told me a lot about you, in fact. About you and Kay."

"Oh? Like what?"

He's looking off toward the mountains now, but his big hand is on Amber's head and that's funny, that he wants to do that, or that such a big guy can suddenly look so tender. "She told me the story of how when you were kids and your mom was drunk, you and her would ride off bareback on your horse. What was your horse's name?"

"Slug."

"Yeah, Slug. Because he walked so slow. And that she'd sit behind you, holding onto your waist, and you'd say, 'Don't worry Tess. We'll just ride off into the mountains and then we'll be free.'"

I laugh a little. "We were just kids then, eight and five or something. Slug died on my ninth birthday."

"That's what Tess said. That your mom loaded up the shotgun and went out and shot her."

"Only because she had colic. She was dying anyway."

"Tess was crying, and your mom said she didn't want to see any of that, and then slapped her for carrying on."

"Well. Yeah."

"Kay doesn't have much room for weakness. That's how Tess put it. I told her, 'Tess, crying for a horse isn't weakness. It's feeling.'"

"Well, Kay doesn't have much room for that either."

Clark smiles at me. "I know the type. There's only so many times a person can bust you up inside before you need to say, To hell with 'em. Probably that's one good reason Tess left."

I know what he's saying, and my answer, if I could say it, would be, Well, it's not that easy, though. At least for me. If I could leave Kay, I would. If I had the money, I'd move into town. Although maybe not. Maybe that's not entirely true. Because you get all bound up in people, and maybe you love them even if doesn't always make sense.

"Tess told me that you've been her mother. A mother that was three years older."

"Yeah?"

"But that she doesn't need a mother anymore." Clark's watching me carefully, so I'm careful not to show a thing, because of course that hurts. "Sometimes a situation gets so messed up, and a person feels so guilty, and there's too much history, and the only way to be free is to leave. Sometimes you have to break a connection to people. For your own good."

Why? I want to ask, but I don't. Instead I stare at the package, which I'm curious about but want to open when I'm alone. Then I look at Amber, who's waving her hands in the air, all disjointed and crazy-like. Clark bends down and nods at her and says, "Hey, hey, hey, little lady." She blinks her eyes at him and opens her mouth like she's trying to say something. Clark says, "One of her eyes is squished down."

"I know."

"That's cute. Looks like she's winking. So you're doing all right with this kid?"

"I guess."

He waits for more, but all I can do is shrug. He says, "Anyway, you're the responsible one. Tess ought to straighten up a bit and you ought to let loose a bit, that's what Tess says."

I pick up a pebble from the blanket and throw it into the grass.

"Although, she says, both of you make bad choices in men. But that's because there's so few choices in this town and so it's

110

not your fault." While he says this, he gives me a look and his eyes hold on to mine.

I laugh a little. "That's true, I guess." I lean my head toward the sun and it feels like it's sending the color red through me, through my eyelids and into my body.

"You've been after her, Tess says, for always befriending the bad boys. The crazy and dangerous ones."

That embarrasses me a little and I wish Tess would keep some things to herself. "Well, I'm not saying that includes you, necessarily."

"Naw, it doesn't include me." Then he winks and says, "No, no. We were never together. Anyway, according to Tess, she knows when to let people go, unlike you. She said she hoped you'd break up with your boyfriend, what's his name?"

"Derek." Now I wish I could take off my sweatshirt, because the sun suddenly feels too hot. Now is the moment when the soft purple of morning gives way to everything that's hard: flies buzzing, heat, noise. Amber starts fussing and I try the pacifier but she spits it out. If only I could take off my sweatshirt, but I don't have anything on underneath, so I sit there feeling suffocated.

"Derek," Clark says over Amber's fuss. "Derek is nice enough, but just not as sharp as you. And furthermore, you don't love him. You're just afraid of being alone. That's what she says." Clark turns his head to talk to Amber. "Tess figured he'd leave Libby, here, because of you, you, you, little sweet gal. We'll see, huh? We'll see if he hangs in there." He looks at me like he knows he's said more than a stranger should, and he's feeling me out for my reaction. I keep my eyes away from his and smile and shrug.

"Well, then. I'm off. Just wanted to stop in and say hi." He rubs Amber on the head again and then gets up, and all the time he's watching me with a certain look in his eye. *On the prowl* is what Tess would say about that look—we used to talk about that, how some people always have their radar up, always looking, always wondering, and now that Tess isn't here I guess his wonder is directed at me. Which surprises me, although I guess neither of us is all that good looking or successful, which means we're on the same level, and it's a fact that prowlers prowl everywhere, but especially in their own league.

I look right back at him and I mumble, "You won't be seeing Tess again? Because if you do, she's supposed to call the father of this baby. And tell her I need some signatures. I'm meeting with social services and I need to get this baby legally."

"I won't be seeing her."

"Well, just if you do."

He raises his black eyebrows and shoots me a different look. "Well, I won't. I just said that. But your sister, she's all right. She was afraid to get out of here, I think. More afraid than she wanted to admit. But she'll make it. She's got her eyes on the big picture."

On his way to his truck, he passes by Kay's old car. Her old lasso is looped around the side-mirror, and he stops to pick it up. "Whose dally-rope is this?"

"Kay's. I guess she was out practicing."

He takes the rope and backs up, then starts to swing the rope in a circle, letting out a bit of slack now and then. The loop he makes gets bigger and bigger, swirling in the air above him. He makes out like he's going to rope the air in front of him, but suddenly he turns toward me and his arm shoots out, right at me. "Jesus!" I yelp, and I duck fast and move toward Amber, so that my body is between him and her. The rope lands in front of me, at my feet.

"Scared you, didn't I?" He laughs and flips his arm up to send the rope back toward him, and he loops it up and puts it back. "Don't worry. Don't be pissed. I wouldn't have got you. I could have. But I wouldn't do that." He looks at me again and smiles. "I was just joking, okay?"

"Okay."

"Okay, then."

Before he climbs in his truck, he stops and stares at our house. I see it the way he does, brown paint that's cracked, junk piled all around, Kay's old car growing weeds and glinting sun off the broken windshield.

This isn't where I should be. Maybe this is true for both of us. I get the feeling that him next to his beat-up truck, and me next to my beat-up house—this isn't where we're supposed to be. And maybe that makes us wonder, more than ever, what's going on behind that junked-up space that separates us, the space that keeps one human from understanding another.

The package from Tess is wrapped in newspaper with a head-line that reads "TESS ESCAPES!" And in smaller print below, "KID SISTER CROSSES BORDER TO NEW LIFE!" It takes me a minute to understand that it's some touristy-thing, a fake newspaper printed with a headline she picked. *Durango Times*, the paper's called. The other headlines are "Tourists Trash Sand Dunes, Jailed for 2 Years" and "Two-Headed Cow Left by Aliens."

A journal book is what's in the package. On the outside is a photo of a baby sitting inside a humungous flower, and the baby has dark, silky, short hair and pudgy cheeks and doesn't look a thing like Amber, although Tess's note says, "This reminds me of your baby girl. Write in this book so that she can read it later and find out what it was like when she was a baby. Draw some of your pictures, too. And tell her about you, so she'll really know her mother."

"Damn it, Tess," I tell the photo of the baby. I hold my head in my hands and push the tears back in with my palms. I sit there for a long time before I can sigh and breathe and look up again.

There's a silver pen tucked into the metal rings, so I take it out and write:

> Dear Amber,
> My name is Libby and I'm your mom. I'm going to try to be honest with you and tell you that some days I am so scared. I never had thought much about my life or what I wanted to do. But now I realize that everyone needs to change for a reason, and you are my reason.
> Here's what I would write if you were one of Baxter's cows:
> Sex: Female.
> Birth weight: 6 pounds, 9 ounces.
> Polled: Yes. (No horns that I can see. Just a halo. Like Baxter says, you're an angel.)
> Coloring: Blotchy red at first. Now creamy white.
> Sire: Unknown. (Well, the truth is, Simon. Simon Frazier. At college—not in the picture).
> Mother: Tess. Libby. You have two. That makes you lucky, I think.
> Tag number: A-M-B-E-R
> Notes: Blond hair, like fuzzy duck. Right eye squishes down, makes you wink. Bubble on your lip from sucking. Healthy. A keeper.

Then I sketch her face. The thing about faces is to get the placement of the eyes right. They go right in the center of the oval, whereas most people are apt to think they're up higher. Light as I can, I draw a straight line for the eyes, and one for the bottom of the nose, and one for the lips, and then an up-and-down arc to help get the angle right. Faces start with these four lines, and then the angle of cheekbone and hairline, and I watch as her face comes alive on paper and it's pretty good, this calm, wide-eyed face looking up at me, much more like Amber than the baby on the cover, and I'm glad that at the very least I can do that—that from nothing except paper and ink, something real gets captured.

When Tess was pregnant, I'd give her presents of chocolate, flowers, a necklace that was on sale at Ginger's Boutique. Also I did the grocery shopping more, because she was always wanting fruit and complaining that Kay never bought enough of it. I bought mangos, oranges, fresh pineapple, bananas, even though they were expensive. I made her drink milk instead of pop, even though that was more expensive too.

Sometimes she'd flash me a smile and a wink, or grab my hand and start a thumb war, which is something we'd been doing ever since we were kids. Or she'd hug me and whisper in my ear, "You're all right, Libby, yes you are."

She made it clear to me that her gift back was the pregnancy. "Good thing this is temporary," she'd say, "because there's no way I'm giving up my life forever." She liked to remind me what she missed: drinking, smoking, partying, pot.

It was at her five-month checkup that I gave her some big shirts, because she was having trouble wearing her old clothes, and because spring was coming and she couldn't wear big sweaters forever. That was when the nurse did an ultrasound and said, "Hmmm, hard to tell, but it looks like a boy, though that could be the umbilical cord." I was so excited, but Tess was lying there with a faraway look in her eye. She didn't look happy or excited or nothing, just faraway. On the drive home, she said, "Some people were never meant to have kids and here I am anyway, with a baby inside, and this was a real mistake."

I tried to cheer her up. "I read in a book that your baby is—"

"*Your* baby."

"Okay, *the* baby is three pounds now, as big as a grapefruit. It can suck its thumb!" I reached over and rubbed her round tummy. "Hello, baby."

She picked my hand up from her tummy and moved it away. "I don't want this baby. I wonder if I'll feel different when it's born. But here's the thing. I don't *want* to feel different. I want to make sure I don't feel different."

"Okay."

"I'm not sure you're going to want it either. You better not be kidding."

"I'm not kidding. I'm going to be so happy, Tess."

"Libby? I'm afraid to know the reason why. Why you wanted to do this."

I shrugged, because I didn't know the answer to that question. And anyway, it was like there was a million answers, not just one, and only with them all together did it make sense, and that made it too hard to explain.

Because Tess didn't really want to have an abortion.

Because it was unfair she'd have to do that, just for a little mistake.

Because it would make her proud.

Because it would make me special.

Because I wanted something to happen in my life.

Because I wanted someone to love me—just me.

Because I knew Tess was about done with high school, and that she was going to leave. And maybe if there was a baby here she wouldn't take off after all.

Because maybe I don't know what my life is about if it's not about Tess. And maybe this was my last-ditch effort to keep her around.

116

E I G H T

Drunk feels good and *melted*, like a candle that doesn't have to stand up any longer, which is a damn *relief* because for once the wax can be soft, it can let go for just a moment—what an amazing *gift*—because when something's that soft it can't *hold* anything. Can't hold anything like scared-hurt-panicked, and that's why I'm so glad to be here, melting, and there's no Amber, and I'm free.

Derek's driving his sister's car, driving like a maniac down the gravel county road, and we're leaving nowhere and going nowhere in the middle of the night, and I'm sitting in the back, just for the hell of it, giggling, because there's this stuffed animal that his sister has on her dash, and it might be a dog but I think it's supposed to be a bear. It looks like whoever made it couldn't decide, didn't care enough to decide, didn't want to decide. Wobble, wobble, all over the place, who the fuck *are* we, anyway, and it looks like one of those cheap things you win at carnivals and I've named it Randy for some reason. And hey, Randy, doesn't it feel good to just *melt* every now and then? I like you Randy. You're cute. Plus you're not screaming at me.

There's a huge full moon coming up into a dark arc of sky, and the wind is blowing at the car, and Derek's cussing the radio because his sister doesn't have a sound system like he does, and he's mad he's got to be driving her car instead of his truck, but his truck has a flat. He stops the dial at some scraping-sounding rock music, just to piss me off, because he knows it's hard on my ears.

"Come on," I say, grabbing his chest from behind and kissing his ear. "Something softer, please."

"Then shut up with your Randy. And get off me! I drive good drunk, but not with another drunk hanging off me." He tries to pry my hands off but I hang on and I'm giggling like crazy till I see the car going off the road and bouncing down the slope, but even that seems funny, like, Whoa, here comes some grass! When the car bumps to a stop, I get thrown forward into the back of his seat, and my nose starts bleeding but it doesn't hurt. The car stalls and Derek turns around and says, "You dumb shit." But he's smiling and I'm smiling back, which is hard to do, because I'm tipping my head up to get the blood to go backward, and I say, "Come on, Derek, tell me the truth. You weren't at the movies with Shelley?" As I'm talking, he climbs into the back with me, so I say, "Aren't you going to get us out of here? You got any toilet paper? You got to get me home. I'm so late. Late, late. Kay's going to have a hissy fit."

"I told you, I was at the movies with guys from work. Shelley was there too, but I wasn't with her."

"Promise?"

"Do you really care?"

While I'm pausing, thinking about that, he leans over to kiss me on the cheekbone. "Listen. This is why I asked you out tonight. We gotta talk. We're at a spot where we gotta decide." He looks at me closely but I shrug and bite my lip. He says, "I don't want to raise a baby. Simon's baby. Is that what you want? Because if you do, I think you need to ask me."

"I'm not asking—"

"But you come with the baby."

"So then, tell me goodbye."

He looks at me hard and for a moment it looks like maybe tears are coming into his eyes even and he says, "I can't."

"Can't it be like my job? Like, I work around your job and you work around my job. Only I've got two—a store and a baby—"

"No, it can't be that way."

"Why not?"

"Because a baby's not a job. It's a life."

"Then tell me goodbye!"

"I can't."

It makes me want to fly apart, this thing. I just want to shuck it off—not Amber exactly, but the whole baby *weight*, it makes me feel like it's smashing me down, and what about *my* life? And I want to shuck off this talk, because I just want to kiss Derek, and I don't want to have to think so much, and I just want to feel, and what's so wrong about just *feeling*?

Finally I say, "You know Hippie Ed? He was out checking his bees and he said to me, out of the blue, 'People just let their lives happen to them, without a struggle, and that's a crime. The crime of not paying attention to your life.' I don't know, Derek. I don't know about her life or my life."

"Well, have you thought about it? Giving her up?"

"I promised Tess."

"She let you promise too much. She knew what she was doing."

"I don't know. I don't know," I whisper. "Can we just— can we just not talk about this?"

"Well, when are we going to talk about this?"

119

"I don't know, but not now?"

He looks at me for a long time, and I lean toward him and kiss his ear, and he kisses back, and his kisses are so soft but they have a power like you wouldn't believe, and he knows that when he kisses me near my ear that my back arches toward him, and when he traces his finger along my arching back, down low, that makes me arch even more. His hands slide up the sides of my body and I can't get enough of his hands either, the way they feel out my body like I'm something special. I love this feeling—I love it I love it, I can't help it—and my hands find his hips and slide beneath his jeans and then we're past the place that cares about decisions and reasons.

The car's too small and Derek slides backward so his knees are on the floor and pulls me toward him, but still we can't quite match up in any good way. When we pull away and laugh, Derek opens the car door and I think it's so that our feet can hang out, but no, he's pulling me outside, into the grass.

He takes off his shirt and puts it down, and then guides me down on top of it. He takes my hair out of the ponytail and pushes his fingers up against my scalp and he says, "The world hasn't wrecked this up yet. You told me that once. That no matter how bad the world seemed, the one thing that was still pure and real was this. I think of that sometimes. It was a true thing you said."

A truck goes by on the road and we pause for a minute, but it speeds by, sending gravel flying against the other side of the car, and then he pushes my clothes off, down, up. I'm going crazy. I need him inside me. I'm using all my strength. I want to be the stronger one, I want to push his body inside me, but he's stronger and holds back for a moment. For once I'm all connected, and my neck and my heart and my mouth all feel the same thing and all I can do is breathe, but just barely.

He pushes himself gently inside me, his eyes locked on mine the whole time, and when he's in deep, he smiles and tilts his head to consider me. I mumble, There you are, and he says, Here I am, and we both close our eyes to feel what we are feeling. Which is good good good. He pauses for a minute and the moon lights up his face, and he presses his face against mine to rest, and then we move together so tight but it feels like space and space and space. And we rock back and forth until everything's twisted and bursting, and it feels so good to have the force of him inside, pushing away the empty, and for a moment I think I'm going to lose it, I can't keep the feeling, it's going to flicker, but I hold on and suddenly I am there. The finest kind of explosion, everywhere, a candle flaring.

I want to thank him but I don't know how, but I make a wish for him, a hope that he feels like I do, which I'm never really sure about but I want so badly for him to feel this joy. What comes out of me, what I hear my voice saying, is, "You're holding me together. You're keeping me warm."

The stars are burning holes in the sky. When we're resting, holding each other, we look at them and talk about them and then Derek whispers, "I know why you wanted to keep that baby."

"Hmm?" Somehow I'm almost asleep and I'm trying to bring my brain awake and toward his words.

"You knew Tess was leaving. You wanted to keep *her*." He whispers this into my hair. "You love her so much."

"Well, I also—"

"It's nice, Libby. That you love someone like that. I wish I had someone who loved me that much."

It's a flood of hurt, right up my throat, but I don't know what to do with it and I'm too hazy to come up with anything, and I push it away, quick, because sometimes I think if we really felt what we felt it would kill us, and the only thing that saves us is being able to turn a little numb.

When we climb back in the car, Derek turns on the heater for me and finds a country music radio station. That's a little gift for me, and I want to give him one too, so I squint at the floorboard of the car and all the junk that's piled there till I find what I was hoping for, a pencil and some paper—an old envelope from a bill. I sit up and reach down for them and put on my glasses. I sketch a picture of two hazy figures, holding hands. I just draw the back of them, so it's like they're walking away. Then I put pine trees all around them.

Derek says, "There's no pine trees out here."

"Yeah, but they're easy to draw."

We're talking real soft and mumbly, like we're sad and worn out. I've got the pencil hovering over the envelope. I want to draw a third figure, a little toddler, walking right between them, but I don't.

"That's real nice." He takes the envelope I'm handing him and folds it and puts it in his jeans pocket. Then he leans over and whispers in my ear, "I don't know if you believe this, but this was such a good thing." I know he means us, not tonight, and I know he means *was* and not *is*, and so I nod and bite my lip. I know there's going to be another goodbye, but this is the goodbye that he means, and it was about the most tender way he could tell me.

Hey, crazy baby Amber,

It's in the middle of the night and you're sleeping right next to me and the stars are so bright. Probably you should be in your bassinet but sometimes we cuddle in bed, I keep my arm around you all night, and I listen to your little puffs of breath.

Listen, I was just thinking. Once Baxter told me: A person's only got so much time and energy—make sure you use yours right.

122

Before you, this is how I spent my time and energy:

1) Finding beer. Drinking it

2) Getting through school

3) Working at the store

4) Hanging out with Tess and Shawny

5) Flying kites, playing dolls, coloring—growing up, I guess.

I'm grown up, now, Amber. I got through school. I'm legal to buy beer. Tess left.

I should have asked Baxter what was worth it and what wasn't. Oh my god, I have no idea about this world I'm living in and no idea about my life.

I think that maybe, my heart never stops talking, but it doesn't know what it's talking about. I talk back to it like it's a stupid person. My heart's always talking about dream-love and you got to teach me about the real kind. Together let's figure this out: What is enough to make up a life?

As I close the book, something drops out. Folded money. Five one-hundred dollar bills, brand new. It's so surprising I wonder how drunk I am and decide to wait till morning to see if what I really see is true.

Kay's standing in front of the dryer looking for her jeans. She's got a big bruise on her thigh, probably from getting kicked by a horse last week. She pulls on her Wranglers while she stares at me. She puts on her shirt, still staring at me, except for the second that green fabric crosses her green eyes. She gets her brush and starts brushing through wet hair, still staring at me.

"I'm sorry," I say.

"If I help you out more with Amber, you're just going to get

123

used to that help. You need to buckle down and decide you're going to do this on your own." She starts a French braid, and I haven't seen her do that in years. I watch the three sections weave through one another. A few white strands fall around her brown cheekbone and I decide to try to draw her sometime soon because all of a sudden she looks more beautiful than I have ever seen her.

She puts her wallet in the pocket of her Wranglers and grabs her keys. "I'll watch Amber while you work, and that's all. And pretty soon I want you to quit the store and work at Baxter's, where you can keep Amber with you a bit more. Do you understand me?"

"I don't feel so good, Kay. I like working at the store. Will you please hold Amber? I have to pee."

"There are lots of times you'll have to pee with no one to hold your baby. Figure it out. Baxter's offered you a job with flex hours that pays more, one where you can work with Amber."

I don't say anything. I look at Amber, who's looking at Kay and flapping her arms in the air. I turn away from Kay and head toward the kitchen, and that's when Kay says, "Simon's parents came by last night."

I turn around and raise my eyebrows.

"Just showed up, unannounced. I could just see them, looking around—"

"Oh, shit. Oh, really? Oh, man. The place is a mess. Did they see Amber?"

"Sure, they held her, asked about her."

"I thought they said we were going to meet in town for lunch."

"Well, they told me they were out this way and just decided to come over. I just wish I—"

"Did you tell them where I was?"

124

"I told them you were out. I called Tess from Baxter's after they left. I was hoping to catch her at work. To tell her we need to take care of the adoption papers. Guess what? She's not working there anymore. She quit. The manager didn't know where she was. Has she called here?"

"She's gone?"

"Have you talked to her?"

"No. She moved?"

"Apparently."

I wonder if I should tell her about Clark stopping by, but I already made up my mind that I wouldn't. Mainly because it's a good idea to keep Kay separate from just about everybody; she'd probably call him up and badger him about driving Tess off, and that will just embarrass me. Plus, he doesn't know anything anyway.

"We need to get a hold of her. For one thing, you need to have Amber legal. For taxes, benefits. You two should have worked it out before she left."

"I didn't know she was leaving! I didn't know!"

"Don't get snotty with me. Plus I'd just like to know she's alive." She reaches out to touch Amber on the nose, and she looks sad. "Baxter and I are going to work on the guzzler. You could come. He'll pay you."

"Where will I put Amber? There's no shade there. It's so hot."

She nods like she doesn't want to agree with me but has to. She turns from me then, and walks away fast—just like she's saying: Yeah, farewell, and this is the start of you getting left behind.

NINE

"Bees *know* geometry," Ed says through a white, goofy-looking hat with netting all around. He looks so ridiculous, and so much like he doesn't know it, that I have to trap a smile behind my hand. "Enough to make row after row of *perfect* hexagons. Here's something else about them: They don't fly at night, they're calmer in the evenings, which is why I'm moving them now. You going on a walk with the baby? Don't come over here now, they're a *little* riled up."

I nod and put an arm around Amber. After a minute, Ed comes walking over, leaving behind him a stack of white boxes with a bunch of bees swarming outside. Farther behind him, the sun is getting low down by the mountains.

Ed lifts his hat off, pushes the glasses to his face and runs his hand through his curly hair. "The alfalfa's *just* blooming," he says, and he holds out his hand and unfolds his fingers. Resting on his palm is a bee that lifts off into the air the moment it's free. "That was a drone. They don't sting. They don't even have stingers. They eat honey and have sex and then die, that's their job. What a life! Hi, baby. Look at your pretty eyes. Hi, dog, yes, yes, you want some attention, huh? If you're going on a walk, Libby, I'd like to go with you."

I glance at him but he's not on the prowl, he's just standing there looking at me all genuine and open, waiting for me to respond. "Well, okay. I was going for a short one, before it gets dark."

He comes alongside me and we walk together, next to the alfalfa, away from the bees and toward Baxter's place in the distance.

"Nicer to walk with someone," he says. "Gets lonely, I think, even for a loner. Once I walked up to a group of friends. Professors of mine, actually. Who were talking outside. People who I liked a lot. This is a story of how something so *little* can change a life. I walked up, and nobody noticed me. Or more like, they just ignored me. I felt so invisible. I've always been that way. I don't know *why;* I have that blind spot about myself. Something's wrong with me. I mean, people don't notice me. So, anyway. I moved to El Salvador. A little village in El Salvador, in the rebel-controlled territories, the FMLN. All because I felt like I wanted to do something that mattered, so that *I* would matter. I snuck in solar powered generators for radios. Long story. Solidarity movement. Long story. Then I got my heart broken."

"By a woman?"

"No, no, the world. Because I wanted to make a difference, a big *difference,* and it wasn't working out. I'm sorry if this is a weird conversation for you, but I'm not all that good at having the regular kind. They're boring."

I try to mumble something about it being a good conversation, but all my words are messed up too, although I get out enough of them, I guess, that he knows what I'm saying, and he nods a bunch of times and smiles.

"Not being able to help, that made me feel small. So I

moved out here. So that I could feel like enough again. And all this because once I walked up to a group of people, and god knows that wasn't *their* fault, they were in the middle of a conversation. The reason I am telling you this is because you're not small. You figured out how to change what's in front of you."

I don't know what to say, so I concentrate on Ringo, who's darting ahead of us, then darting back, tongue out, tail swooping in huge circles.

"The reason I moved myself to El Salvador, I think, was because there I wouldn't be invisible. Because I was different; I was the white guy, for one thing. Do you think that's why Tess left?"

"What? Tess?"

"Yeah, Tess."

"I don't know, Ed. I don't think you're invisible. I don't think Tess was invisible. Why would she be less invisible there? People *do* like you. You're just different, is all. I don't think Tess was invisible. People noticed her. She's beautiful."

"I never noticed her. I noticed you though."

"Oh."

"This is not a come-on, by the way."

"Okay."

"You're female and I'm male, and god knows why but the world we live in made it nearly impossible for us to have a real conversation."

I glance at him and smile, because I'm realizing that here is a person who's just going to say things, and that already makes him more interesting than most of the world. Nobody else I know says stuff like this, just honest stuff—something other than cars, or gossip, or the weather, stuff that just gets closer to the heart.

"My sister's gone. Just suddenly gone. From Durango. We can't find her."

"Okie-dokie. Yep," he says, nodding. After a bit, he says, "Some people, they *want* to be invisible. At least for a moment. So they can move from place to place without being seen, for instance. Only then, because they're *trying* to be invisible, they're *not*. For example, most of the illegal immigrants get nabbed because of routine traffic stops. Did you know that?"

"No."

"And most of *those* were caught on Highway 160, between Durango and Alamosa. More illegals are caught there than any other place in this country."

"By Durango? Is that true?"

"Yes, it's true."

"Ed, I'm sorry. I'm not very smart. I'm not just saying that. It's a fact. I'm telling you this because I need to—because I'm trying to talk with you for real, because you are and I don't know what the hell you're saying. I'm sorry."

He looks at me and smiles. "Okay, what I mean is, most people spend their *whole* lives trying *not* to be invisible. This is what we all want, right? To be seen by someone? Someone who matters to us?"

This part makes sense to me and I nod.

"I don't mind telling you, because I feel like I know you well enough—well *actually* that's ridiculous, because I don't know you so well, but I'm willing to take a risk, and anyway, some-times you just look at a person and it seems that you know her—but anyway, *anyway*, I just picked up some *ilegales*. In a little town outside Durango."

"What?"

"These people needed to stay invisible so *la migra* didn't get them. And your *sister* was supposed to pick them up."

"*What*?"

"But she didn't—"

"My sister? Tess? I—"

129

"*I* don't know that for a fact. But I'm operating on instinct, and my instinct is pretty good. Instinct and gossip. I keep an eye out, and that means I just know about certain things. Your sister was the contact, I think. A girl drives, less suspicious. Girl driving on a Sunday, when fewer INS agents are out—good thinking. Girl driving an old pickup with a tarp on top, or an old van, no problem. Okay? But something happened to her and she didn't show. Luckily, one of the fellows had my name and number and so I drove up to get them."

"I don't know what you're saying."

"I'm getting there. A *coyote* arranged their transportation. You read the news, right? Semi-trucks hauling illegals, sure, there's that. But also young female drivers, who don't look suspicious. And this was Tess's job, but she didn't show. You don't know anything about this?"

"No."

He looks at me to see if I'm telling the truth, and then nods to himself. "Well. I'm sorry to surprise you with it, then. Luckily, I have a VW bus. Very handy for some sorts of things. Orange, even. That's a fact, for sure. The more obvious you are, sometimes, the less people see. You put something right in front of them and it's too *there* to be noticed."

I stare into the alfalfa. The little purple flowers are bobbing up and down in a breeze. "Let me get this straight. There were some illegals that Tess was supposed to pick up, but she didn't, but you did. And they're here now? They're safe?"

"Yes."

"Miguel's group?"

"No."

"Tess was doing this as a job? For money?"

"It's good money. Very good. One of the best ways to make money out here these days. That's a fact."

"Well, where is she now?"

"She's fine, I suppose." He pushes his glasses up. "Listen. There's two routes for people coming here. One's through Texas, up to Kansas. The other, for people crossing in Arizona or New Mexico, brings them to southern Colorado, through the mountains. Through Durango. She was a stop, transportation from a store called El Mercadito. But she backed out, or there was a miscommunication. If she was smart, she got the hell out of there, quiet. *Extracted* herself. You see what I mean?"

"No. Yes. She's good at that, disappearing."

He smiles. "Pretty sly, huh? It's one thing to be invisible. And another to be a *pelagato*—a nobody. It's a fine line. But that's a little bit off the topic, isn't it?"

"Ed, what do you know about my sister?"

"I got word that she left. Just left. And I would know if it was something else."

"Something else, like what?"

"Like, you know what else."

I put my hand on Amber's head. I realize I have the money my sister got paid but maybe didn't earn. I realize that I don't know what kind of world I live in. I realize that all this time I've been not seeing. It makes me feel sick.

"Ed? If you picked them up, then nobody's mad, right? And she's safe, right?" It comes out as a whisper.

He nods. "That's what I'm hoping."

"Thank you, Ed."

"You're welcome. But I didn't do it for you. Or for her. I did it for *them*."

"Okay," I say. "*Qué bueno.*"

He smiles. "*No sabía que hablas español.*"

"*Estudio el español un poco.*"

"I think we should all be living more dangerous lives. We have to be careful, yes. But when we get too fearful, we become small."

For a while, we walk in silence, past the alfalfa and into pastureland. Amber stares ahead and kicks her legs and does this new thing, which is to make a soft little coo, which has got to be the prettiest noise, especially when you compare it to the screaming she usually does. I think I'm paying attention to it because I don't know what to do with Ed, or his words, and I can't think yet about my sister, and so all I can do is focus on something simpler.

"Tulip gentian." Ed points to a purple flower.

"Tulip gentian," I say.

"I think humans are only capable of *small* moments of honesty. Then they get tired and back away. It's something to foster, this ability to keep it for longer. How to keep being honest and aware. Is that what you're thinking?"

"Yes, sort of. Actually. I can't keep up with you."

He turns to me and smiles. "Yes you can. You're meeting me head on right now. I appreciate it. Cone flower, there, see that yellow one? Baxter's field is in good shape."

"People say that. He's a good rancher."

"I wonder if he lets the cattle in this pasture. Not for a while he hasn't. There's scarlet mallow. We become invisible to each other, and we fight to become visible again. It's a constant battle, and it wears us out. And the only thing I've figured out is that we stay alive to each other if we can stay honest and aware."

"Scarlet mallow? I've always wondered. Because that's my all-time favorite." The flower is peach colored and the leaves have a tint of sagey color to them, and Ed knows I'm not just listening to the flower names, he knows that I'm listening to it all.

"Yellow-headed grackle," he says, pointing to a bird sitting on a bush.

"It's pretty."

"You seem like a strong person. Like maybe someone who can absorb a lot."

I snort-laugh and give him a look like, Whatever.

"No, really. And that's something I'd like to learn how to do. Face things better. Be a little more sturdy."

"I don't think I'm so good at that, actually."

"You're brave like the *ilegales*. You move forward and you do it. You take a baby, you raise it. You don't make it complicated, you just do it."

"No, really. You don't know—"

"Well, we all see strengths in others, and we use them to teach ourselves. I'm a pretty happy guy. But sometimes—this world, it's being ruined. But look, look, all we see is this grass and sky." He swings his arm over Baxter's pastureland. Up ahead is a gully, its bank lined with bushes and tall grasses, and far beyond that a small rise of red rocks. "It's why I moved here. To be in a place where I felt it less. Felt the pain less. Because otherwise I think I'd put a gun to my head."

Something about his voice tells me that he means this. It's the most fragile thing about him, and he wants me to know it. I can't just say nothing, so I finally blurt out, "Jeez, Ed. Don't do that. Please don't do that." Then I add, "I had a gun to my head, once."

He looks at me, surprised but steady, and his eyes won't let go of mine. "Did you?"

I reach down to pick a scarlet mallow flower to press in Amber's book. "It was my girlfriend who put it there. She wanted me to feel what it was like, to be feeling that kind of pain. Ed, are you far away from that place now?"

"Far enough." He's looking ahead and he's scared, because we're talking about something real. And then I feel him smile, in his body, because he feels found by someone, and he feels that I feel it too.

And isn't it funny how if one person speaks for real, then the other person can too? We just did that. We just became friends. It's just a matter of finding the right person and crossing that barrier together, almost like you're holding hands, but really you're holding the most tender place inside you.

It's the dark morning hours before the sun comes up, and Amber's up and I'm so sleepy I start to cry. I cry while I put on her diaper, make her a bottle, and the tears drop down onto her tiny body and into the fuzz of her hair, and I'm too tired to be angry, I'm too tired to be anything. I flop on the couch to feed her and I flip on the TV. Nothing good is on, so I settle, finally, for a show where a man's painting an oil-color and telling me how to paint the exact same picture. Half an hour, I watch him, and watch his painting unfold, and I'm glad for Ed but not for what he told me, and I think about Tess and how she's been lying to me this whole time. Why didn't she just tell me she was running illegals? It makes my cheeks burn, and I've been seeing the world in such a simple way, and I never wanted to believe that about myself, but now it's so true, not even I can miss how stupid I am.

Somewhere along the way, Tess knew she was going to leave this baby, and that she'd need a way to make it, and that she was going to run illegals, and that even though we'd told each other everything our whole lives she decided to keep this a secret. And Clark lied, and maybe Miguel even knew. Maybe I did too. Because what was I thinking when she gave me that money out of nowhere, when I knew Clark hauled alfalfa? Who knows and who knows and who knows, but now I feel myself sinking down, too far down, where it just doesn't feel safe.

Tears are sliding down my cheeks—stupid me—and I hold myself so still and I watch the painter's hand add ultramarine blue above fading down into cobalt, and he says that in the early paintings of the West people didn't believe the artists, didn't believe the sky could be that color. But it *is* that color, and that the people of the West understand something about the color of blue and its variations, more than most people.

I try to pull myself up and out of this buzzing sadness by staring hard at the TV. I think maybe the artist has been out this way, because he's painting a stretch of dry grass and an earth-red ridge, but mostly he's painting sky. His painting is good but not great—even I can see that. Because it looks like life, but without the spirit. Without something underneath. But I like the title of it. He calls it "Sky Bridge."

He says that only in a place like this could a person touch sky. He says a person doesn't move into the blue on a mountain or a skyscraper—no, those places actually push the sky farther away. Only in a place like this do earth and sky come together in such a way that they bridge into one, and in such a place a person could put up her arms and find herself in heaven.

When Tess picked me up at work that same day she told me she was pregnant, I was smiling. It had only been a handful of hours, but I had spent all those hours thinking and dreaming. Tess was driving Kay's truck, and she leaned over the seat to open the door for me. "You got to get your car fixed, Libby. Kay says she wants thirty cents a mile for all this extra usage of her truck on your account. She's sort of kidding, but not really." When I didn't say anything, she added, "I know. I know what you're thinking. How come we got stuck with *this* life—broke all the time, cars not running, living in the middle of nowhere, with Kay as our mom. But at least you're not pregnant. Right?"

"Tess, I've got an idea."

"At least you don't got that hanging over you too."

"Tess, just listen. I got an idea. How about this? How about I keep your baby?"

She laughed. "No way. Are you crazy?"

"I'll raise your baby."

"No."

"You won't have to get an abortion. I'll move to an apartment in town. I'll raise it. I mean, you can help if you want. It'll be so cute, don't you think? Do you think it's a boy or a girl?"

"It's not a baby yet, Libby. It's nothing."

"It might be. It will be. It will be something."

"Have your own baby."

"Well, maybe I will. Someday. But now is now, and now you're pregnant."

"No."

"Yes. I can just picture it, me holding a little baby."

"No. If you don't want to take me, I'll take myself." She got all pissed off then, bitching about how at a moment like this she thought at least her sister would help. As she talked, I looked out the window at the nighttime sky and there were stars shooting through my whole body.

I was thinking of Shawny. She'd died just a few months before. That's not why I wanted the baby, though. I wanted the baby because Shawny had been wrong about things. And I was sorry that she didn't feel this way much—that feeling of buzzing with energy and excitement, with life. I figured that if I faced it, it would be all right. That's what I was feeling, and it was so damn strong I knew there had to be some truth in it. I knew I should be brave enough to brace myself and reach for something terrific while I had the chance.

TEN

There's a place inside us that knows something before we know it. I'm cleaning the meat room when I see Derek walking down the chip aisle toward me and words fly into my mind: *Oh, Libby, steady now, don't let this hurt.*

Derek pushes the swinging metal doors open and walks right into the meat room at the same time I'm taking in a big breath to brace myself. The meat grinder is only half clean, but I put down the rag and pull off my yellow gloves. My eyes sting from the cleaning chemicals and I squint at him as I put my gloves in the sink. "Hey, you. But you're not supposed to be back here."

"Ah, Frank doesn't care."

"You want to go outside? I need a smoke anyway."

"Naw." He looks around the room and nods a couple of times, like he's agreeing with himself, and then looks at me. "Listen, Lib. Listen here. I'm sorry."

I let out a long breath and stand there, nodding.

"I said all along this was coming. I meant to tell you the other night."

"You did."

"Not clear enough." He puts his hand at the back of his neck and lowers his head to rub his neck and keeps his head lowered while he looks up at me. "Look, Shelley and me *were* at the movies. I know you've been trying to make it work. But keeping me and Amber separate, trying to show me that my life won't change, that's not right. I was waiting for you to do this. I figured you'd leave me. I think you want to leave me, but you won't say it. And I think maybe it's for the wrong reason. And I don't know if I can stick around if I'm not sure you love me. I guess I've never been sure."

I nod to it all, because how can I disagree with any of it? What I finally say is, "Okay. Don't worry about it. But remember our deal." Our pre-breakup agreement, I mean, which is that we'll run into each other in this little town and the least we can do is be nice to each other.

"Yeah, I'll remember it."

I rinse my hands off in the sink and unclasp a necklace he gave me last Christmas.

"You don't have to give me that necklace."

"I want to." I drop the gold chain in his palm. He has a cobweb of faded black lines from the oil he can't ever seem to wash out of the creases on his hands, and the chain looks striking there in the instant before he closes his hand and plunges it into the pocket of his jeans.

"Libby, it was you who came up with that deal. You know that, right? You were protecting yourself all along." When I don't say anything, he adds, "In any case—hell, I ain't got what it takes to be a decent father. And how'm I supposed to be your boyfriend without being her father?"

"You'd make a good father."

He stays silent for a minute, then says, "Someday, maybe. I do love you, though."

I smile at him, because how can I help it? He's looking so honest and sincere and sorry.

"We had some fun times, though," he says. "I'll say that. Right?"

"Right."

"Okay, then. You okay?"

"I'm okay."

"I want to tell you something. People are always talking about good hearts. So-and-so has a good heart. But there actually aren't that many. Good hearts. Because people've got their own goals and selfish things to worry about. But you, you got an actual good heart. You really do."

I stare at him for a bunch of heartbeats, and then I finally say, "Jeez, Derek." And I'm thinking, why didn't you ever tell me this before? But all I say is, "Well, jeez."

"I know your life isn't so great right now—"

"It's my own fault."

"—but what I'm saying is— If you need someone—"

"I don't need anyone." I'm surprised at how soft my voice is, so I clear my throat and say it again, louder.

"I realize it's a bad time to leave, maybe."

"No," I say. "It's a good time. It's the right time. I'll see you around, Derek. I'm okay."

"Yeah?" He reaches out to touch my cheek. He turns and then pushes the swinging door open, and I watch him leave through the big glass window that separates the meat room from the rest of the store. His cheap, dirty jeans, T-shirt, the hand that's still rubbing the back of his burnt neck.

The tears that are on their way are gonna be a relief, because they'll wash out the sting. I go to the bathroom and let them come till they're done. Then I test out my voice. "Hey, hey! How are you?" I say to the mirror, at the ugly, stupid me that's looking back. I want to make sure my voice doesn't sound quivery. I want to make sure I can hold it steady. "I'm fine," I say. "Just fine."

I make faces at myself. To cheer myself up, maybe, or maybe to disgust myself even more. Maybe because I don't know what else to do. I jut out my lower jaw, then squish up my lips, lower my eyes, stick out my tongue, and then lift my eyes up and smile.

"You jerk," I say. I don't know if I'm saying that to myself or to Derek or to the world, and it doesn't even matter. It applies to everything and everyone.

I finish cleaning the meat room, restock a few gallons of milk, mop all the aisles. Right before the store closes, I go to the Employees-Only part of the store. I'm watching my hands and I swear it seems as if they're working on their own. I'm right next to the palettes that hold all the pop and beer, and I watch my hands pick up a twelve-pack of Coors Light and throw it in the trash. Into the big, gray trashcan that sits next to the break room. I just heave that beer right in.

Man oh man, I tell myself, what the hell am I doing here, and how'm I going to explain this to Frank?

I'm trying to figure that answer out as I dump the bathroom trash in the trashcan too, looking in to see if it covers the beer. I see some of the wads of toilet paper filled with my snot. I'll say, Frank, I don't know how the beer got there. Huh, who knows? I'll say, Frank, I've stole from you here and there before, and that's just the way it goes. I'll say, I needed some beer and I was broke. I'll say, I just fucking feel like shit.

I finish gathering the trash and walk up front to see what Frank and Arlene are up to. I can see outside through the glass door, and the parking lot is dark and deserted and there's no sign of Derek's truck—he's not blinking his lights at me to show he's waiting. Arlene is clipping coupons from the newspaper, which she sends in to the manufacturers even though no customer ever used them, and I think that's sort of illegal and so she's a crook too. Frank is in his office, tallying up numbers or whatever he does up there. So I go straight to the back and

140

haul the big plastic bag out to the dumpster. It's hard to throw a bag that heavy in, but I manage to get it over the edge.

Right as I'm ready to punch out, Frank comes back and stands in front of the pop and beer crates, but I know he's only tallying up how much to order. I keep busy, hanging up my apron and getting a plastic cup of ice from the icemaker because I like to crunch the ice in my teeth on the drive home. Probably Frank cheats on his taxes. Probably Arlene takes a dollar or two from the till now and then. Or puts a steak in her purse on her way out. She hasn't had an easy life, and she needs to make concessions too. When life is shitty, it is so easy to be shitty back.

Arlene's already left and Frank's locked the door, so I have to wait till Frank comes up with his keys to let me out. My eyes hurt, so I keep closing them. My feet hurt from standing all day so I shift from one to the other, one to the other. Frank finally comes up, holding my paycheck. "You want me to cash it?"

"Please."

"Figured. Already counted it out."

I sign the back of the check and he hands me two hundred and ten dollars back. As he opens the door for me, he says, "You ought to get a bank account, a savings and checking account."

"One of these days I'll go."

"It's not hard to learn."

"One of these days."

"If you want me to help you out with that, let me know. I'll walk over to the bank with you. Okay?"

"Okay."

"Night, Libby."

"Night, Frank."

He watches me walk to my car. He always waits for it to start before he gets in his own truck, because he knows there's

141

a long history of it not starting, and he's been known to jump-start this piece of junk or give me a ride home. He does this because he's a good guy. But not good enough. Apparently.

My car starts and I pull away and head down the road. But after a while I pull over, turn around, and drive back to the store.

I have to climb all the way into the dumpster to get to the bag. Trash-picking, Tess and I called this, and we used to do it all the time, mostly for beauty magazines the store threw out, or sometimes the little bouquets of wilting flowers. I find my twelve-pack and balance it on the corner of the dumpster as I climb out.

I drink four beers on the way home. They're warm, but what the hell, and that's a lot of beer for me, but what the hell. And what the hell, why is it that even when you know something's going to happen in your head and then it does your body feels snapped to pieces anyway?

I never know what Kay will be doing when I come home from work—if she'll be sleeping, or pacing with Amber, or drunk-happy, or drunk-pissed-off, or Gone Berserk. Sometimes she's some mix of these, like happy drunk and cooing over Amber, or asleep on the couch with Amber on her stomach, or glaring at me as she thrusts a newly made bottle at me and heads for bed. So normally I'm not surprised at anything, because the possibilities are endless. But what I do see makes my eyebrows shoot up, because there's Kay, sitting on the couch with Amber awake in the crook of her arm and Baxter beside her, and all of them are watching TV, and all I can think is, *I am really damn drunk.*

"Hey," I say, because they're looking up at me.

"Howdy, Libby." Baxter's got his feet up on the table. He's wearing a white undershirt and jeans and white socks. I don't

142

think I've ever seen him sit like that before, and I can't believe he's just sitting there, relaxing, right next to Kay.

"Amber's been up for a good two hours," Kay says. "This is the unsleepiest kid in the world. You'll want to feed her before you go to bed."

"Okay."

"Her rash looks like it's clearing up."

"Okay."

"We're watching a movie," says Baxter, nodding his head at the TV. "I was over here anyway with the swamp cooler. See?" Now he nods at the window and, sure enough, there's a big gray box stuck there. "Does it feel cooler?"

Actually it does. I hadn't noticed it till now, although how I could have missed it with all that noise is beyond me. I'm pretty tipsy and so I'm concentrating on seeming anything but.

"Yeah," I say. "Wow. That's real nice. Wow."

"Did you do those drawings, Lib?" He points toward the two I've just taped to the wall. One is my version of the TV-painter's "Sky Bridge," but in charcoal, blended together so it's soft and hazy. The other is a new watercolor, a whole piece of paper filled with one scarlet mallow flower, and the thing I'm most proud of is that I got the white space right, which is something that's tricky to do with watercolors, since you can't ever get the white space back.

"Ever since she was a kid," Kay's saying, "always demanding art supplies for birthday presents."

I'm still standing up in the doorway of the living room, so Kay scoots over, closer to Baxter, and pats the couch. "Have a seat. How was work?"

"Fine," I say. I don't want them smelling the beer, so I stay standing where I am. "I think I'll get a glass of water. Either of you want something?"

"Nope," Kay says for them both.

143

"Guess I'll head for bed."

"Come get your baby." Kay hands her to me and I hold my breath as I grab her. But Kay doesn't notice nothing; she goes back to watching TV, which is what Baxter does too, so I walk to the bathroom.

Kay hasn't had a boyfriend since the summer I was sixteen, which is the summer she was fixing fence with Baxter and the barbed wire came springing loose from the fence stretcher and caught her across the throat and there was a lot of blood. I wasn't there but I heard about it, how Baxter got her to the hospital just in time. Later, Tess noticed that Kay hadn't gone out with anyone in a while, hadn't been drinking so much. Tess was complaining about it, because she liked it when Kay left so she could turn up the music and dance around the house, but I was happy because it was just us after that.

Maybe I shouldn't be surprised. But damn, Baxter? He's older and too clean cut and too much of a friend, although I guess none of that really matters. But what does matter is that he knows who Kay is already, and he doesn't have to go through that process the others did, at the end of which they all packed up to leave.

Kay's picked up the bathroom. Our tampon box and toothbrushes have been put away and Kay's wiped the sink clean and brushed out the toilet. It even smells like glass cleaner.

I stand there, looking at this clean bathroom until finally I realize I have to pee, and so I put Amber on the floor and sit on the toilet.

The one good thing about when Kay had a boyfriend was that she paid attention to things. But there were bad things too, like trying to tell if her new guy was a nice one or a mean one. Figuring out whether he liked beer or liquor, whether he'd stay one night or a few weeks or a year. Baxter I already know, so there isn't that much to watch for.

Maybe he just put in the swamp cooler and decided to stay late to watch a movie. Maybe. But something about the way they were sitting makes me doubt it. As I wash my face, I think, *Well, what the hell. At least one of us will have a boyfriend. And maybe Kay will rise to the occasion.*

I was six and Tess was three, and we were sitting under the table at a bar, and on one side were Kay's legs, her jeans and boots, and on the other side there was some man's legs, also jeans and boots, but bigger. It smelled like beer and the floor was sticky, and we were sitting on brown paper towels that Kay had put down there for us. I had a loop of string and I'd just learned how to make a Jacob's Ladder, and I was trying to show Tess but she was too little and so she was just batting her hand against my string, which didn't bother me. We'd all been out to eat, which was special, and we were allowed to order dessert, which was even more special, and I had a strawberry sundae and Kay had reached out and put some whipped cream on my nose, which made Tess laugh, and now I was sitting under a table playing string games with my sister.

When we left the bar, it was just the three of us, and Kay was carrying Tess in her arms. When we got to the truck, I climbed in and she put Tess on my lap, and Tess's eyes were open-closing the way they do when a kid's just about to fall asleep. When Kay started to drive, she also started to cry, which confused me, maybe just because I was a kid or maybe because when you're happy you tend to think other people are too. She said something like, "I'm sorry about yesterday, Libby," and I said, "What happened yesterday?" and she looked at me, surprised, and said, "That wasn't yesterday, was it? I'm going crazy. That was years ago. It's the thing I'm most sorry for. I kicked you across the kitchen. I guess you were only two.

Wasn't yesterday. Sorry, I'm drunk. Who was I then?" She wiped her nose and smiled at me. "I am pretty damn drunk. And you were looking up at me with this confused face. That's what made me stop. Was your face."

And I remember saying something to her along the lines of "I'm not confused now, Mom."

That only made her go back to crying. "Yes you are," she whispered. "I've lost it with Tess a few more times, I know that. Because then there was two of you, and I was alone, and everybody was always yelling at me, wanting something. Once I held her under cold water in the bathtub, just to get back at her for crying so much."

I looked down at Tess's face on my lap and watched her little mouth breathing. She was wearing a blue velvet dress with a lace top, a dress that I'd loved when it was mine, and it was sticky and smelled bad, but still it was beautiful. I tried to picture her as a baby, flailing in a tub of water.

"I'm so sorry," Kay said. "I'm so sorry I did that to the both of you. I was so tired. And I wanted my own land. And I wanted my time. For me. And I wanted a boyfriend. And I didn't want you."

I looked out the window, at the dark passing fields moving by. We were almost home when I asked her, "Mom? But why'd you kick me?" Because all along I figured that's what she was trying to tell me and her story was never getting there.

"Oh, just because you wanted chocolate milk. Coco milk, you called it, and you stamped your feet and screamed, 'Coco, coco. Bad Mommy,' and you threw your milk glass at me and I kicked you across the kitchen and said 'For-the-millionth-time-we-do-not-have-chocolate-milk!' I was so afraid someone'd see the bruises. But I kept you at work with me, you and me and Baxter and Adeline working and pretending nothing was wrong, until the bruises were gone, and I remember thinking,

Don't kick her again, and one reason was because I didn't want to be hiding bruises. That was the reason. Jesus. It was just so hard. You don't understand. I know you don't understand. It's okay if you don't understand. It's just that I'm sorry. I shouldn't be taking you to a bar with me at night. You shouldn't be the mother to your sister."

I told that story to Tess one night when we were older, even though I promised myself I wouldn't. I was drunk, though. We were both at a party, standing around a fire and a keg, drinking beer from plastic cups. She was standing next to me, dancing a little in place to the music. She listened and said, "What a bitch," and walked off. Later she came up to me and said, "Probably that's why I hate water," and walked off again. Later that night, she touched my arm and said, "We got stuck with a stinkhole of a ma, didn't we?" And on our way home, sitting in the bed of a truck with a bunch of other kids, being driven by some senior who thought it was fun to peel around the corners of old dirt roads as he took people home, she had to yell so I could hear her and she said, "Probably everyone loses it every once in awhile. It don't mean she doesn't love us."

"She loves us, sure," I yelled back.

"I don't like kids, either. I just want a different kind of life. Nothing wrong with that. What do you think about kids, Libby?"

I shrugged, but I wanted to tell her something and couldn't find the words. It was something about the way kids love. For some damn reason, they operate under the assumption that if they love enough the world won't be so confusing. If they love enough, good things will happen. I guess that's it. It's just that kids love too much. They haven't grown out of it yet.

ELEVEN

"*Adiós*, Lib, *Ad-i-ós.*" That's what Kay says every night when I come home from work. I walk in the door and she walks out. I watch her truck's headlights swing away, and listen to the tires crunch gravel, and if I walk out the door a bit I can see her drive all the way to Baxter's.

Nobody's said anything. Kay and Baxter, together. It just hangs there, like something so obvious that nobody needs to point it out.

Most nights, after she leaves, I sit on the couch and have a beer. I'm on my third stolen twelve-pack and I'm drinking too much—even I can see that. Sometimes I flip through the channels and sometimes I close my eyes and listen to the cicadas and crickets and wind. I don't like the swamp cooler after all—it doesn't feel familiar—so I turn it off and open all the windows. Then I feed Amber, put her in bed, and fall asleep myself.

I wait until I'm totally exhausted, because otherwise I can't sleep at all.

Now that Kay's not here, I hear things. I think about all the crazies that drive by on the highway. Every little thing makes me jump. I have nightmares about running with Amber in my arms, trying to get away from evil, which is not a person but a force, like wind, and it catches us anyway and tears us to pieces. When I wake up, I have so much fear caught up in my throat that I can barely breathe. So I daydream the night away, dreaming Tess back into my life a million different ways, and men falling in love with me a million different ways, and me proving to Kay that I'm not going to turn out like her after all, and me proving to all of them—to the whole damn world—that I'm strong and sure and worthy.

So much for brave Libby, who can't even sleep in a house by herself. So much for the put-together me. What am I supposed to do? Say, Kay, can you quit going to Baxter's, because I'm afraid of the dark? Fuck me.

If I was braver, I'd call up Ed, but I like him too much and I don't want to fuck up whatever nice feelings he might have about me. And Miguel's working all the time, extra hours, because he's got this plan to buy a house in Lamar for him and his cousins, because he's ready to be out of Shawny's old house. I can't even talk to Arlene, or Baxter, or Frank. When I try to talk about how hard it is even to take a shower, or how much Amber cries, they act sorry but really they're not. Basically, they're glad to see me growing up, which means getting smashed down.

Amber, though, doesn't scare me like she used to—she's sturdier—but she's still confusing. Like, I don't know how someone is supposed to ignore cries when the baby is just two feet away. She usually wakes five times a night and I know that's too many and that I should let her fuss a little so she'll go for longer stretches. That's what the magazines say, but I think most of those magazines are written by people with a lot of extra time on their hands, and help, and some space in their house. One article said that after the baby came I should start letting things go a bit—for example, quit folding underwear, and take myself out to the spa once in a while, which just made me laugh and think, *What a bunch of fuckers.*

Mornings are the only good time. The world seems safe and Amber splashes in the bathtub, and when I try to figure out what was so scary about the noises I heard, or what was so terrifying about my dream, nothing seems dangerous at all. And Amber is a cute, wiggly baby who waves her arms in slow motion, like she's floating in the air.

You find out a lot about babies when you stare at them all day. Like how she's learned to bring her tiny hands up to her face and suck at her fist. Like how, in the bath, when her arm or leg touches the water she crinkles her forehead like she's trying to figure out what that feeling is. She also tilts her head and tries to get some water in her mouth, and I'm always saying, "Now, Amber, don't do that, you're going to drown." I always tilt her head back up, but she always wants to turn her face toward that water, and I wonder if it reminds her of being inside Tess. Maybe she's fighting to get back to what's familiar.

Then there's the rest of the day, which is mostly a lot of work. I do laundry and clean and shop and cook, or if I'm too tired I hold Amber and watch TV or lie on a blanket outside. Every once in a while, I go through me and Tess's clothes and our back shed, looking for extra stuff to give Miguel's family. Sometimes I spend a few minutes drawing, and sometimes I flip through magazines. Mostly I'm just tired. Good thing she's sleeping more, because then I can take naps myself, curled up next to her.

I wait till the clock moves to three. Then I take a shower and get ready for work. I drop her off with Kay and head into town. Then I can breathe for real. Up ahead is a cool store and lots of people. Driving to work seems like the opposite of a dark, long night.

On the way, I watch clouds boil up over the mountains, far off to the west, and hope for rain. Everything is too dusty and pale and brittle, except for the few irrigated sections like Baxter's alfalfa. It's like the heat has knocked the whole world flat. Even the people seem tired—everyone complains about it, but in a slow way, like they've given in to the heavy, uncomfortable weight of it all. I hear that churches have moments of silence to pray for rain, and that some rancher hired an Indian to come in and do a rain dance, and the news is all about wildfires and thirsty cows. Ed, when I see him, tells me that more of that carbon dioxide stuff has been released into the air in the last thirty years than in the million years before, and that we've ruined our sky. I imagine what Derek would say, if we were talking, about how hot it was out on the rig. Baxter worries about the wildlife, and Miguel worries about illegals crossing the desert—not his cousins and girlfriend, who are still waiting at the border, but others—the anonymous, but not anonymous to themselves, since this is, after all, their one life.

The days move on, and to my right someone's baling a second cut of hay, and to my left someone's herding cattle. I try to pay attention to what blooms when, and what sorts of birds fly up from the grass at the side of the road. And I wish there was someone to talk to about the deep inside of me, and I wish I wasn't so scared about life, and I spend a lot of time telling myself, *Now, Libby, isn't this nice? Things will work out, Libby, don't you worry, something good is coming your way.*

GOT JESUS? That's what the bumper sticker says. And sitting on the bed of his old blue truck is Simon, his feet dangling down in front of his bumper sticker, staring right at me.

He's just like I remembered. Short blond hair, jeans and a bright rodeo shirt, cowboy boots that are too fancy to be useful, and a belt buckle about as big as a postcard.

As soon as I park, he walks toward me. "There she is." He bends down and cups his hands around his face and peers in the window of the car.

"What are you doing here?"

"Wow, she's blond."

"Yeah."

"Wow, she does look like me."

"Yeah."

"Wow. Can I hold her?"

"She just fell asleep. Maybe you could let her be for a bit. What are you doing here?"

He says, "Amber. She's real cute. She doesn't look like I expected. I figured she'd look like Tess."

"So did I."

"I don't know why I thought that. Maybe because Tess is so strong. Like her genes would win or something. Wow." He turns around and leans against the car and looks at me. "My parents made me leave for Alamosa. When they found out."

"They didn't *make* you."

"But I've been talking to them. I told them, W-W-J-D."

"What?"

"What would Jesus do?"

"What?"

"I said to my parents, 'Well, what would Jesus do?' And my parents said, 'Well, Jesus wouldn't have gotten a girl pregnant in the first place.' They got a point there. But humans are weak. I was weak. But God's been telling me not to run from my mistakes, my weaknesses. So I've been talking to them."

"Simon, what are you doing here? What are you talking about?"

"Well, about being involved with this baby. Raising it right. They've agreed to help. They want to be a part of this baby's life. We were all wrong. And for that I am sorry."

I stand there a long time, squinting at him. I'm so tired today that my eyes feel like broken glass and my brain feels like it's weighted down with heavy air.

He waits for a bit, and when I don't say anything, he says, "My parents say, and I agree, that this here isn't the right sort of situation to raise a baby in. And to have a kid raised half the time with my beliefs, and half the time with—well, what would Jesus do? He would take care of his baby. Raise it right. I don't want someone else taking care of my mistake, I don't want my daughter calling someone else Dad. Plus, this house, this place isn't any place for a baby to grow up." His face is turning blotchy red, and his eyes start darting all over the place. "My parents were right. Amber deserves more than this. We called a lawyer."

I blink at him, trying to catch what he's saying. "What? No you didn't. What?"

"Yes we did. My parents said the least I could do was tell you that. So I'm telling you. That's what I'm here to tell you."

I breathe out, tilt my head, and stare at him. "You're telling me what?"

"That I'm going to take Amber. Legal."

He rubs his hand on his cheek and stares behind me, at my car. "I'll tell you one thing right now. I've got legal rights. This baby is half mine. And I'm not going to have her be raised by, well, you, and a drunk grandmother—"

"What?"

"—I have all kinds of things I can use in court when I take you there. All the stories Tess told me about Kay. Try to see it my way. Why would I want my baby being raised here?" He kicks his feet at a cigarette butt buried in the dirt. "It's not like I want a baby. Holy cow, how's a single guy going to raise a kid? But I got an obligation. And I got a sort of community that you don't. My parents are helping me. With her, with the

153

money. Like I say, we're getting a lawyer." He nods to himself, proud that he got this all out, and turns and walks toward his truck. Over his shoulder, he says, "So tell Tess that I'm taking this baby, I'm getting her away from you." He passes right by my car, but he doesn't stop to look in at Amber.

I can't open my mouth. Not until he's gone, at least, and then I yell at the place where he just was. "You never talked to Tess once, Simon, not once, after you found out she was pregnant, you never asked how she was doing, you never came to the hospital, you get the hell out of here, you never come back! If there's a hell it ought to be for selfish people. It ought to be for people who look down on me like you do! Because at least I was there, Simon. I was *there*!"

I kick the cement birdbath lying in the dirt, but it hurts my toes so bad that I kick at the marigolds instead. After I get one plant kicked out of the earth and I can see the roots, I stop. Then I reach down and heave that damn birdbath up, and it's heavy as hell but I get it upright and balanced. It sits there, empty and dusty, and right away it tilts and pauses and falls, and there I am in the driveway again, my knees on the gravel, crying like crazy and looking at the empty space and trying to figure out what's going on in someone else's eyes.

"*Amiga*, dance with me." Miguel holds out his hand at the same time I tell him I can't dance, I really can't, and I'm still all teary and upset, but Miguel says he doesn't care, and he holds out his hand. There's something about his eyes—sad at the edges but still trying-for-happy in the middle—something about all that makes it possible for me to stand up and let him guide me to the dance floor.

We're at the Big Timber Steakhouse & Saloon because I went to Miguel's house, crying, after Simon left. I told him about Simon, and I almost told him how light I felt, how relieved I was, that the very possibility of someone taking Amber was at first a surprise that was good, and then bad, but good first and what did that mean? But at the last minute I stopped the words, put my hand at my lips to hold them there—although Miguel was waiting for them, but when the words didn't come, he said, "Lib, go home and get ready, because we're going dancing."

I put on the only thing I have that looks decent, my Rockies jeans and a white shirt that actually fits, and some makeup, and here I am, feeling like this country song is trying its hardest to transform me.

"It's not you, Miguel, it's me, I can't," I whisper, but he has taken my hand and is pushing me forward in that gentle, listening way that comes with dancing.

"It's a two-step, see? One-two, one. *Ya ves? Sí, puedes.* One-two, one. You got it. You can too dance."

Something about his voice can turn from regular-sounding to more full, and I look up because I can't help but wonder what's going on inside him. I don't know what it is, but it's a fact that there's more inside Miguel than in other people.

He's wearing black Wranglers, Ropers, a white shirt with a narrow collar. He's a good dancer, weaving us through the dance floor, which is so crowded I figure half of the county must be here. He turns me round and round and something about this makes me feel pretty, which is ridiculous but for this moment I am, and that seems like enough.

As we dance, Miguel talks about Alejandra. He prays for her. He prays for his cousins. The water, the danger, the baby inside her, and when he says the word *prayer* it sounds more like a real wish, a hope, and it sounds beautiful.

"Did you know, Miguel, that Tess was running illegals? Is she picking up your group?"

He pulls back so that he can consider me, and show me his surprise. "I didn't know. I guess it doesn't surprise me, though. *Híjole,* I hope she's careful."

"You didn't know?"

"No." He says it softly and holds my eyes with his to let me know that he's sorry for this, and then he sighs and pulls me closer.

After a while of dancing, I say, "I didn't know about it either. I just found out that she's involved, somehow. She'll be bringing your cousins, I bet."

He's thinking, and nodding, and I know he's not going to speak, so I change the subject and ask him the other question I've been considering. "Do you think you and Alejandra—how will that be, exactly?" I try to ask it in an off-hand way, like it's not something I've been wondering about for a while.

He shrugs. "It's going to be however. I don't know. I don't need to know."

"Maybe it will be love."

"Maybe."

"And if it's not—?"

"Then we'll just wait till she's a resident."

"And in the meantime, you'll raise her baby?"

"Yeah. Juan will be a brother."

"And it won't bother you that—"

"No, it won't."

"And the real father of the baby?"

He shrugs. "I don't know."

"You can do that?"

"I can. I can for a short while if that's what happens. And I can for a long while if that's what happens. I can because I don't think too much, which is a good thing."

I laugh. "I know, you've told me before. You think us *gringos* are too cold, too careful."

"I don't, I don't. I just know this is something I want to do." Then he adds, "You'll be Alejandra's friend, okay? Help her feel happy here. You can do that."

It's not a question, it's a statement, so I don't have to answer. As we swing around, I see Arlene standing over by the bar, holding Amber. I'd called her to see if she wouldn't mind watching my baby, and she said, "Hon, I got a better idea, I'll go too and make everybody stop their smoking and dance with that kid and teach her a thing or two about country music."

It was a good idea, because every woman here, and even some of the men, have been standing over that baby, taking turns holding her, cooing and flirting, and there's only one grouchy-looking old guy in the corner smoking, turned so that he doesn't have to see Arlene's fierce glances.

All that, I see in a second. As we turn, the next thing I see is the windows, how the rain flies down from the sky. People keep glancing outside to watch the sheets of water come off the roof, and the room buzzes with the joy of it, the relief, and also with the echoes of thunder rolling across the earth.

When Derek walks in, then, he's soaking wet, and smiling because of it. Somehow our eyes meet right away, and I wave to him before he can have a reaction so that my reaction wins, or gets everything out of the way. It's a happy wave, like, It's good to see you again, and he winks and waves back on his way to the bar, and then I can't see him anymore because Miguel has moved us to the other side of the dance floor.

"I built a shrine where you and Shawny used to play," Miguel says. "In the ditch bank. It's my way of hoping, of praying."

Miguel surprises me, how he'll say something that makes him seem fragile, but how he doesn't care.

"They'll come, Miguel. They'll make it."

He nods. "Did you know that along the way, through the desert, there are shrines? So carefully tended. I don't know if you *gringos* can understand what's inside those people who cross. The hope, the faith, the whatever-happens-happens attitude." Then he shakes himself free of this worry he has and smiles. "They work hard, and they play hard. Let's do the same," and he laughs and starts dancing with a bit more energy.

Right as the song ends, he leans back a little so he can look at me. "You and Shawny. You grew up together, I know. I imagine you two as girls, making your way through all those years together. I'm sorry I took her from you. She shifted away from you and toward me, I know that. And I'm sorry she left for good. I'm sorry that that's gone."

A truth spoken softly like that has so much power. I keep my eyes on the dance floor as we walk off. Because it's a great kindness for Miguel to say that and for someone, once, to know how much I miss her. But also I keep my eyes down because I'm realizing that this, maybe, is what falling in love is like. For some reason I believed that if you fell in love it was a guaranteed thing that your path would cross with his, and I never wondered how it would feel to fall in love with a man whose future just couldn't include you.

I can look Derek right in the eye. All these years together and finally we're dancing. It's not as smooth as dancing with Miguel, but it's more comfortable because I don't care how bad I am. After I tell him about Tess, he says, "I told you so," and after I tell him about Simon showing up and wanting the baby, he says, "Now *that's* a surprise."

"I never thought they'd want to take her."

"You know, I saw Simon's parents just the other day. In Lamar, at Big R."

"Did you talk to them?"

"No. Looked like they wanted to, maybe. Looked like they couldn't decide. They knew who I was, though. That I was your boyfriend, or ex-boyfriend. I mean, that I was—"

"The guy hanging around their granddaughter?"

"Yeah. I was getting a crescent wrench and a can of WD-40. They were checking out when I walked in, buying a whole slew of stuff. Looks to me like they're fixing fence. They almost came over to me."

"Almost. The world is full of almosts."

"Well. They're probably trying to figure out what good it would do. Some things aren't worth the trouble." After a bit, he says, "I'm sorry. About Simon. If you find Tess, you'll get it worked out. Or at least, that's the first thing you need to do. Find Tess. And you know what else you need to do? You need to talk to Simon's parents. From their point of view, which is far off and wrong, you look like an iffy mother."

"I do not!"

"Shhh. You do. You're single, and broke, and living with a mom that has—well, a reputation at the bars. Or used to. Just show them. Explain to them. And then they'll be satisfied, and go away."

"Derek, today I was feeding Amber and she reached up and touched my cheek. Usually she touches her cheek, but this time she touched mine. I thought, *Oh my god I love this kid.* Then I thought, *I can't do this, I'm too tired.* I'm always worrying about something. Like, is she drinking enough formula? And if she did, then how come she's crying? Or how come she's not crying? I'm tired of worrying."

"You need a friend. A mom friend."

"I don't know any."

"After Shawny, you never had any friends."

"I did have friends. I had Tess, I had you. And what am I supposed to do? Drive all the way into Lamar and stand

159

around looking for other moms?" I lean my head against his shoulder. I don't care if he doesn't want me to, I can't help it.

He pulls me a little closer as we dance. "I've got a story for you. My dad's horse died a couple of days ago."

"Really? Old Spirit? That's terrible. Why didn't you tell me?"

That last question makes us both uncomfortable, but luckily he ignores it and starts talking. "Listen to this. Old Spirit died right next to where that new banker built his house, and the banker's wife called, and she said she was so happy to finally be out of Denver and they sure loved it out here and they had such a nice view, but you know, there was a horse carcass out there with birds picking off the flesh and their little dog—one of those little yippy things—came home one night with a chunk of horse skull and was gnawing on it and, well, why was that dead horse there and could it be moved?

"You know what my dad said? He said, 'Uh-huh, that's part of the package. You city folk want to come in here and have us provide a free view. I'm not in the business of free views. I'm in the business of managing a ranch, and sometimes that includes dead horses.' And he hung up on her.

"So then the banker calls and says, well, something has to be done. And Dad said, 'Your ugly house has ruined *my* view. Your ugly house is equivalent to *my* dead horse. Only I'm a better neighbor, because mine is temporary. Now we're even.' Isn't that hilarious? I think that's hilarious."

He looks so happy telling this story that I can't help but smile.

"Dad ranted for hours about these new folks coming in, complaining about pigs smelling and slow tractors on the road. Why did they move here in the first place? This is the country, for godsake. Dad's right. But anyway, the horse is not officially violating any codes, so Dad's not going to move it. I told him, if your horse had to go, man, at least it went out causing a ruckus to the end. Because that was an ornery, mean horse."

160

"He wasn't so bad."

"Remember when we went riding? Bucked us both off."

Derek smiles, because that was a fun day we had years ago, riding around bareback, and it's nice to share a memory like that, a different version of us, floating, in its own time.

The song ends, but we stay on the dance floor and wait for the next one. When we're moving again, Derek says, "Dad's always going a bit overboard, but he's got a point. He says, 'Nobody ever unplows a Wal-Mart. Nobody ever gets rid of a subdivision. When this land is gone, it's gone forever.' It made me think, if I had some land I'd stay out here. But I don't. I don't want to be spending the rest of my life on the rig. I think I ought to get out of here."

He sometimes says that; everyone around here says that occasionally. I don't know what to tell him that I haven't said already. So I say, "You know what Baxter told me once? He told me that every person, to be happy, has to create something that doesn't die when he dies. For a rancher, he said, that's easy. He leaves the land. A teacher leaves something important. An artist leaves something. But for the rest, it's hard. They have to find something to create that matters, they have to do something beyond their own life."

Derek leans down and whispers in my ear. "What's that supposed to be for me, Libby?"

I turn my head slightly, so I can whisper into his ear. He smells a little like salt, like familiar skin. "I don't know. For me either."

We dance for a while and then I say, "Derek? Can I tell you something else? There was a message on the machine. Simon called while I was getting ready to come here tonight. He said he forgot to tell me something. I'm supposed to bring Amber to the hospital. They need some of her spit. They take some of Simon's too, to prove he's the father."

Derek looks at me and nods and waits.

"I'm not going to take her to the hospital. Not yet. I gotta think."

Something flickers in his eyes, and he shakes his head at me, no. "You can't delay everything, Libby. Make a decision."

I bite my lip, because I know what he's saying, and I owe him that much—I do. An answer—for him, about him. I owe him an attempt to speak the truth, the same sort of truth I wish I would've gotten from Tess about whether or not she was going to stay. So I say it. "Derek, what would you do? Say you got along with someone, and you had terrific sex, and you had enough in common and were friends and all that, but it wasn't love? It just wasn't? What would you do? How long would you stick around?" And as I say that, I move closer to him, because I can't stand to say something that's real but that hurts, and I can't stand to see him react.

The song winds down and our hearts beat and the dance floor feels quiet. Derek does the nicest thing, then. He leans forward, he whispers in my ear. "Okay, thank you. That's enough."

When we get back to the table near the bar, Miguel hands me my glass of beer and reaches out to shake Derek's hand, and somewhere in between there, between all the motion, the glass slips. It happens during the silence between songs, and I don't even realize I've dropped it till I hear the smash of glass on the hard floor.

Everyone in the room turns, and I'm blushing and trying to figure out what to do when some rancher at the next table over stands up and says, "Ah, what would all the glass makers do if nobody ever broke a glass?"

That makes everyone laugh, and then a woman at the next table stands up and yells, "Yeah, and better a broken glass than a broken heart."

Everyone cheers at that, and the music starts up again. Before I even get a *sorry* out, the bartender's come and gone with his broom and dustpan. Derek's smiling at me, and Arlene brings Amber over. Pretty soon she's talking to Derek and Miguel about the tornado that passed through Limon a few years back, how it tore up all the gravestones and took away the cemetery office and its maps, meaning that nobody quite knows where anyone is anymore, and the other story about how there was a woman living in a trailer, and her son picked her up to get her out of there, and as they were driving away part of her trailer landed in the back of the very pickup they were driving.

Amber's listening to it all, taking in this news of a world that spins cows into feed stores, and feed stores into silos. For some reason, she's as happy as can be. Seems like the more chaos around, the quieter she is.

I look away from them to find Frank walking toward me, fast. "Libby," he says, and before I even have time to be surprised, he grabs my arm and pulls me a step away. "Listen, Kay left a message at the store. Baxter had a stroke today. She's taken him to Pueblo. Well, first to the hospital here, and then to Pueblo."

"Pueblo? He had a stroke?"

"Get the details from Kay. She's with him. She'd fed the animals already, but for the next few days you're in charge. I got it all written down. Bulls, horses, calves up front, canary, roosters, donkey, peacocks, chickens. How many animals does Baxter have, anyway? Can you do all that? I'm glad I saw your car out front. Thought Arlene said something about coming here. Listen, you take off whatever time you need from the store, of course, and you'll have to leave early to feed at night."

"I'll figure it out. I can do it."

"Well, ask for help if you need it."

163

"I will."

"Here's the list of chores. Also the number at the hospital, and a number at a hotel where Kay's staying. Why don't you come in for a half day tomorrow? If you can find someone to watch Amber, that is. Or bring her in. Anything you or Kay need." Then he bows his head, but he keeps his eyes on mine. "Because I owe you, you know. I owe your family. So ask."

I nod. With our eyes, we're talking about an unspoken thing.

It was my father who found Frank's fiancée, Dawn, twenty years ago. My father was driving back from a bar one winter night, and he saw a car going fifty down the highway slam right into a semi-truck the very second that it started to jackknife on ice, and there wasn't a thing either driver could have done because it was just one of those split seconds where a person can't see what's coming and no amount of preparation or careful driving would have made a difference.

Kay said my father was pretty worried about getting in trouble himself, being drunk and all, particularly since he had several DUIs, but he stayed standing by the car, by Dawn's mangled body, until the police got there. The truck driver had a concussion and was slumped over in his truck, but he was fine. "That was a nice thing your father did," Kay told me. "He reached in and kept his hand on this young girl's bloody head until the police came, because it just wasn't right to leave a body like that alone, even if it meant he'd go to jail. Every once in a while, he did something decent."

There's so many people who die out here in their cars. Cancer or cars. Every once in a while, there's news of a farm accident, or a heart attack, or a drowning at the dam, but it seems that most people die in their cars, and the only thing that makes the stories different is how the cars crashed—was someone taking a corner too fast, or hit ice, or came across loose gravel, or got hit by a snowplow?

164

I didn't know Dawn, of course, and I didn't know my father much. But I think about my father and her sometimes, and her blood on his hand. It's incredible that a life can just end, just disappear from you, a snap of your fingers and it's gone, and all that's left is some wispy connections.

I look out the window, into the raining-down sky. *Please don't let this happen to Baxter*, I ask of the clouds. *Don't let him wisp away before I had time to love him the deepest that I could, which is not something I've done yet—I never even tried—but I will, I will, I promise, if you don't take him from me yet.*

I'll figure out how to be truer: to let people go if they need to be let go of, and to hold on tight if that's what's called for. I will pay attention, so I can cross each human heart that comes across my path, cross it as true as I can.

Kay doesn't have much to tell me. I call her from Miguel's place, since he's got long distance, but all she's got to say is that Baxter's alive and tests are scheduled.

She's more interested in giving me the details of chores: to check Luz's left front foot, to spread the bulls' hay all the way down the trough or they'll fight for it, to make sure I turn off the water when I'm done filling the water tanks, to make sure the canary gets new water and seed, and water later in the day because he sometimes likes to take a bath in the first water, do I understand?

By the time I hang up, Miguel's half asleep on a futon on the floor. He was trying to be polite, not going to bed and all, but he was tired. As I listened to Kay, I watched him come out of the bathroom changed into sweats, check on Juan, sleeping in his toddler bed, and then on Amber, who's sleeping in, of all things, a cardboard box, which doesn't bother me since it's clean and looks about as cozy as a bassinet. Then Miguel put down a futon mattress and a blanket and fell asleep himself, though as soon as I hang up he wakes up enough to motion me over.

"Tell me," he mumbles. "Baxter okay?"

I sit next to him and tell him what little there is to say. There's a silence, then we speak at the same time. I say, "I want to sleep here tonight," and he says, "Just sleep here tonight."

He pulls me down onto his chest with one arm and holds my hand with another. Something about the way he does this tells me he doesn't want to do anything but sleep, and in a moment that's exactly what he's doing. His body jerks a little as he drifts off, first his leg and then his shoulder twitches, and with about every third breath he makes a small grating noise. That makes me smile, because it makes him more human, to see him this way. But I know staring at him might wake him, so I turn my head back down, toward his chest.

I bite my lip and sigh and think, *No, Libby, don't. Don't go there.*

But I make myself a list anyway: One, I'm curious. Two, I want to see what love is about. Three, I want to know what there is besides Derek. Four, I just want to throw the dice and see how it turns out. And five, he is somebody, he's a man, and now that Shawny is gone and Derek is gone he's not so off limits.

But don't, I tell myself. Don't try, because it will mess up this friendship. And don't do it because you'll get turned down. I gotta trust what I know. Which is that Miguel is not interested, he's just not. In that secret, silent way that people talk to each other all the time, Miguel has already told me that we're going to be friends, and that's all, and I need to listen to that.

I'm about crazy for someone right now, though, that's the truth. And in the morning, I'll probably still try to catch his eye

166

to see if he'd like to sleep with me in another way. I wonder how he'll signal to me that that's not what he wants. And then we'll make some breakfast, and we'll talk kid talk, and I'll try to be glad for this friendship, and we'll both start our days.

Because that's how I know it's going to go, I prepare myself for it, and then I fall asleep. All night, I wake up to find us holding on to each other, our legs or hands touching, and then I drift off again, sleeping a deep sleep, a deep sleep that comes with feeling safe, with having another body next to me. Somehow, I know I'm sleeping with a smile on my face, and I know I'm sleeping with the feeling of the deepest thanks, and that even if I want more, this seems like a lot, and this one night is going to last in my heart for a good long while.

TWELVE

"Whatcha doing?"

When I hear Frank's voice, an "Ooohhhhfuck" comes out my mouth before I can stop it.

Frank cocks his head. "Libby?"

I don't even try to find the words that will explain why I've just thrown a twelve-pack of beer into a trash can.

"Libby?"

"Oh. Hey, Frank."

We speak at the same time. I let down the trash bag so that it rests on the floor, and then my hands fall to my side.

"Well," he says after a moment. "I think I understand."

I look up for just an instant, then look right back down.

"Well, I never would've thought." He doesn't say what he never would have thought, though, and for some reason him not saying reminds me of all those times he used to say "noble."

He just stands there for a long time, looking at me, and me looking at the floor. I imagine what he sees: me with my jeans, baggy T-shirt, blue apron, glasses, frizzing hair falling out of a ponytail, trash bag at my feet. After a while, he walks over to the black plastic bag, bends over, and takes the beer out. He puts it back onto the stack behind us. Then he walks out of the room, leaving the bag at my feet, wads of toilet paper and scraps of trash tumbling out the top.

I walk to the bathroom. I sit on the toilet for a good long while, mostly thinking nothing and then trying to think what to do. Finally I take off the apron and hang it on a peg. I rinse my face and glare at myself in the mirror.

Amber's been here the whole time. There's nobody to watch her and so I figured I'd just get in as much work as I could while she was napping. And get some beer while I was at it. She's in her car seat, sleeping still, and I pick her up in one hand and grab a cup of ice in the other.

Frank and Arlene are talking to each other up front. That's what makes me sick is seeing Arlene turn and look at me. It takes everything I've got to look up at her. She's not giving me a you-lame-ass look, though. She actually looks sorry for me, and like she's trying to smile at me, secret-like, so that Frank won't see. That look means everything. It means that she understands, at least a little bit. It means that for some reason she's willing to let it go.

I walk right up to them and turn to Frank. "Sorry," I say. "I really am."

"Surprises me, Libby."

I nod.

"If you're having hard times— I mean, I know you're probably having hard times now. But I don't think I understand. I've never had a kid work like you do."

"Sure," I say. "I guess I'll be leaving now."

"Libby, I don't know what to say—"

"Thanks for everything you've done, Frank. And I'm sorry. Really sorry. See you around, Arlene."

I push the glass door open and push myself through it.

Strange, to be leaving work when the light's still shining, without my eyes stinging and feet aching. I swing Amber's car seat a little as I walk to my car, and I look up at the blue, hard arc of sky.

The letter is on regular white paper, with no return address.

>Dear Libby, listen to this: sticky spruce, prickly pine, friendly fir. Get it? You can tell the type of tree by the needles. Spruce needles are sticky, pines are prickly, firs are friendly. Neat, huh?
>
>Well, I'm moving.
>
>I lost the weight the baby put on me. And my boobs quit hurting! I think it's all over now, I'm feeling better. For a while, I felt low. But I learned something from you. Remember how once you were standing below Baxter's barn window and I was trying to open it to throw out a rope to you and I pushed on the pane of glass and it fell right toward you and I yelled, "Heads!" and you ducked just in time and the glass broke on your head and shattered all around you and you looked up at me and smiled and said, "Well, that was exciting," and that's how I'm trying to be. Just duck when I need to and stay calm, and smile. You were a better teacher than I ever realized. I love you, Tess.

I sit in my car outside the post office and find my notebook and write like crazy.

>Tess, I don't have your address. And why won't you tell me anything real—where are you and what's going on in your life? This letter won't get to you. We've

170

been trying to track you down, and Kay's called the police, she doesn't know that you're driving illegals, which I do know, so watch out.

Please come back and help me figure this out.

Do you want Simon to have the baby?

Will you be mad at me if I give Simon the baby?

At first Amber just slept and cried and went through the diapers. When she sucked at the bottle she reminded me of a baby pig, which I mean in a complimentary way. Now she makes cooing noises and I call her my little pigeon. When she opens up her mouth wide, she reminds me of a hippo.

Some days I don't know what I feel. I feel nothing. I feel numb. Some days I feel panicky, like I got to get her and me out of here. My heart is beating too hard. It's going to explode. Some days I think I hate you. Some days I think I hate Amber.

I feed her when she's hungry. I shake a rattle when she's awake. I take her outside, I take her on walks. I'm trying to be a good mom, but it's too hard.

Kay and Baxter have something going. Maybe they had something going all along but had to keep it secret till Adeline died. Or maybe it's new. Who knows?

That hippie guy, Ed, he has his bees out here and sometimes he stops by and we talk. I never knew anybody like Ed, exactly. I think he's lonely. I think he gets sad. I think he needs a friend like I do. He just comes by to hang out and that's weird because I know I'm just not all that interesting.

Derek and me broke up. It's hard to be so alone. Clark stopped by once.

I miss you.

Nobody ever talks about this: how you need someone.

And how that fact makes all your decisions for you.
Everything you do is based on that fact.

I will do fucking anything to have somebody
around. I don't even care if it's love. I just need somebody.

I don't know why I can't be alone.

I can't.

I'm trying. I can't.

Tess, you took two suitcases and said, 'I just need to
get out of here for a while.' What does that mean
exactly?

There's a girl coming up from Mexico. She's pregnant. She'll have the baby here. It's called an anchor
baby. It will have rights here. Miguel's going to marry
her anyway, though. You should pick her up, Tess, if
you said you would. Remember how sick you were
during those first months? What if you were that sick
and escaping your country at the same time? And what
if nobody picked you up?

I looked on the map for Oaxaca. It's so far away.
Miguel says that the border is a place of intense evil
and intense good, side by side, which makes it one of
the most interesting places on earth. Oaxaca, border,
Durango, here. Or start here, then Durango, then border, then Oaxaca. The world keeps zooming in and out
on me.

Why do I keep hoping you'll come home? Just tell
me that you won't and then I'll quit hoping. Just tell
me what's going on in your heart and then I won't have
to wonder, and I won't have to feel like I'm zooming
back and forth, and I'll feel settled.

I leave Amber in the car while I run into the post office. I plan on dropping the letter in the slot, except the mail carrier is there and I don't want him to see me dropping in piece of paper with no address, a letter that we both know will get nowhere. So I just keep the letter in my hand and walk right back out, as if I know where I'm going. As if I'm not feeling a little crazy, like maybe I'm starting to crack apart.

THIRTEEN

"Interesting procurement methods," Clark says after I take my hand off the steering wheel, hand him a beer, and tell him how I got it. He says the word *procurement* like he knows I'm not smart enough to know it and he wants to teach it to me.

So I say, "Yeah, I *procured* it illegally."

"Well, I might have to tell Frank about his fine employee, stealing beer." He winks at me and then leans over to jab me with his elbow. "What you going to do to keep me quiet?"

"I'm going to give you a beer, that's what I'm going to do." I don't tell him that Frank already knows about his fine employee; I'm not ready to tell him that part of the story.

"A beer's good enough, I guess," he says.

We're heading out for a picnic. Amber's with Arlene, who agreed to watch her for the evening, since it's Sunday and that's when the store closes early. I think maybe Arlene has made enough mistakes in her life that she doesn't feel ready to judge anyone else, which is why I called her. And Amber seemed happy enough, when I dropped her off, waving her arms in slow motion like an astronaut in space. The way she moves makes me think that's how it would feel to live in the sky. For a second I felt sorry for being pissy around her all day, but she was fussing and is it too much to ask to have a minute to yourself? What a relief it was to have someone take her from me. But now I'm feeling bad: I didn't even kiss her goodbye.

I did the chores at Baxter's this afternoon, except for the irrigating, which some other rancher is doing. And Miguel offered to do chores tonight, and since everyone seemed willing to help, for once I'm going to take them up on it, and I'm going to find out something about my sister.

Ed said we should all be living more dangerous lives. I want to find Tess.

I want to find someone for me.

I want a new first kiss.

I can't take doing nothing anymore.

I'm not like Tess or Kay—I'm not going to be with just anyone—but on the other hand I might as well try to start looking. Anyway, the only connection I got to Tess is Clark. Plus I remember that look he gave me. Plus he could be all right. Plus there's not that many other choices.

So I called him up and said, "Hey, I was thinking about going to the dam for a picnic, want to come?" And there was a pause, and then he said, "Sure, I got nothing else to do, but not the dam, because I got a better place." And in his voice was already some sort of hope, or uh-huh, here we go, and I said, "Fine, let's do it then," and he said, "Okay, then come get me at Sammy's Garage in Lamar."

He looks like he doesn't belong in my car—he's so big that his legs are bunched up even though he pushed the seat back as far as it'll go. He looks like the kind of guy who should always be driving a big truck and anything else just isn't going to fit him right. He's wearing the same Rockies ball cap he always wears, with his black hair sticking out underneath, and he's chewing on a toothpick.

We've already talked about the weather, and that's about it. I kept the conversation off Amber, since me being associated with a kid is the last thing I want, at least right now. I want him to see *me*. I also kept the conversation off my job, since I don't have one any more, and I noticed that he kept the conversation off himself completely except to say that he's been real busy.

Now there's a silence. We're driving south from Lamar and there's lots of pale green and blue sky and too much heat being held between the two. I'm just going to say something about the heat when Clark starts talking first. "So, you heard from your sister?"

"Yeah, sort of. She sent a letter. But it didn't say much. It didn't say where she was. It just said she was moving." I glance at him, because I know there's a truth he could tell, and I'd like for him to tell it.

But all he says is "Yeah," and he doesn't say it like a question, he says it like it's information he already knows. "I'm delivering some alfalfa in Durango next week. Maybe I'll run into her."

"In a town like Durango? You'll just run into her?"

He shrugs. "It's a possibility."

"Clark, can I just come right out and ask you something? And be real honest? Because I need to find her. Amber's father wants to take her from me, and there was a message on our answering machine from a lawyer. I haven't called him back. Kay says we got to use delay tactics till we find Tess. I never got Amber legal. And maybe I *will* give her up—I mean, I don't know *what* to do. I need to talk to Tess. To see what she wants. So you see, I really, really need to find her. Can you tell her to call me?"

"If I see her." But his voice is hollow and distant, so I know he doesn't mean it.

"Tell her it's really important."

176

"I will."

"All she has to do is call. Please."

"What are you going to give me?" He laughs and stares at me. Then he shrugs the moment away. "I'll tell her. If I see her. I was a little in love with your sister, you know. She just pulled me in. She has a way of doing that."

"Yeah? That's true, maybe."

"I'm over her now," he says, looking at me. "But if I see her, I'll pass on the message." Then he looks out the window. "We'll have our picnic at this ranch. Good arrowhead hunting around these parts. That's what we're going to do. This rancher lets me on his property as long as I shut gates and stay away from the animals."

"What do you find?"

"Arrowheads." He says it like it's a dumb question. "Well, and scrapers, couple of shards of pottery. I've found a few big caches. One of these days I'll make a display with black velvet."

"Aren't you supposed to tell someone if you find stuff like that?"

"Naw, they don't belong to the government of Colorado, or to some dumbass professor sitting in an office, contrary to what they'd like to believe. The guy from Colorado State tells me that he frowns on that type of collecting, all that information lost. He tells me they take twenty-seven measurements for every artifact they find. I called him in good faith, wanting to tell him what I'd found. But all he did was be condescending to me. He's never going to get his ass out here and wander across all these ranches." He finishes his beer and sets it on the floor of my car and smashes it with his boot. I hand him another. "Turn here."

I turn off the highway onto a county road, then through a gate. Next to the bumpy road, a prairie dog colony has turned the pastureland to dirt.

"Assholes," Clark says to the heads poking out of the holes as we drive by, and then he flings an empty beer can at one of

177

them. He searches in the car for the other empty cans we've produced and wings those out too.

I finally say, "A friend of mine, Miguel, helped me fill out some applications. To the community college. I could become a nurse."

"Which hospital you want to work at?" he asks.

"There's only the one in Lamar."

"Well, that's what I'm asking. Whether you had plans for, say, Denver or New York or whatever, or if you planned on working here."

"Here, I guess. Well, no. I've always pictured living somewhere else, but I don't know where."

"Your sister sure hated it here. I like it, though. Not too many people, cheap to live, lots of sky."

"Tess ran away a few times. Once she met a guy and his girlfriend, on their way to California. She just asked to go along. Can you believe that? She's always been brave. She was only fifteen. When Kay found out where she was, she drove all the way out there and brought her home. Kay told her to stay until graduation and then Tess could do whatever she pleased. And Tess always said that the minute she was done with school she was out of here forever."

"She told me the same story," Clark says. "She said she was glad Kay came and got her. Because when she got to California she realized she had some thinking to do, to figure out how somebody makes it on their own. Because you've got to be smart about that. Have a plan. Maybe all this time, she's been thinking."

"I guess so." After a while, I say, "Kay would freak if she knew I was with you. I know it's not your fault, but she still wants to beat up the guy who drove Tess away. I won't tell her about you, though."

"I'm obliged." He leans over real close and whispers, "I like being a secret. And speaking of, where's Derek? How come you're not going out with him?"

"We broke up."

"Ah, Tess guessed right, then."

"I'm happy. It's for the best." I smile at him and then look out the car window. "It's Tess that I miss." Who knows why I say that, and now it seems like I've got to say more, so I add, "It surprised me, you know, her leaving the day she got out of the hospital."

"I bet it did."

"It was so soon and all."

"She asked me to get her out quick. At least you've got her baby."

"That just makes me miss her more. That baby wears me out, sometimes. I don't know how to say it."

He says, "Drive down into that draw there. Love is hard work, isn't it? I had a girlfriend who said that to me. She said, 'Clark, we're not meant for each other, because you're basically lazy and love requires hard work and, you know, you're not up to it.'"

I smile "Naw, love's not hard work. Otherwise it's not love. Love is magic, that's what I think."

"Nope. It's work." He gives me a look like I'm dumb. "Every kind of love is work. I love arrowhead hunting, for example. It's work, but I love it. I like the thought it takes, the challenge. You got to read people, even though they're long dead. It's like figuring out where somebody is. Like, where was that Indian when he left this arrowhead? It's like *people* are hiding, and it's my job to hunt them out. It's a rush, man. Probably you could care less about this shit."

He looks at me like he's pissed off, even though I didn't say anything. I know what he's thinking: that I'm one of those people who are easy to figure out—not as complicated as arrowhead hunting, for example. He's bored with me, and he wants me to see that. It's sort of like a challenge.

I shrug and look away. It hurts to feel people decide that about you, that's a fact. I'm not Tess, after all. I have nothing to hold a guy long enough to show him who I am. Maybe that's what beautiful people have going for them—a few extra minutes of attention to announce themselves.

"Actually, I *am* interested. And I bet it's harder than people think, isn't it? Everything looks simple from a distance. Then, the more you look, the more you see. And *that's* when you have to rise to the challenge. Isn't that right?"

Squint and shade my eyes. That's the first thing I do when I step from the car, and the first thing I notice is the buzz. Maybe it's some kind of insect, but it seems more like it's the land itself, buzzing with heat.

Dry land stretches to the west, pretty much nothing except sagebrush and short grass, and the only thing that interrupts the view is a windmill and a watering tank and a cluster of cattle. But to the south, about a mile away, are green trees bordering the Arkansas River and I follow the green line with my eyes until the land dips down and blends in with the horizon.

Clark stands there looking around for a minute, too. "Pretty, huh?" He kicks at the dirt. "It's windblown here, so it's a good place to find stuff. The ground gets exposed. Indians would've camped up high, on a south-facing slope with water nearby, which this is. See, here's a dry creek bed." He points to a sunken spot in the earth. "It's got water in the spring." He starts walking in the direction of the river. "Now's a good time to look because it rained. Things get washed up. Look on ant hills or prairie dog mounds, too. Clues everywhere, if you know how to look."

I walk alongside him. We're looking at the ground, and I'm wondering how my eye is supposed to pick something out of all these rocks. Big rocks, little rocks, pebbles, clumps of hood-in-needle grass, yucca, cactus, and more rocks.

Every once in a while, I glance up at him. Sometimes when I

do I find him looking back at me. Maybe he's not so bored with
me after all.

Derek's the only man I've slept with. I don't know whether
or not I want this thing to be in the air. Clark doesn't quite
seem like the one. But I want *some*thing. And maybe I should
give him a chance. Wobble, wobble, all over the place. I feel
myself getting nervous, like electricity's in my stomach and it's
shooting out everywhere.

"The trick is looking for shiny rocks," Clark says. "Could
be any color, anything from red jasper to brown to quartzite.
But, see, rocks that make good arrowheads are similar to glass,
chemically, so they shine in the sunlight." He stops to pick up a
piece of rock and then throws it sideways into a bush, and
throws his beer can right after it.

I'd like to go pick the beer can up, which is something Ed
would do, but on the other hand Ed would say you gotta live
life, take chances, move forward, and anyway, I don't want
Clark laughing at me, so I just say, "Shiny in the sunlight."

"You wanna learn something? Conchoidal fractures." He
looks at me hard and raises his eyebrows. "Certain rocks make
conchoidal fractures, just like glass does. You know how a glass
fractures when you shoot a BB gun in it?"

"Why would I shoot a glass with a BB gun?"

"On the close side, you get a hole the same size as the BB.
But on the other side will be a perfect cone. Because the glass
fractures conchoidally."

I don't know what he's talking about, but I never thought
before about how rock shatters, or even how people have
known for a long time which rocks to break, and how. There's
so much I don't know.

As I walk alongside Clark I finally try to talk about the
other thing that's making me nervous. "Clark? Don't get mad,
but I know you and Tess are running *ilegales*. I know she was

supposed to pick up some people and she didn't. I know all that. But that's all I know. I really need to find her."

He stops walking and stares at me. "Goddamn. How come people can't keep their mouths shut?"

"Tess didn't tell me."

"Who did then?"

I'm not letting Ed's name out. "Just people, you know. Who are expecting some guys. And who put two and two together."

He walks up to me and stares at me, hard. "How can I impress on you how dangerous this is? If Tess or me get caught, we do jail, big time. It's a felony. *Felony.* It's supposed to be a fucking secret." He picks up a rock and wings it hard into the distance.

"I can keep secrets! I don't want Tess to go to jail, for one thing. Clark? I don't care what you're doing. But I really, really need to talk to Tess. Just about Amber. Please tell me where she is."

He considers me for a minute, and he's calming down. "No. But I'll tell her to contact you." He pokes at my shoulder and we both see how the skin goes from red to white. "You're getting burned."

I know I am—I can feel my skin tingling with too much sun. "I forgot sunscreen. Clark, Kay called the police. If the police get involved, it's going to get bad, isn't it? But Kay doesn't know about the *ilegales*. She's just looking for her daughter. Now there are police looking for Tess. I wanted to tell you that. You should know that, right?" He looks angry again, his face still and red. "Look, tell her I need for her to come help me get Amber legally and then I'll let her go. Just ask her to do this one last thing. Don't let the police find her." Still he doesn't say anything, so I say, "Was she supposed to pick up a group, and she didn't? Are you mad at her? You seem mad."

"She and I will work it out."

"Please don't be mad." When he doesn't say anything, I add,

"Listen, Clark. Please. Do you want money? Because I can get some. I know you're pissed. I can see it."

He looks past me. "Libby, I'm probably fucking pissed off that she didn't love me. I'm probably fucking pissed off that your sister led me on and then laughed me off. I'm pissed off because of our arrangement. But none of this is your business." He walks off with just enough speed that I know he wants to be left alone.

Flies are following me and some are the biting kind, so I keep slapping at them, and rubbing the sweat at my neck. I'm too tired to walk so I sit down and stare at the cows and windmill.

If I was brave enough to speak to Clark, this is what I'd tell him: Tess is good at making people love her and then not loving them back. She flirts until she's got them to move from Not Interested to Interested, and then turns her back. Maybe it's her way of getting back at the world.

And maybe I'd even say: I'm the opposite. Or at least I want to be. Seems to me that, given a chance, I love like crazy. Or I used to, at least. I loved Shawny. I loved Tess. I want to fall in love with Amber. And if I couldn't love Derek more, it wasn't neither of our faults. At least I'm open to the possibility of love. It's my way of getting back at the world, to love stronger than ever, to love the way I wish somebody loved me.

When I look up, Clark is staring at me with a face that's blank, or gone somewhere else. I jerk a little, because I didn't know he was there—either I must have been zoning out or else he's pretty quiet.

I'm sitting on the ground and he's standing to my side, holding out his hand. "Here you go," he says, opening his palm. Inside his cupped palm is a perfect arrowhead and one tiny, thin rock. "Nice arrowhead here. And a chip. Chips are mostly what I find. It's a fragment from the process of making an arrowhead. It's just trash, really. Somebody else's trash."

He puts them in my hand. "See this arrowhead? It's got a scarring pattern there. Indians used two types of striking, not that you care. Percussion flaking and pressure flaking. Probably you could care less about this shit."

"I care."

"This is percussion."

"Who made it?"

"Arapahoe, I bet. It's probably a couple hundred years old."

"They're pretty."

"They're for you."

"I can have them?" I look at him because he's acting weird and I don't want him to be angry. I want to say something about how nice that is, but he's already talking.

"This might have killed something. Who knows what. Human, deer. Maybe this little rock ended a life. I love thinking about that."

"Hey, Clark? I'm getting really burned. Maybe we could get in the car, or find some shade?" What I want to do is go home, but I don't say it. What I want to do is bring up Tess again, and make him not mad at her, but I don't know how to say that either. I don't want to push too hard. So I look up at him to see where he's at inside.

His eyes are holding onto mine. There's a heartbeat of a moment when I know what's coming, and wobble, wobble, I can't decide. "Let's go to the car," he says, and he takes my hand and leads me off.

Clark has a different kind of kiss than Derek—harder, with less give and more force. He bites my lip a little, and I sit up in the back seat of the car and he pushes me back down and he says,

"Shhh. Sorry, sorry, sorry. Come on now." He's saying this to my shorts, which are stuck on my hips. He pushes me backward so he can slide them off, and then he pushes my shirt up and pushes my jogging bra up and leans down.

If I lift my head, I can see Amber's car seat over his shoulder. He unbuckled it and threw it out of the car so there'd be room for us. Next to it is the picnic basket I'd put in the back. My glasses are still on, which is why I can see them. Unlike Derek, who takes my glasses off, Clark is just kissing around them, nudging them up with his forehead so that they're crooked and pressing against one side of my face.

"Hey, Clark?"

"I don't have AIDS or none of that shit. Do you?"

"No. But Clark—"

"Birth control?"

"What? Yeah, but Clark—"

"Okay, okay. Shhh."

My mind races around, trying to catch onto a daydream of a moment like this. I want to feel what I feel in the daydream. I picture me in a blue dress, a man watching me, that feeling rising in my chest, that crazy feeling down low, my body waking up.

Clark twists himself out of his jeans and throws his ball cap to the side. I try to sit up, he pushes me down, turns himself toward me and pushes himself in me, and it hurts because I'm not wet yet and it hurts because he's not gentle.

"Please," I say. "Wait."

"Shhh," he says.

"Don't," I say.

"Shhh."

"Clark! Fuck, that hurts!"

"Libby," he says, leaning back so he can look me in the eye, "I said to shut up."

185

And that's when I know. That this is going to happen.

My mind races for a new daydream, because there have been dreams of a man who has power, and in my mind it felt good, but it didn't feel like this. In my dreams, it didn't feel like the man was angry. It didn't feel like he hated me. It didn't feel like he wanted to hurt me so much.

"Clark, I'm asking please."

He turns me over. One side of my face is against the seat and it smells like dirt and fabric and maybe even I can smell the tears that are just starting to fall.

"Mmmm," he says. "Good. Oh that's good. You fucking bitch."

Past the water in my eyes is a pebble resting on the seat, and as my body rocks back and forth, the pebble falls to the floor. I watch where it disappeared over the edge, the little patch of fabric where it once was, and if I stare at it long enough, then this will be over.

In dreams the only hurt I feel is in my heart. I didn't know how the body could hold so much hurt. I didn't know. I didn't know it could hurt like this. I forgot to know this about life.

I beg my mind to help me. I close my eyes and concentrate, hard. And I'm searching for a dream, and searching, and finally I catch on to one. There's me and a little girl, playing in a yard. Me and a little girl, and she's got blond braids, and we're reaching out to each other, and there's green grass and blue sky, and we're laughing. Me and a blond girl, coming together, arms all tangled up in a hug. I can hold her inside me. I can.

My clothes get tossed on top of me. I pull them on and climb in the passenger seat. I stare ahead as Clark throws the car seat and picnic basket in behind me. I stare ahead while Clark drives us back, across the fields, through the gate, down the highway.

I keep my eyes on my daydream, so that it can grow and shoot out everywhere: me and a blond girl, we're coloring together, on our tummies on a wooden floor, crayons scattered in a slant of sunlight. We're walking down a road and laughing and jumping on each other's shadow. There are tears I can wipe away and sadness that I can soften. There are dangers to protect her from. I can hold her in my lap. I can hold her in my heart. I can love her a million different ways.

The car door slams and Clark is walking from the car to Sammy's, and the keys are dangling in the ignition and all I need to do is drive home. I'm teaching her to fly a kite and the string gets tangled and the kite crashes in a field and I know enough to laugh at this, and bend down so that I am at her level, and I hug her. On the way home, when I lose the dream I just speak out loud: "Girl, blond braids, we're laughing together," and when I say this, a new image rises in my head and I hold very, very still so that I can listen to the story unfold.

A buzz roars in my ears, a buzz like the land, a buzz from nothing.

I'm showered, changed, cried out. I'm standing in the kitchen doorway, smoking and looking out at the alfalfa.

Had it coming, my brain tells me.

Didn't want it.

Didn't say no.

That's not what I wanted.

Had it coming.

Did not.

Did too.

Kay is back. She must have come home from Pueblo in the middle of the night. I didn't even hear her come in. But this morning I heard her moving in my room. In an act of mercy, I think, she took Amber, came right in at five-thirty when Amber started crying, picked her up, fumbled in the drawers for a diaper and a change of clothes, and walked out of the room. I was too tired to ask when she got home or where she was going or how Baxter was. I think I whispered a thank you that she didn't hear and I fell back asleep. The note on the kitchen table said they'd gone to do chores together, and then to the store.

I watch Kay pull in the driveway, lug the car seat up and put it at my feet, start unloading groceries.

"Thanks for your help," she says.

I follow her and unload plastic bags from the car.

"Look at Amber," Kay says. "Look at her look at you. Her eyes are following you now. Her eyes are changing color. Turning brown. Take her inside, it's too hot out here."

I move Amber, still in her car seat, to my bed. She's still looking at me and, yes, her gray-blue eyes have speckles of brown near the center.

Before I leave my room, I pull at my shirt and look at my breast, my shoulder. It seems like there should be blood, but there isn't, just the circles of bruised skin. There's fingernail scrapes down my stomach, and my anus hurts where he put in his fingers.

I look at Amber. *Kid, I'm a piece of shit and I can't take care of you because I can't take care of myself. It was wrong and I went along with it. I'm my mom all over again, and you deserve better. I tried, and look what happened. It's not what I wanted, but maybe it's what I had coming. I can't rise to the occasion of you. You're going to be so beautiful, though. So beautiful.*

I leave her sitting there and walk out to the kitchen. *Keep the words inside*, I tell myself, *keep them inside.* Because Kay won't treat my words right, but still they want out, these words, so I keep my hand over my mouth.

"The police call?"

"What?"

"Did the police call?"

"No."

"No word from Tess?"

"No word from Tess."

"Nice of you to ask about Baxter. He's not doing so great."

I put milk in the refrigerator, apples in a bowl, formula in the cupboard.

Kay says, "He'll be back in a few days. This formula is so damn expensive. I don't know why they take the thing that's most important to an infant and kill us with the price."

"Who?"

"Them," she says, her hand flying around to the outside world. "Hand me a knife, will you? Can you get the margarine from the fridge? I'm making me a sandwich, you want one?"

I nod, hand her a knife, get out two plates and two glasses of water. My hands put away the groceries until the bags are empty. I sit down in front of the grilled cheese sandwich, put the sandwich to my mouth, take a bite, chew.

Kay slides into the seat across from me. "Baxter's fine and he's not fine. They took all kinds of pictures of his brain, gave him all kinds of drugs. He seems fine now. Except that he's scared." Her mouth has bits of toast falling from it. "He's emptied out a little. Have you ever noticed that sometimes in your life you're willing to die? I hope that for Baxter. That he's willing to and able to at the same time. It's not so easy, getting to the end of your life. When the end is in sight. You'll be there someday. So will I. It's a hard thing to stare down. Where's Amber?"

"In my room."

"Sleeping in her car seat?"

"I guess."

"You guess?"

"Yes. She fell asleep."

She brushes a strand of gray hair behind her ear. "You did the chores like I said?"

"Yes."

"Are you incapable of speaking more than two words, or what is your problem?"

"I did the chores. I did them Saturday morning and afternoon and night and yesterday morning and afternoon and Miguel did them last night. I went on a picnic. An arrowhead hunt."

She looks at me. "With who?"

"You don't know him." I stare at my sandwich.

"Don't know why you wanted to waste an afternoon looking at the ground, but whatever." She rubs at her nose and sighs. "You girls have always specialized in dumb ways to use your time."

I put a bite of grilled cheese in my mouth. My plastic plate has a ring of black on it from where it got burned by something, and scratch marks from a hundred forks and knives eating on it. I remember eating from this plate when I was a little girl but I don't remember when that mark appeared.

"Baxter says I just got to let you girls go. Step in as a guardian angel when necessary. That's not my job though. I'm not a damn angel."

She looks tired, but even so her green eyes seem calm enough. She's in one of her good moods. She says, "I tell him: 'Baxter, these girls, they don't need help.' And you know what he says? He says, 'Cream does indeed rise to the top. But not if it's always being shaken up. And anyway, a lot of milk can go sour in the meantime.' And so we gotta find Tess."

I look at her. I feel dead. I don't think I care about finding Tess anymore. I think, *I tried, and it didn't work, and maybe that's good—that I got to a place where I don't care anymore.*

"What's the matter with you? You gotta wake up," she says, standing up and batting me on the side of the head.

"Mom? I'm glad about you and Baxter."

She scowls at me and then looks away, and then looks at me again. She starts in on the dishes and while she rinses them off she says, "That was nice, thank you." After a minute, she adds, "When your father left, so did my dreams about my own land. This job saved my life, because at least it gave me something real to do meanwhile. While I shifted from one dream to another. Which is a hard thing to do. As you know. I always cared for Baxter. I always thought a good deal about Adeline, too, but she died. She died. And one day Baxter leans over and kisses me. Surprised the hell out of me. You were surprised, too?"

"Yeah."

She smiles. "I figured."

"It's nice, though. It's nice to find someone."

"I think so too." Now she's looking at her feet, smiling. "I'm heading over to Baxter's. I'll see you tomorrow. *Adiós*, Lib."

As she steps out, she's framed for an instant in the kitchen door and there's a huge field of dark green behind her and I say, "It's not dumb, Kay. It's not dumb spending time finding someone to love."

I take a breath before I pick Amber up again. "Come on, Amber, quit crying." I put her on my bed and rub her tummy. I whisper, "Amber, shhhh, my name is Libby and you are Amber I am Libby and you are Amber. We'll be okay. Neither of us feels so great right now. Libby, Amber, Libby, Amber. We'll be okay."

It's been two hours straight. That's how long it takes me to try everything I know: a bath, holding her in front of the TV, pacing inside, walking outside, a short drive but not too long because I'm low on gas. "Oh god, no more, shhh little baby, *ay, mi amor, tranquilo! Híjole! Qué tienes?* It hurt so much and I didn't stop him. Please kid I'm asking you to shut the fuck up."

I get out the little bottle of medicine for gas and I try to put a dropperful in her mouth. Most of it comes running out her lips. I give her some Tylenol and she chokes on the dropper and starts hollering again.

I change her diaper, but it's not that wet. I put her sleeper back on, zip it up over her tiny red stomach. She's so tense, her little fists clenched in the air, her legs flying around like they're trying to kick out some pain. I put a pacifier in her mouth and she spits it out and so I pick it up and do it again. But it doesn't work, so I walk with her and I trip over Ringo and I fall forward into the counter and knock over the new can of formula and crack my wrist against the edge, which makes me want to kick Ringo but I don't, I kick the bottom cupboard instead and fuck, fuck, fuck, why won't anyone help and shut*up*shut*up*shut*up*!

I can't do it anymore. That's all I know. Tomorrow I'll take her to the hospital so they can get her spit. Tomorrow, I'll call the lawyer and social services. I don't deserve this kid. She doesn't deserve me. But right now I can't take it anymore. And right then her eyes close, open, close, open, and then close for good. The both of us sink into bed, worn out from crying and each other, and I drift into the deep, dark place of sleep and the minute I get there Amber's wail shoots into my face.

My body does this: my hands push her hard, hard, too hard into the car seat. My hands pick the car seat up. My feet step, step, outside, out to the car. I open the car door, and shove that car seat inside, hard, and slam the car door shut. I open the car door, slam it shut again, harder.

I go inside, to my bed. I sleep. I sleep until I can open an eye to see the red numbers on the clock. It's 5:12, they tell me, and

192

with 5:13 comes an understanding. Amber's not in the room with me. She's in the car. There's no space inside me to care. I sleep again. My eyes come back open and see that it's 6:00. I start to drift off again, but this time I keep them open. "Please," I say. "Please keep them open." The red numbers of the clock fade in and out and I start to see their pattern, blotches of red that really don't exist, all around my room. I look at them and listen to how quiet it is—so quiet that it seems like nothing's alive and maybe never was.

Ringo follows me when I get up, her feet padding on the carpet. She whines and touches her nose to the door.

Outside, the sky looks dark wet, and a mist is rising from earth to sky. Maybe I should be flying apart from feeling, but the fact is I'm not. I'm nothing inside.

The gravel of the driveway cuts into my feet, the same way cold air cuts into my body. I let it hurt. I keep moving until I see Amber's head through the glass window, a fallen-forward head, eyes closed.

When she's in my arms, I run my fingers over her hair, her cheek, my lips touch her brow. I hold my breath until I hear hers and it's raggedy, broken up into hiccups, and her stomach rises and falls, a slight movement under the light fabric of her shirt. I breathe out.

I've done it.

I've done this.

I've left this baby. Left this baby alone. She could have died.

"Amber, wake up."

She doesn't at first, until I scream it loud, and then she startles awake. She doesn't cry, but she opens her eyes. Then her tiny hands curl around my shirt, grabbing tight. "No," I say. I pry her fists open and pull my shirt away. She curls her fingers in on themselves then, making tiny fists holding nothing.

FOURTEEN

Ed's standing at his door in a white T-shirt and boxer shorts, his glasses tilted, his eyes trying to blink themselves awake. I come into focus and time slows down, because I'm watching so careful, because this is important, and he does what I'm hoping for, which is that he smiles. From the way the smile comes to his face, from the place underneath where it comes from, I can see that it's not the smile of a man looking at me as a woman, and not of someone being put upon, it's the smile of a friend, of one human being to another.

It cracks me apart. Because if he hadn't smiled, I would have turned around, gotten in my car, and driven to the hospital and left a baby girl. Funny how such little things can change a life.

He backs up to motion me inside. Still, I stand there until he says, in the quietest, softest voice, "People have such a hard time asking. Come in."

I nod but I am so empty inside that I don't even know how I manage to move. I hand Amber to Ed. "I left her outside most of the night." I can't get my voice very loud. "I don't know if she was crying that whole time or what. I don't know if she's sick or what. She was crying forever. I can't do it. She seems okay, but I don't know. I don't know. You can't just leave a baby crying by herself in a car all night."

He holds Amber in his arms. It looks like he hasn't held that many babies in his life, because although he looks willing enough he just doesn't know how she should fit against his body.

"I was that way too," I mumble. "Just a month ago."

"What way?"

"Not sure how to hold a baby."

We sit on his couch. He puts Amber up against him, and then shifts a few times to get her situated. I'm dead inside but still I can see: His house has regular-looking walls, but it's so empty, so clean-looking, and he has this weaving of a bird in flight, in soft colors, and a painting of birds, only they're not really birds, they're brushes of paint that look like they're in motion. I wonder where they're going.

"But you do now. Know how to hold a baby."

For a long time he listens, and I never felt like such a jerk in all my life, sitting in his living room and crying and talking in bits of sentences and blowing enough snot to use up half a roll of toilet paper. Everything comes out in fragments: Tess and Simon and dancing and Baxter and wanting someone and Clark, except that I leave out the important part and just say that our date didn't work out so well.

When I'm done he knows he needs to say something and he fumbles around for some words. "Probably it was the smartest thing you could have done. I mean, putting her someplace *safe* and getting *away.* There was some wisdom there. We can get her to a doctor to get her checked out, but she looks okay."

I look out his window because I don't know where else my eyes should go. "I don't want to be *me* anymore. Because if I was a different person, I could do this. And I *want* to do this. I just can't."

When I glance back over at him, he's looking down at Amber. He's got her in the crook of his arm, gingerly, and is considering something about her. He says, "Libby, teach this girl to be gentle with herself." Then he adds, "Who do you want to be?"

For a long time, we sit in silence. I don't have an answer to his question. I fall asleep, and when I wake up, he's in the same spot, holding Amber. I fall asleep again. When I wake up, I see that he's feeding her, which means that he must have gotten Amber's diaper bag out of my car and figured out how to make up a bottle. He's changed her diaper and her outfit. I close my eyes again because I need to think, and in that in-between of sleep and wake I try to think about different paths, and different versions of me. I get still. I hold that stillness in front of me. I ask it: *What do you want?* But all I can think of is: One thing about love between two people is that you should both deserve it.

When I open my eyes, Ed says quietly, "She looks fine. She was awake and now she's asleep, and maybe she spent a night in the car, but I think she survived it, and I think you will too."

I nod and start to cry, just the tears, and I keep the rest of myself still and quiet. He brings me tea, which he must have made with one hand, because he's still holding Amber, and then sits down next to me.

"I have a *theory,*" he says in his quiet voice. "But this one I'm not *so* sure about, so take it with a grain of salt. Okay?"

He waits until I mumble an okay before he goes on. "The best way to handle *danger* is to move right toward it, before it has time to maneuver itself. Go *toward* things. Right at them. We're going to go find Tess. And then we'll find Simon. Listen to me. They're both coming toward you. Meet them before they get there."

"I wish Tess was moving toward me." I shift my eyes to the window. "She's out there somewhere."

196

"No, she's been coming toward you. Actually, she's already here."

Sammy's Garage has a room in the back, a dark, cool place that has a certain feeling to it—a trace of all the humans that have ever been there, like they left outlines of bodies or remnants of dreams. Cots are lined up against one wall, piled with blankets, and there's an old yellow fridge and some cardboard boxes with clothing spilling out over the edges. It's a way station for the illegals, Ed's told me, and as I stand there I think of all the hundreds of lives that have passed through, and meanwhile my eyes make out more shapes and shadows in the dark. Then Amber lets out a soft gurgle, and with the noise comes motion, and a figure jumps up from a cot, bolting up and stepping back as we step forward.

Ed pulls a string that turns on an overhead bulb and there are her eyes, Tess's eyes, seeing me. Her eyebrows shoot up and her mouth opens in an O, and then her eyes flick from me to Amber to Ed and back to me. She says, "Libby? Libby! Jeez, what are you—?"

"Hey, Tess."

"Shit, Libby, you really scared me."

She's just come out of sleep and she's fighting to get out of that soft and confused place into the hard, real world. I see her eyes move from person to person, and they also move from fear to confusion, and then—and this is the part I'm watching for—her eyes tense and she's trying to close herself up.

"You look beautiful," I say. She does, too. Her hair's pulled back into a dark, shimmery ponytail, she's wearing a simple hemp necklace around her tan neck, and she's in jeans and a black tank top.

I pick up Amber's little hand and make it wave up and

down, and I say in a high voice, "Hi Tess, I'm Amber." And then, because she's looks from Amber to Ed in a worried way, I say, "And that's Ed, and don't worry, none of us are here to cause you trouble."

"Well, shit," she says, finally. "How are you here—? Why are you here—?"

"Don't worry. All I need from you is a bit of time—signing papers, working some things out. I need to get Amber legally."

"So you know what I'm doing?"

"About the illegals? Yes."

"Well, I did it," she says. "I brought them."

"Was it Miguel's group?"

She nods.

"Are they safe?"

She nods again. "They're with Miguel."

"You were driving here yesterday?"

"Yes."

"Clark knew that?"

"Yes."

She comes forward to give me a hug. "I'm not staying, though," she whispers into my ear, and as she says this she tilts her head and looks at her baby girl. "I can't."

"You're staying long enough to help me."

She looks unsure, so I say it again, and then I say it another time, which is when I feel her give in.

Ed steps out of the room so that I can talk with Tess alone, and since I've already gone and written her a letter, the one I didn't send, I know everything I want to tell her, and as we stand under a single bulb of light I talk fast. Tess makes snorts and occasional remarks, like, "All Kay wants is the ranch. Baxter ought to consider her motivations," and "You and Derek were never in love, let him go," and "Simon can go to hell," and "Amber sounds great," and silence when I tell her about Clark, and more silence when I tell her about leaving Amber in the car, and dark eyes that finally get serious and look a little sorry.

Finally we go outside because there's nothing else to do, and when we walk out we're blinded and we have to stand there, squinting and adjusting to the sunshine beating down on us. When we climb in Ed's orange van, he turns to consider Tess. They nod to each other like they're old friends, although Tess says, "So, you're Ed," and Ed says, "So, you're Tess."

He starts driving us home. I sit in the back of Ed's VW bus with Amber on my lap, which is illegal but sometimes the people who make up laws are just way out of the loop on what actually occurs. Tess sits up front and looks back at me. There she is, right in front of me, and all of a sudden I have nothing I want to say. The only thing that's tumbling around in my mind, in a lazy sort of way, is that if Amber is gentle with herself, then maybe she'll be able to fall in love with her own self, and won't that be nice, to grow up that way?

Tess clears her throat and says, "Clark keeps them there, at Sammy's, till whoever pays up. Payment on delivery."

"Who paid Clark? Miguel?"

"Yeah, he paid for them all. Man, he was pissed off at Clark, because at the last minute Clark changed the price. Clark shouldn't have done that. They spent about an hour bartering. They almost got in a fight. Clark told him, *Chinga tu madre, pinche cabrón*, fuck your mother, you fucking goat. That made me laugh, but Miguel about punched him."

"Why'd you let him?"

"Who, Clark? Change the price?" She shrugs. "Not my deal. I'm just driving."

"Tess—"

But she holds up her hand, no. "Lib, you and I got different ideas on how this world operates. Uh-uh, I don't want to hear it. I don't want your lecture."

199

I close my mouth and stare out the window at the fields flying by. I wonder what I'm actually seeing. At first I wasn't seeing much. And then I saw a little: Miguel and the immigrants and the things people do for each other. And it made me brave. And then I saw other things, like Clark's face and Tess's lies, and then I felt small. I don't know how the world operates, or how brave to be, or how many chances to take. But some things are coming into focus, finally. Like Tess. Like Amber. And as I stare at the pale grass flying by the car, I hold myself still so I can feel what I'm really feeling about them.

After a while, Tess clears her throat. "I want you to know that I'm staying in this business. But I guess not with Clark. Not after what you just told me." Her voice sounds soft and tired. "I guess I'll have to figure out some other way. I know some other people. I got other connections now. When I went south, into the reservation, to pick up these guys at a stop, I did leave food and drinks and a box of shoes. You'll never believe this, but I even bought a bunch of those cheap plastic rosaries and I left those." Her voice gets thick but she holds steady and says, "I do realize what's going on, I do see how hard—" She shrugs. "What am I supposed to do about it? There's different levels of bad, you know. I didn't know about Clark, that he would do that to you. That he would hurt you like that. I'm sorry."

There's a big, long silence. I stare out the window and then my eyes flick to Ed for a second, because I wonder what he's thinking. I never told him all about the Clark part, but he's listening and he looks very still as he drives, like maybe he's deep inside himself thinking about something. Tess is staring at Amber, and she's still and thinking, too.

Finally, I look at Tess and say, "I imagine that they could do a lot worse than you."

Tess tilts her head at me. "I hope that's true. Big sister, I just got my own life to make." She smiles a sad smile. "And making it isn't so damn easy. I won't charge them extra, I won't take advantage." Her eyes flicker right to mine. "I've done that before, and it doesn't feel good."

I look hard at her, so she'll understand that what I'm about to say is next is very true. "I wish you would have told me you were leaving for good. I wish a lot of things. But maybe they don't matter anymore. Because in the end, here's what I wish. I wish I wasn't so alone, but still, I wish Amber was mine. I do. So don't feel bad any more. You gave me a gift. A life. Now help me keep her, all right?"

When I come out of the bathroom, Tess is sitting at the kitchen table, cocking her head down to hold the phone between her ear and shoulder. She's writing and concentrating too hard to look up, but after a bit she raises her eyes and winks.

"Where's Amber?" I mouth. I'm brushing my wet hair. I took a shower because already this seemed like a long day and all the tears and snot and life needed to be rinsed away for a minute, and now I feel like maybe I can start again.

Tess jerks her head toward the door. I look out and see Kay holding her in one arm and talking to Ed, who dropped us off and then, apparently, decided to just stick around. I can barely see Amber's face, but I see that her eyes are open, and I see an arm flail in the air.

Finally Tess hangs up. "Holy moley, the world is complicated. I didn't know how hard it is to live. I think that surprised us both, didn't it?"

When I don't answer, she says, "Amber is— It's been hard to be without her. Harder than I thought it would be." She jerks her head and clears her throat. I've got rid of tears the exact same way, so I know what she's doing.

"Is she okay?"

"Amber? Yes. Still no fever, no nothing. Kay took her to the clinic this morning. She's fine—"

"I was just so tired—"

"A healthy baby, just like the doctor said. She'll be out of the colic period soon."

"So tired and—"

"—You're a good mom, Libby. It's not the worst thing."

"But it's something."

"It's a one-time thing."

"I don't want to be Kay."

"You're a far cry from Kay."

We both sit back in the kitchen chairs and look at each other. "There's a lot of things we could talk about," Tess says finally. "We both want you to be the mother of this baby. And Simon says he wants her. And she is half his."

"Is that who you were talking to?"

"No. I was talking to social services. I was thinking that Simon could be involved, but then he said he wanted full custody. I talked to him right before I called social services. First thing I did was to tell him he was a fuck-head. That he was the biggest mistake of my life, except that he made me love my big sister even more. I told him that Amber wouldn't be alive if it wasn't for you, and that he had no right to come showing up, acting like you and this family were so low. But then I had to ease up, because I had to talk to him, you know? Because I had to play him right, so that we can get this baby."

"And what did he say?"

"Full custody. He said it like such a baby boy. 'Full custody or else you'll be hearing from our lawyer' is what he said. He wants to take Amber on the road. He wants to quit school, join the rodeo, and lead the Cowboy Christian Coalition, and take Amber along with him. In that way, he says, she'll learn the ways of the Lord. So you can see, I don't really prefer that as an option. What a fucker. I can't believe I slept with him."

"Neither can I."

"What a mistake."

Kay walks in from outside, holding Amber in her arms. Amber's facing out, looking around the kitchen, flailing her arms and making a sort of happy, buzzing noise. She looks around the room and then her eyes rest on me and she wiggles.

Kay sits down at the table and cuddles Amber next to her. "Ed just left. Funny talker, that guy. Bees, bees. He made Amber a present. Look at this." She holds out a dreamcatcher, a circle filled with some sort of twine, and with feathers hanging from it. "He's heading over to Miguel's place. Apparently he's helping out some illegals, which you girls know something about." She stares at us hard, and we look back at her, blank.

"Social services said Simon could take us to court if he wants," Tess finally says. "The baby's his too. He wasn't named on the papers, but he could ask for those tests and all." She scans the page of her notes. "But we got some things on our side. He wasn't there for emotional or financial support during the pregnancy, birth, or first months of Amber's life. Basically, he abandoned her. If he takes the DNA test, he'll have to own up, and pay for the next eighteen years of child support. If he's going to be a part of this child's life, he has to be there with money too." Tess looks down and traces a zodiac sign on the table with her finger, then clears her throat and looks back at me. "He won't do it, Libby."

Kay hands me Amber. I hold her away from me so I can look her in the face. She looks right back at me, waving her arms. I hold her to me, her chest against mine.

"So what I should do," says Tess, "is to put Amber up for adoption. To you, Libby. I put her up for adoption, and I name you as the adoptive parent. Okay?"

"Okay."

"But here's the trick. In that case, Simon can intervene. I can't give her up for adoption without his consent."

Amber starts fussing, so I get up to start the water boiling and measure out formula, but it's not soon enough, because a wail fills the room. Tess waits till I'm sitting back down, feeding her, before she starts up again, and then she has to talk louder over Amber, who's still fussing.

"What I can do is—wait, let me check my notes—what I can do is relinquish my parental rights and give custody to you. In the papers, I can add that if Simon tries to disrupt the adoption in any way, then the relinquishment is null and void." She looks up. "Do you get it? If he doesn't step in, it's easy. She's yours. And if he does, the adoption doesn't go through and she's mine."

"But you don't want her."

She shrugs. "Simon won't come through in the end. He's too lazy. He's a coward. He just wants to feel like he tried, that he gave it a shot. He just wants to get Jesus off his back."

"Jesus is smarter than that," Kay throws in.

"The money, the lawyer, the fight, the diapers," Tess says. "It's too much. He won't even go so far as to give his spit. Because his spit will confirm it, and then he's stuck for the rest of his life. He'll let you legally adopt her. That's what you want, right? Is that what you want? Be very sure. I'm willing to take the chance, if you are."

There's a long silence in the room before Amber wails again. Over the sound of her cry, I think I hear Kay. I think what she whispers is, "We can do it, Libby. This time, I think we can do it right."

But I don't need her to say that. Already I'm nodding, because some things are bright and clear in my mind.

FIFTEEN

The most beautiful blue dress I have ever seen appeared in the window of Ginger's Boutique. It's the color of sky and made of the softest material, and it feels like air.

There isn't a damn dry cleaner in the vicinity, that's what Kay said when she saw it. Then she wanted to know how much it was, and I wouldn't tell her. Meanwhile, Tess was taking one long look at it and said, "Yep, that's the perfect dress for you."

It is perfect, and I stand in front of the mirror and look at myself for longer than I have ever done before. Amber is down below me, on a blanket on the floor, kicking at the air, and sometimes she stares at me. We spend a long-ass time just staring at each other, which I figure is as good a way to start a relationship as any—a real relationship that is.

My only regret is that Derek didn't see me in this dress before he left. He stopped by on his way to Denver, and even though his truck was all packed up I had the feeling that if I'd said the right thing he would have stayed. But instead I hugged him goodbye, and I said goodbye like I meant it, and he leaned over and kissed me with one of his soft kisses and then I stood there, waving and smiling, and watched him drive off. It turned out just like I imagined and it felt right, only I wish I'd been wearing this blue dress.

I pick up Amber and walk to the kitchen door and lean against the doorframe, looking at the field. "That's alfalfa. Alf-alf-a," I say to her. "It's a deep green with purple blooms, and I think you should know that."

Isn't it typical of a kid that she's not listening to her mother at all? Amber's not looking at the alfalfa, she's staring like crazy at the marigolds. "All right," I say. "Mar-i-golds. Let's water them."

I turn on the hose and realize, suddenly, how big they've gotten. All those spindly stalks have turned into bushes, and each is full of yellow heads bobbing up and down in the morning breeze. I remember planting them on the day Tess was at the hospital giving birth, my hands putting the dirt over the thin seeds, and that seems like a lifetime ago. Water splashes up from the ground and splatters across my blue dress, but I don't care. In fact, they look fine next to each other, floating blue and bright yellow and sparkling water, each dancing with each other in the wind.

From atop the ladder, where she's straining to reach the eave of the house, Tess says, "We're running drugs too."

"Holy shit, Tess." I stare at her. "I don't think that's a good idea."

"I know. Thanks for saying it. I'm not going to listen, but it's nice that you said it."

She's dripping paint everywhere. This is her goodbye gift, she says—the one thing she always wanted to do was to turn this brown into something a little more inspiring. Me and Amber are going to have the only purple house in the middle of a field in the middle of Nowhere, Colorado—of that I am pretty sure.

"Tess, you're dripping paint everywhere! Drugs—that's too much. That's too dangerous. You're going to get arrested."

"I'll take my chances."

"You could get killed."

"I doubt it."

"Well, shit."

"Well, I wanted to tell you. But I won't be working with Clark anymore. I didn't know—" She turns to look at me, and as she does a long line of paint falls from her brush to the grass below.

"Don't drip so much! I didn't know, either."

"I'm sorry."

"Well, we didn't know. Quit being a slob."

"You went arrowhead hunting on Sunday, the same day I was driving. Maybe he was nervous. I don't know. I don't know why he did that."

"Tess, please quit putting so much on the brush."

She ignores me and turns to slop on some more paint. She looks ridiculous, wearing my clothes, which are way too big for her. And there's purple paint in her hair and on the lawn and all over the ladder.

"Clark decided we might as well be efficient. Run two things at the same time. That first pick-up—that first job of mine—it wasn't my fault. There was some trouble over the drugs, a cop was following me. I did just what Clark said to do, which was stay away."

"He was never mad at you?"

She shakes her head, no.

"And Ed picked up the illegals?"

"I guess. He's not part of the picture. He was acting on his own free will." She looks down at me so I can see her roll her eyes. "Those saviors of the world." But she says it like she doesn't mean it.

"But you got this group fine? And Clark knew all along that you were coming?"

"Yes." She tilts her head at me. "I think he regretted it, asking me to join him in this. Because he hated it being out of his control. He hated that he had to let it go and leave it up to me. He was all nervous. Jumpy and pissy on the phone. And I was teasing him about it, which made him madder—"

"And then I called him up and asked him on a date?"

"I guess. I'd just pissed him off—"

"It's not your fault." I know that's what she wants to hear, and anyway it's true. I'd like to tell her, though, that my sunburn hasn't healed up yet, and neither have the scratches and bruises, and that noises make me jump and at certain moments I get washed over with this fear that's so huge it makes me sick. But I want to keep those words to myself for a while. Plus I believe somehow that Clark won't be coming around anymore. And on top of that, I feel enough life inside me to know that sometime soon I'm going to feel better.

"Libby, I'm leaving tonight. I can't stay."

I look down at Amber, who's is sleeping in her car seat, and I touch the soft blond hairs on her head. She twitches underneath my finger, but she keeps sleeping.

"You're going back to Durango?"

"Yeah. Waitress, drug runner, *coyote*. My new job description."

She's trying to make me smile, but I'm not in the mood so I just look away. "What you're doing is so dangerous—"

"I know."

"The stupid kind of dangerous."

"Maybe."

I watch her paint for a while and I'm offering up Miguel's kind of prayer, hoping that she stays safe. Finally, I say, "Tess, I miss you and I love you. And Tess?"

"Hmmm?"

"Can I just say one other thing? And it's not about you, it's about them. Don't forget you're dealing with humans." I feel stupid and shy saying this, but I want to get it out. "Don't forget to pretend to be them sometimes. So that you can realize what it feels like. They're not numbers. They're not money. They're not even a 'they.' You know?"

Tess looks down at me, ready to give a smart-ass reply, and I look right back at her. She's the one with the beautiful body and shiny hair and straight teeth and a life away from this town. But the one thing I got going for me, I figure, is that I've spent a lot of time in my mind, and that's why what I'm saying makes sense to me and maybe doesn't to her, and I wish I could give some of that to her, but I can't. See people, I want to tell her. *See them,* and especially see them if at first you don't think they're worth noticing.

Tess mumbles something about me needing to lighten up, and I tell her to bug off, and we laugh because it's nice to feel familiar again, although of course I'm feeling lousy too, because I love her and she's going to leave. And because I know we're going to talk of smaller and smaller things. We're going to go backward, from love to not-knowing, and I don't know how to stop that.

Amber rustles in her car seat. I look from her to Tess and back again. One thing is for sure, I'm not going to make the same mistake with Amber that I did with Tess. I'm not going to fill up my life with her. Because truth be told, she isn't enough. And that isn't the job of babies, anyway. And it's not the job of a mom to depend on them to do that.

But I am going to love her, and watch her, and see her. And won't it be interesting to watch her figure out how to fill up her life as I go along figuring out the same thing?

Amber rocks her head, back and forth, back and forth, just coming out of her sleep. Her eyes drift open, and they haze around for a moment before they settle on me. She makes a movement then, kicking her arms and legs, running with joy.

When Frank called and said, "What, you don't eat anymore, don't need to do any grocery shopping?" I agreed to do what he wanted, which was to come in and talk.

When I walk into the store, Arlene winks at me, which is nice, because I'm nervous as hell and because I'm not feeling all that great in that place in my stomach. Just like houses have standing spots, those spots that reach out and hold you—well, the body has those too. Spots where certain feelings hang around—like how sadness is in the throat, and love is in the chest, and guilty is in the stomach, which is where I'm feeling it now.

Arlene is busy ringing up a customer, so I wander around until I find Frank. He's in the meat room, slicing ham. I look into the window till he sees me and waves me in.

"About time," he says. "I've been waiting for you to come in here. I've got a few things that folks have dropped off for Amber. Hey, kiddo." He looks down at her. "You're getting big."

"She is."

"Also, I want to talk to you." He takes off his thin plastic gloves and turns to face me. "Libby, you are a fine person. I always wondered how you turned out so fine, in fact, considering. From a distance, I could tell it was hard. And if I'd looked closer, I'd have seen more."

He clears his throat and runs his fingers down his big mustache. "Did you know your dad was the one who found my fiancée?" He sees me nod so he goes on. "I always felt like I owed your family for that. Which is not why I hired you. I hired you because you seemed like a good worker, and you were. There ought to be room for mistakes. There ought to be more times where we get to try again. Because if the world was set up that way—room for mistakes, chances to try again—the woman I was going to marry wouldn't be dead. Right? Or I would have had the chance to say goodbye. Right?"

He waits for me to nod before he goes on. "There ought to be breaks, especially for the rare kind of people with a goodness inside of them. Like you. So what I'm saying is that you're welcome back here any time. I'd hire you back in a flash." He must see my eyebrows shoot up, because he smiles and shrugs. "I hear Baxter wants to hire you full-time, though, and that might be the better thing. I know this isn't the best job in the world. And I can't promote you because there's only room for three, and unless Arlene quits there's nowhere for you to go. But at least don't avoid the place. I need your business."

I smile back at him and then sigh. "Frank, I probably took seven twelve-packs. I lost count after a while. I don't know why I did that. Just to see, I guess. Just to do it. To feel what it feels like. I don't know." I shrug.

"Well, you never collected your last paycheck. How about I subtract some from there and give you the rest before you leave today?"

"Okay. Thanks, Frank."

"So do you want to come back? Right now Arlene and I are doing your job, but that can't last forever. I can start looking for someone else."

I look around the store. "I liked it here. I'll say that. But I'd like to give Baxter's a try. I want to go to school, too."

"Well, we'll miss you."

Maybe he sees that I'm trying to say something, but I don't know how to say it. Maybe he knows what it is and doesn't need to actually hear it. He waves me out of the meat room and says, "Do some shopping, then. You don't need to be in this smelly room any more."

As I walk down the chip aisle, I feel his eyes on my back and I realize how funny it feels to be walking away when you know someone is watching you go and wishing things could be different.

Hasty Lake has its usual crowd: the migrant workers having a picnic, guys in ball caps fishing, families in beat-up RVs cooking out on the grills.

I meet Miguel and Alejandra near a shady area on the beach. She's short and thick and keeps her head tilted down, and she's smiling. She's not showing yet but she keeps one hand on her stomach.

"*Hola, mucho gusto. Soy* Libby."

"Alejandra," she says, reaching out to shake my hand and then she backs up a little and pulls herself upright, and she's dancing between feeling shy and unsure of a new life and finding her strength at the same time. Miguel's got a smile in his eyes, and of course he can see it too: all of us struggling to bring our lives together, being unsure, and being sure, and trying to be true with each other.

Amber and I sit in the sand next to Miguel, with Alejandra on the other side. We all watch as Juan runs in and out of the water. He's too busy playing at the shoreline to even notice that I've arrived, and I'm happy for him, that he can be that absorbed in something that makes the rest of the world disappear. Amber touches the sand with her hands, pulls them back, touches again, and I figure she's in the same place.

"Caught a wiper already," Miguel says to me. "White bass-striped bass mix. Got it in the ice box. Along with my Enjoy Polar Ice! bag, and I asked that bear if he remembered you." He smiles at me, his eyes teasing, because once I told him about talking to those bears. "You wanna fish? I got an extra pole." Then he whispers at me, "Her English isn't so great and she doesn't talk much anyway. But don't worry. She'll come forward. But right now, you know," he shrugs at me, "just let her be."

I nod and smile at them both. After a bit, I say, "Miguel, I have to ask you something. Did you know all along that Ed had left the dog?"

"*Híjole*, no."

"He came to visit me this morning. He said he left Ringo and was hoping I'd adopt her, and knew I would, in fact, because I seemed the adopting type. Wanted me to have a dog around. He'd just found her abandoned, and he can't have a dog because he has pet rabbits running all over the place, and he was driving back, past our house, and probably he knew about Tess being involved with Clark and all, though he didn't say it. What he said was, 'And I thought, *Libby*, that Libby person needs a dog.' So he left her. And I said, 'Why didn't you just drop the dog off in the daytime?' and he said, 'Ah, things work out better when they're more random.'"

Miguel blinks at me. "That's weird, man."

"I know. He was going to come back and get the dog if nobody found her. But it worked out, just like he planned. After he left, I figured something else out—the alfalfa, his boxes of bees—it was never so much for the honey. You see what I mean? He knew what Clark and Tess were doing and he was worried. That's funny, Miguel. Someone was watching *me*."

Miguel's eyes are good listening eyes. They're just taking everything in like, Hmmm, ain't that interesting? He says, "Does that creep you out?"

"No, it was a good kind of watching. But I do think Ed has too much time on his hands. There should be better things to do than watching out for some girl you don't know. Although, come to think of it, that's exactly what he would say. That we should take the time to watch out for someone we don't know. But anyway, now we do know each other, I'm going to teach him how to watercolor and he's going to teach me something about photography."

I watch Juan, who's on his hands and knees, stabbing the sand with a stick. Amber's in my arms, watching him, or the water behind him. Alejandra is hugging her knees, looking even farther away.

I look across the lake, too, at how the sun hits water. A blue heron stands on the far shore, as still as can be, watching. And behind him, the faint outline of mountains, which is where Tess is now.

"It was Kay who told me that Shawny died," I say. "When she told me, she was so hard. She said, 'Your friend, she went and shot herself in the head, through the mouth. Dumb kid.' I think Kay's so hard because she's been hurt so much. For such a long time, I didn't believe her. I believed Shawny was still in California. But then you came back without her. I have trouble believing what's real, I guess."

He laughs softly. "Man, don't we all."

"Shawny told me something once. That killing yourself didn't have anything to do with reasons. It had to do with something extra, beyond. She was going to fight this thing for as long as she could. It wasn't you, and it wasn't the baby."

Maybe he knows this. But I want to say it anyway, just in case it helps him to let go. I glance over and he's clenching his jaw, tight, fighting back tears.

To help him out, I start talking again. "Derek left," I finally say. "I asked him, 'Derek, do you remember that night I told you Tess was pregnant?' and he did, of course. What I remembered was the sky, because it was so cold that day and everything seemed so bright and frozen, even the air. The branches were frozen with frost and you could see all the crystals. Way back then, I thought the baby was going to be a boy. He said he didn't remember the sky at all, he just remembered thinking that I wouldn't do it. Not really. And so I said, see, for both of us, it's true: Things never turn out like you think they will."

Miguel nods. He's found his voice and he's got the tears back where he wants them. He says, "I never figured I'd be a single father. Or that then I'd be a father of two. I suppose Alejandra here never figured she'd be living in Colorado."

"Kay never figured she'd be helping a group of *ilegales*— she's busy finding them all jobs, now. Baxter never figured he'd be putting his land into a—what do you call it?—conservation easement. I never figured I'd be in Ed Monger's garage, centrifuging honeycomb."

"*No sabemos lo que está a la vuelta de la esquina,*" Miguel says.

"You got that right." But I'm thinking: It's more than that, too. I keep seeing how everybody's pushing ahead, looking for a place with enough space for our dreams. The illegals. Tess. Derek. Me. Moving forward, trying to cross those invisible boundaries so we can find the place where we're the most free, and the most full.

I glance at Miguel, and his brown, steady eyes are considering something far away. Someday, I decide, I'm going to tell him how much I see inside him, that I think he's a higher-up class of person. I don't know what he's going to do with that piece of information, or if it will matter to him, and I don't even really care. I just want him to know. What I say now is, "So, are you gonna invite me over to your house in Lamar sometimes?"

"*Ay, mi amiga.*" He tilts his head toward Alejandra, who looks at me and smiles. "We will. Our kids are going to grow up together. *Y nosotros también.*"

I feel so alive that I can't help but laugh. We will. We'll

show ourselves to each other. We'll become friends. We'll become human to each other. We'll love however we can.

Kay walks in the kitchen door and pauses, then looks back outside and pauses. I've got all the old furniture moved outside so that I can paint the walls, and it looks like a crazy mess, stuff piled everywhere. She scowls at me and my two new chairs, which are the only furniture in the room. They're light pine, and they were on clearance at K-Mart because they got scratched, but still they're simple and pretty. "Good god," she says. "You've got no sense."

She leans sideways to look into the living room at the walls I have painted, and if she asked I'd say that I picked a color called sage because both the color and the name are beautiful. She doesn't know it yet, but there's new tan carpeting on its way, which Baxter sprung for in honor of his new helping hand, and a peach-colored couch I picked up second hand.

I'm braced, ready for whatever nasty thing comes out of her mouth, but all she says is, "Brought you the mail." She hands me a large envelope. "Thought you might be interested in this."

I don't have to open it to know what is inside. It's the start of a long process, one that will involve lots of paperwork with Tess's signature, and mine, and all the pages of type explaining what those signatures mean.

There's also a letter from Tess addressed to Amber, just like she promised. That letter is also filled with words about those signatures. The envelope is pretty thick, so I guess she had a lot of explaining to do. Sometimes it takes a while to say goodbye in the right kind of way.

I'll put these letters in Amber's box, along with the letter I put there yesterday—the one from Harold and Dottie. What they wanted more than anything, they said, was for Amber to feel loved. They said they didn't want to fight over custody, and that, after all, a baby needed a mother, and no arrangement they could figure out would take the place of that. Plus Simon had prayed and had decided that his future shouldn't include a baby after all. But didn't I agree that a baby needed a set of grandparents? They'd like to be involved with her somehow and—forget the court system—could they have her visit now and then? How about one day a week? Because that way they'd feel a part of Amber's life and I could get a break. And Amber could grow up knowing the other side of her family, because they imagined that having one half missing created a gap that would be hard to fill, to which I could only agree. Which is all nice, although I'm not dumb enough to think it's going to be heaven, because they also threw in a "God bless you both" at the end, and an invitation to join their church, which was, as they put it, quite a soul-saving station. I figure I'll just take that one as it comes.

In that box of Amber's are also an arrowhead and a chip. Someday I might tell her what they mean, or maybe I won't, because it seems like one of a mother's jobs is to protect a kid from the hurt of this world. Maybe it would be better if she held them in her palm one day and wondered, and smiled at the possibilities, and I'd let her believe in them.

Kay opens the refrigerator and scans it, and then starts to make herself a cheese sandwich. "Whaddya have here to drink?"

"I hear you and Baxter are getting married."

That makes her turn from the fridge, and she looks at me, surprised.

"Small town," I say, and shrug. "I hired Ed to do the photos."

"Jeez, I was going to tell you myself. Word spreads faster than I thought. And who said anything about photos?"

"I did. They'll probably cost a lot of money."

She blinks at me. "Don't be a brat. Yes, we're getting married.

I'm staying over there every night anyway. This is a little town, people talk. There's that to consider. Plus he asked me."

"I didn't ask you to explain yourself."

"Don't be smart with me."

"I hear Baxter's not doing so great."

"He's not."

"I'm glad you're marrying him."

"Well, this is a small town."

"Could it also be, that you love love *love* him?"

Kay makes a face and then turns back to the fridge. "Quit sounding like a schoolgirl. You're supposed to be grown up now. And for godsake, I don't want any photos." She makes her cheese sandwich, grumbling about my lack of good sense, or any sense at all, and how she'd be satisfied with even one tiny-itsy-bit glimmer of sense, and why am I sitting while she does all the work, and why's she always got to be the one doing so much, and why aren't I out helping them with the haying, because people have been carrying on with babies since the beginning of time, and it's easy enough to drive a truck with a baby, and she expects to see me out there after lunch break, and am I listening to her?

I stay where I am, seated in a patch of sunlight. I've got my feet propped up on the other chair and Amber's propped up on the slant of my legs. She's staring straight at me and smiling.

It's a new thing, her smile, and it's something I'll write in her journal later, that her first-ever smile happened the same day it looked like she was really going to be mine. I'll tell her, Amber, this is what it looks like: It's a smile that starts real slow, spreads gently across your face, and then ends up shy-looking, like you're not so sure about it but think you might like to try.

And I'll also tell her about her eyes, how flecks of brown are crossing into all that blue. Soon they'll change color for good, I know, but what a moment, this in-between stage, this bridge.

ACKNOWLEDGMENTS

Thank you:

To James Pritchett, for countless kindnesses. His constant and generous encouragement made this book possible.

To my readers, who helped guide this along: Lauren Myracle, Libby James, SueEllen Campbell. To the members of my writing group: Tracy Ekstrand, Teresa Funke, Jean Hanson, Kathy Hayes, Luana Heikes, Paul Miller, Karla Oceanak, Leslie Patterson, Laura Resau, Todd Shimoda, and Zach Zorich.

To those who answered my questions: Bo Andrews, Jim Brinks, John Brinks, Julia Davis, Alan Dean, Andy Dean, Mary Dean-Reynoso, Cliff Richardson, Steve Silva, and most of all, my parents, James and Rose Brinks, who have been answering questions my whole life. Also, to the anonymous waitress in Indiana whose conversation started an idea.

To teachers who made a difference: John Calderazzo, Jan Carpenter, Richard Henze, Eric Hermann, David Lindstrom, and Jane Neth Thompson. You taught me about books and writing, and then I could live better and feel more.

To the U-Cross Foundation for time and space.

And finally, to H. Emerson Blake, for believing in this book.

AUTHOR BIO

Laura Pritchett is the author of *Hell's Bottom, Colorado*, which received the Milkweed National Fiction Prize and a PEN USA Literary Award for Fiction. For *Sky Bridge* she received the WILLA Literary Award and was a finalist for the Colorado Book Award. She is the editor of two environmental anthologies and writes frequently about conservation issues. Pritchett lives with her family in the foothills of northern Colorado. Her Web site is www.laurapritchett.com.

MORE FICTION FROM MILKWEED EDITIONS

To order books or for more information, contact Milkweed at (800) 520-6455 or visit our Web site (www.milkweed.org).

Visigoth
Gary Amdahl

Katya
Sandra Birdsell

My Lord Bag of Rice:
New and Selected Stories
Carol Bly

Crossing Bully Creek
Margaret Erhart

Pu-239 and Other Russian Fantasies
Ken Kalfus

Ordinary Wolves
Seth Kantner

Hunting Down Home
Jean McNeil

Roofwalker
Susan Power

Hell's Bottom, Colorado
Laura Pritchett

Cracking India
Bapsi Sidhwa

Water
Bapsi Sidhwa

Aquaboogie
Susan Straight

The Empress of One
Faith Sullivan

Gardenias
Faith Sullivan

Montana 1948
Larry Watson

MILKWEED EDITIONS

Founded in 1979, Milkweed Editions is one of the largest independent, nonprofit, literary publishers in the United States. Milkweed publishes with the intention of making a humane impact on society, in the belief that good writing can transform the human heart and spirit. Within this mission, Milkweed publishes in four areas: fiction, nonfiction, poetry, and children's literature for middle grade readers.

JOIN US

Milkweed depends on the generosity of foundations and individuals like you, in addition to the sales of its books. In an increasingly consolidated and bottom-line driven publishing world, your support allows us to select and publish books on the basis of their literary quality and the depth of their message. Please visit our Web site (www.milkweed.org) or contact us at (800) 520–6455 to learn more about our donor program.

CPSIA information can be obtained
at www.ICGtesting.com
Printed in the USA
LVHW04s0410110818
586441LV00001B/2/P